GIVE OUT CREEK

Library and Archives Canada Cataloguing in Publication

Toews, Judy, 1946-, author
    Give Out Creek / JG Toews.

(Stella Mosconi mysteries)
Issued in print and electronic formats.
ISBN 978-1-77161-305-7 (softcover).--ISBN 978-1-77161-306-4
(HTML).--ISBN 978-1-77161-307-1 (PDF)

    I. Title.

PS8639.O33885G58 2018   C813'.6   C2017-906799-0
                                            C2017-906800-8

Published by Mosaic Press, Oakville, Ontario, Canada, 2018.

MOSAIC PRESS, Publishers

Copyright © Judy Toews 2018

Printed and Bound in Canada

Cover Design by PolyStudio / Interior Page Design by Courtney Blok

Quote from *Our Little Secret* by Roz Nay © 2017 & 2018. Reprinted by permission of Simon & Schuster (Canada) and St. Martin's Press (USA). All Rights Reserved.

Author Photo courtesy of Lisa Seyfried Photography

ONTARIO ARTS COUNCIL
CONSEIL DES ARTS DE L'ONTARIO
an Ontario government agency
un organisme du gouvernement de l'Ontario

We acknowledge the Ontario Arts Council
for their support of our publishing program

We acknowledge the Ontario Media Development Corporation
for their support of our publishing program

Funded by the   Financé par le
Government   gouvernement   Canada
of Canada   du Canada

MOSAIC PRESS
1252 Speers Road, Units 1 & 2
Oakville, Ontario L6L 5N9
phone: (905) 825-2130

info@mosaic-press.com

GIVE OUT CREEK

J.G TOEWS

 mosaicPRESS

"All love stories are crime stories and all crime stories, love."

- Roz Nay, *Our Little Secret*

1

"PUT THE GUN DOWN." The sound of a bullhorn rebounded off the walls. "Come out with your hands up."

Clutching at blankets Stella, struggled to sit up. A sliver of light between the curtains confirmed it. A SWAT team had the place surrounded.

Wait, a Swiffer commercial?

And… snoring?

So Joe had fallen asleep in front of the TV again. And now she remembered the full moon, got up, and pulled back the curtains to reveal the source of the mysterious light. It was a monster, bigger than anything she'd seen when she lived in the city. Bright enough to cast an eerie glow inside a lakeside cabin normally pitch dark at two o'clock in the morning. Before startling awake she had been dreaming, blundering down dark corridors after a shadowy image she was never going to catch. But Stella Mosconi didn't dwell on dreams. With a husband, two kids, a job, and a mortgage, unsettling dreams were way down her list of things to worry about.

Stella turned off the television and spread a knitted afghan over her husband. She tiptoed in to check on their sons -- Matt on the top bunk, arms flung wide, at nine her big boy. On the bottom, seven-year-old Nicky curled around his greying, no-longer-plush sheep. She straightened Matt's tangled-up blanket, swept Nicky's soft brown hair from his eyes.

Before going back to bed she closed the curtains against the moonlight. Then, stretched out under the covers, staring up at a wood-beamed ceiling that had seen better days, she began to second-guess their decision to leave the Coast of British Columbia for a small town in the Interior. Joe had campaigned long and hard to make it happen. When the right teaching job came up at the high

1

school in Nelson, he'd jumped at it – just as he jumped with both feet into the local mountain culture the moment they arrived. Having spent his childhood in an apartment on Vancouver's Commercial Drive, Joe had a city boy's fascination with rural life.

Stella's expectations were more prosaic. She had grown up in Nelson in a less than peaceful household, her mother living for her own personal happy hour, her dad shifting from one workplace to another. He left them when she was twelve. Her mom hung in until Stella graduated from high school, after which neither of them could get out of town fast enough.

And now Stella was back. Living in a cabin on the lake with Mr. Outdoors and their two young sons, working as a reporter at the local paper, and missing Vancouver like crazy. Granted there were compensations, not least the pleasure of cycling to work along a scenic lakeside road as opposed to dodging city traffic. Yet at times all she wanted was to get lost somewhere no one knew her name, her history, every little misstep. Fully awake now, she switched on a lamp and rummaged for a sewing kit on a shelf in the closet. With a scrap from Joe's worn-out Speedo swimsuit, she patched a pencil-eraser-size hole in the seat of her bike shorts, and finally called it a day.

* * *

Morning came too soon. Stella Mosconi got her husband and sons up and out the door with no more hassle than usual. She was running late when she pulled on the patched bike shorts and a reasonably clean red jersey and set out for the newspaper office.

Wild lupines wept dew all over her legs as she shoved her bicycle up a steep, rutted path to the road, mentally shifting into work mode. She needed a fresh story idea, a grabber with a local angle. That was key at the *Nelson Times*. The only way a small-town paper survived in today's plugged-in world was to mine the collective psyche, let folks read about people they knew, see their kids' pictures on the sports page.

At the top of the hill a deer turned tail and bounded into an old apple orchard. Overhead an osprey rode an air current out over Kootenay Lake where a rowboat drifted, light hull and dark gunnels reflected on the still water. Nothing unusual about a boat on the lake on a clear, late-spring morning, except this one looked empty, oars trailing in their locks. High above, the osprey hovered in place then swooped down and landed on the bow, lingered a moment before lifting off with a high-pitched cry.

Stella patted her pockets and rifled through her handlebar bag. No phone. She must have put it down when she stopped to cut a wad of chewing gum out of Nicky's hair. A day without her cell phone did not bode well.

The early-morning chill raised goose bumps as she pumped along the lakeshore road toward Nelson. A loaded logging truck whistled by – the draft nearly threw her off course – then a voice from behind yelled, "On your left," and a guy in spandex streaked past on a carbon-fibre racing bike.

On the roadside up ahead, Stella spotted a parked police car and an officer training serious-looking binoculars on the empty row-boat. And hey, it was Ben McKean, someone she hadn't seen since high school. Rumour had it Ben had gone north to get his start in policing and returned with a wife and child. Would he remember her? Doubtful. Especially not in all her cycling gear.

"So, what do you think?" she said, skidding to a stop. He hand-ed over the binoculars, which might have seemed familiar had he actually looked at her. Did he even know she was back in town?

"First escapee of the season," he said. "Lake comes up fast with spring run-off. You'd think people would have the sense to secure their boats." Benjamin McKean, Sergeant McKean now. With a name like that he should have been fair-haired and clean-cut, for-ever boyish. But even as a teenager Ben's chiselled features had been distinctly un-boyish, and now the blacker-than-black hair was grey at the temples, his complexion too weathered for a man not yet forty. He still had that fleeting smile that never quite reached his eyes, a smile that had once fed Stella's pathetic adolescent day-dreams.

When she adjusted the focus on the binoculars, the boat's name appeared: MY LIFEBOAT, uppercase letters stencilled in black. "Oh, man," she said. "I know the owner. It's Lillian's. Lillian Fen-niwick, a friend of mine from across the lake. It's not like her to be careless." Stella knew Lillian to be anything but careless. She was prudent and meticulous – retired lawyer, member of the hospital board, elder of her church. She was also the driving force behind a

book club that had provided Stella with a ready-made social group
– no small matter in a town as cliquish as Nelson.

"I've called for a motor launch," Ben said. "Should be here in
fifteen, twenty minutes. Do you know your friend's number?"

"Forgot my phone. The number's listed though – Fenniwick
with two Ns." Stella lifted the binoculars again.

Ben made the call in his cruiser and wandered back. "Housekeeper answered." He glanced at his notebook. "Nina Huber. Says
Ms. Fenniwick rowed to a neighbour's place last night. The housekeeper assumed it got too dark to row back so she stayed over. You
sure that's her boat?"

"Positive. She must have gone to Vanessa's. Vanessa Levitt. She
lives on the other side of Give Out Creek." Stella handed back the
binoculars and put her foot on a pedal, ready to push off. "Don't
be too hard on her, will you? Lillian, I mean. As I said, it's not like
her to be lax."

A non-committal grunt from Ben McKean.

"Well," Stella said, "guess I better get going."

"Guess you better." He looked at her now. "Somebody has to
bring us the news of the day."

* * *

Downtown the air reeked of scorched coffee beans from the arti-
sanal roaster two blocks up, a smell no one seemed to mind. Not
when it meant the best fair-trade brew this side of the Rockies, a
point of pride among the locals. That was Nelson: every little aspect
of daily life bold and in your face. Stella locked her bicycle to a
wrought iron stand in front of the old railway station that was now
home to the *Nelson Times*.

Editor Patrick Taft was already at his desk when she entered the
newsroom. "Nice of you to drop by," he said, eyes fixed on his
computer screen.

"My pleasure." She was what, ten minutes late?

He glanced at her over steel-rimmed glasses. A tiny crumb had
gotten trapped in his wispy blond goatee. "Do you think you could
at least pretend to be intimidated when I do my gruff city desk
thing?" he said.

"Sorry, boss." She dropped her helmet on her desk. "You look tired, Patrick."

"In case you've forgotten, Stella, pregnant women don't sleep. Ergo, their husbands don't sleep."

She almost said, good practice for when the baby comes, but thought better of it. "On my way in I saw an empty rowboat on the lake. That new cop was checking it out. I should do a piece on how fast the lake is rising this year, what with the sudden hot weather and more snow than usual in the mountains."

Before he could reply, Patrick's phone rang. He picked up. "Newsroom. Taft."

Stella sat down and checked for messages. Lillian Fenniwick had called at 5:30 p.m. the previous day. Stella's return call went to voicemail, as did an attempt to reach Vanessa Levitt. Presumably Lillian's housekeeper had tracked her down at Vanessa's place and now they were gabbing about the runaway boat.

Stella opened a list for the story meeting on her computer: new season openings for Art Walk, skate park expansion – nail down opposing sides. Oh, and City Council meeting tonight at five. She texted the babysitter to ask her to stay late and emailed Joe to remind him to be on deck for dinner. She printed her list and was scribbling notes on it when Patrick gave her the high sign and ended his call. "Leave that with me and take a run down to the City Wharf," he said. "The cops are bringing in a rowboat from up the lake. Could be the one you saw."

"That's weird. I told them it belongs to my friend Lillian. Why wouldn't they just tow it back to her place on the East Shore?"

"Something must have piqued their interest." He frowned at her chicken-scratch notes on the story list. "Guy on the phone said there was something in the boat but he couldn't see it. Cops wouldn't let him get that close in his kayak."

"That doesn't make sense."

Patrick looked up. "Well, you on it?"

"I'm on it." In her haste, she smacked her hip against the corner of her desk. *Take it easy*, she told herself, *calm down*. There was sure to be a rational explanation. Lillian and Vanessa had probably knocked back a couple of glasses of wine and lost track of the time. Roads were few and far between on that side of the lake and the ferry stopped at midnight. Maybe someone needed a boat pronto – a kid who missed the ferry, say. Lillian probably hadn't even noticed the rowboat was gone until people started calling.

Stella mounted her bike and pedalled hard past a blur of historic buildings lining Baker Street. When she ran a red light, a white-haired woman waved a Nordic walking pole and yelled, "Where's the fire?"

"Sorry," Stella called back.

She stopped at the approach to the big orange bridge that spanned the lower end of Kootenay Lake. Down below, two patrol cars blocked vehicle access to the City Wharf. Sergeant Ben McKean and a couple of other officers waited for the boat on the police float connected to the wharf.

Stella was torn. Go down to the float or cycle partway across the bridge for a bird's eye view when the boats passed under? She decided on the latter and chose a good spot on the bridge deck. In the distance, a rescue vessel approached. Without her phone, there was nothing to do but wait. Too bad she couldn't ring Lillian and give her a play-by-play of all the drama.

She considered her next move. The police boat would soon pass under the bridge and she'd have to beat it down to the float to see what the cops had found so interesting in the rowboat. On the opposite side of the bridge deck, a stairway led to the wharf-access road.

The rescue vessel was almost there, the boat behind it still not visible.

A gull flapped onto the railing and Stella reflexively edged away. During that split second, the larger craft disappeared under the bridge and the rowboat slid into view.

No.

2

FROM HER PLACE ON the bridge over Kootenay Lake, Stella steadied herself against the railing, swallowing to tamp down the sour taste rising in her throat. Directly below, in a small wooden rowboat, a barely recognizable woman sprawled on her back as if dropped from a height. Head at an awkward angle. Long narrow feet splayed, a pale blue Birkenstock sandal dangling from one of them. The legs were unnaturally thin, as if they belonged to someone else, the whole thing a mistake. Except the dress, a cotton print in a delicate tone of apricot, now twisted indecently high above the knees. The dress was Lillian's.

Stella half-ran, half-stumbled across the bridge and down the stairway, sprinted to the wharf and clattered down the ramp to the float. Before she could get to Lillian, Ben McKean caught her arm. "I just need to straighten her clothes," she said. To her ears that sounded reasonable. "She'd hate for anyone to see her like that."

"You can't touch her, Stella."

His hand on her arm was firm and warm. She looked up and met his eyes, reined herself in. "No, of course not. I understand." Spoken as one professional to another.

"You okay?" he said. "Can I call someone to take you home?"

"No, no, I'm fine. But Lillian..." Ben blocked her view of the rowboat now, but she'd already seen her friend's red, puffy face, the eyes empty and naked without the trademark wrap-around sunglasses. And flowers – lupines, irises, lilacs, others she couldn't name – scattered like pick-up sticks, only limp and wilted. "She has this amazing garden," Stella said, lamely. As if that explained anything.

* * *

7

Nina Huber stared out the window at Kootenay Lake, the phone still clutched in a willowy hand now rough and red from when she had scrubbed the bathroom like a mad woman. First there had been a call from the police, the dull heartless voice of a Sergeant Mc-Something to say a rowboat was adrift on the lake. Lillian's boat, a witness had said. A witness. They did that, the police. Made a simple observation seem suspicious.

Yesterday after an early dinner Lillian had insisted on rowing to Vanessa Levitt's cottage, a significant effort for a woman of sixty-four. Not that Nina would have called attention to Lillian's age, or to the twenty-odd year spread between them. Instead she said, "Night will fall before you know it. With your eyesight..." But that had been a mistake – to allude to Lillian's eye condition. The rowboat was her only means of independence. She could no longer drive a car or manage the house without help. Macular degeneration: awful medical lingo that smacked of helplessness and despair. Lillian favoured the term "low vision." With a bright lamp and high-powered magnifying glass, she could still read a little. And she could still handle the small wooden boat.

After Nina's slip of the tongue, Lillian was more determined than ever to visit Vanessa. Lillian was stubborn. Then, insult to injury, she wasted more daylight stopping in the garden to pick a bouquet. For Nina, that had been the tipping point. That was when the argument started.

Later she scoured the bathroom tiles and fixtures with a bleach solution until thin layers of skin on the back of her hands peeled away and bled. By then a full moon had risen ominously over the mountains. Lillian always said a full moon amplified everything, good and bad alike. But Nina was never fooled. She knew the meaning of the word "lunatic."

Morning came and the policeman called. What else could she do? She rang Vanessa and asked to speak to Lillian. "Lillian?" Vanessa had sounded surprised. "Why would she be here?" When Nina explained, Vanessa began to screech and carry on. "If she was headed my way she certainly never made it. Why in the name of God did you let her take that boat out at night, Nina? You'd better call 9-1-1. We have to find her."

Now Vanessa was on her way over and Nina would have to repeat the policeman's words to more screeching and carrying on.

She looked at the phone with distaste before pressing nine, then one. She hesitated over the button for the final digit. The dispatcher at 9-1-1 would ask her full name. Huber is a common surname in Austria and Germany, probably as popular as Smith or Jones in North America. But here they say, "How unusual – what nationality is that?"

The 9-1-1 operator, likely based at some distant regional centre, would have no time for such foolishness. Still, Nina always dreaded the possibility someone might recognize her name and connect her with Max. Even with her husband far away in prison, she never felt truly free of him.

* * *

The Chief of the Nelson Police Department stood in front of his office window, back to McKean, eyes on Kootenay Lake and the deep forest beyond. A calming technique no doubt suggested by his therapist. "Nasty business," the big man said. "Who identified the body?"

"Reporter for the *Times*, Chief. Stella Mosconi. She was upset though – a friend of the victim. Eberly and Lewis went out to talk to the housekeeper, determine next of kin and take a look around. When they're done, the housekeeper will meet me at the morgue and confirm the identity."

"Talk to the housekeeper and anyone else who can help us put together a victim profile, but be careful with that reporter. She'll twist your words. The last thing we need is speculation in the media." The Chief had a talent for stating the obvious. "What did the coroner say?"

"He's calling in a forensic pathologist from Vancouver."

"Good." The Chief turned to face him. "Keep me informed."

Back at his desk McKean reviewed his notes. Top of the list: the housekeeper, Nina Huber. German accent. The surname rang a bell but he couldn't place it. From the start, she'd sounded nervous on the phone, even before he told her about the body in the rowboat. Now why was that?

Then there was Stella Mosconi. The boss wanted her kept at arm's length but he didn't know Stella. Back at school she was always first to shoot up her hand, pressing the teachers for answers, annoying the hell out of the slackers. She had a pretty good bull-shit detector too. It seemed she hadn't changed much in the twenty years since then. Same ready smile and earnest way of talking, same long, silky hair and nice body. It had thrown him to see her again, all shiny and breathless on her bike. Tight red jersey, bike shorts with a little patch on the back that made him have to look away. Later at the wharf, the gravity of the situation steadied him; he didn't hesitate to restrain her. Still. To touch her, to sense the shock coursing through her – the whole experience had left him unhinged.

He told himself to get a grip and emptied the dregs from his coffee pot into a stained mug. Back in the day he and Stella had run in different circles. She likely didn't remember him. No surprise he remembered her. There had been a time he couldn't get her out of his head.

3

BACK IN THE NEWSROOM after the shock of seeing Lillian's body, Stella let Patrick fuss over her a little. Two restorative cups of tea later she surprised even herself by powering through her assignments, including an above the fold story on the mysterious death of one of Nelson's prominent citizens. But by the end of the day a kind of survivor fatigue kicked in as the adrenalin waned. An officer at the scene had offered to transport her bike to the police station but she was too tired to walk over and claim it. She took the bus home.

Bike-less the following day, Stella caught a ride into town with her husband.

For the duration of the twenty-minute drive, Joe obsessed about a barely audible engine noise in his prized WRX-STI Subaru. Stella tried to care but her thoughts kept turning to Lillian. They'd first met at a benefit for the Women's Centre, Lillian linking arms with her to plough through the crowd, leaning in close like a girlfriend with a secret to share. Not that she had confided much in Stella, come to think of it. No, it was Stella who tended to unburden herself during their all too brief friendship. Lillian – mother figure/ father confessor rolled into one – had been a good listener.

Stella snapped out of her reverie as the car approached the bridge into town. Three sailing-club dinghies skimmed lazily under the span. Two shirtless kids played hacky-sack on the City Wharf. No police tape, nothing to suggest a body had been recovered the day before. Stella pointed out the place on the bridge deck where she'd left her bike in the chaos of the moment.

"Huh?" Joe asked, barely listening. "Gone. Stolen, most likely. This noise really pisses me off – I just had a service."

"The bike wasn't stolen. I told you the cops promised to take it to the station."

"Shh, quiet a second," Joe said. "Did you hear it that time – kind of a subtle ping?"

* * *

The Nelson police station was a modest, flat-roofed building that stood sentinel-like on the hillside above downtown's main street. Stella had to show two pieces of ID to reclaim her bike. Information about Lillian's death was harder to come by. The receptionist said Sergeant McKean was unavailable and no one else could comment on the incident in the rowboat. "After the investigation is complete the Chief will make a statement," she said, as if reciting by rote.

"So, there is an investigation."

"Routine. Don't read too much into it," the receptionist said.

"How about the coroner – where is he in all this?" Stella said.

"Like I said, when appropriate, the Chief will issue a statement."

Stella cycled to the office and started an online search on the role of the British Columbia Coroners Service. "Listen to this," she called over to her editor. "If the coroner suspects death by natural causes he'll contact the physician of the deceased. The medical history often points to an obvious cause. I assume that conversation has already taken place."

Patrick Taft rolled his chair over to her desk. "Here's the thing. I have a guy says there was a big huddle down at the wharf yesterday. This would have been after you left, yeah? Cops in uniform, cops not in uniform, police photographer – whole ball of wax."

"Juicy." Jade Visser interjected from her desk across the newsroom. "Sounds like a story I could run with."

"This one's mine," Stella said, almost baring her teeth. A few days earlier she'd let Joe talk her into buying a used canoe from Jade. Stella had arrived at the meeting place to find the two of them out on the water, whitecaps roughing up Kootenay Lake and Joe in the stern showing how it was done. He hollered something and Jade laughed then squealed as *whump, whump, whump,* the red canoe bounced over the wake of a sea-doo, Joe hooting like a bronco rider. Stella would have been petrified out there, but not Jade. Despite the little girl shrieks, she seemed right in her element. Coming ashore she sprang into the shallows and hauled the bow onto the beach in one smooth motion, the picture of competence and self-assurance in a soaking wet T-shirt, auburn hair a riot of damp curls.

Stella had to stop thinking of Jade as a girl. She was twenty-something, a reporter with a college diploma in journalism. Yet despite the friendly canoe transaction, Jade could be a pain. Beyond flirting with Joe every chance she got, she was always nipping at Stella's heels to get a story. Patrick fought an ongoing battle with the publisher to justify two full-time positions in addition to his own, and Stella never forgot she was the newbie, still on probation. She turned back to Patrick. "So, you think they're treating Lillian's death as suspicious? Why would –"

"Wait." Jade again. "You know the victim? How can you be objective?"

Patrick held up his hand. "For now, the story is Stella's. If it has legs you can help with the follow." He wrote a name and number on a Post-it and handed it to Stella. "Go talk to Lawrence Ho."

"Retired cop, right?"

"Retired Identification Officer for the RCMP. You'll probably find him down at the rowing club tinkering with his boat on a day like this. Yesterday he was on the lake when the cops brought in the body. Lawrence is a valuable source, Stella. Don't waste his time. Make sure you get your questions straight in advance."

* * *

On a stump outside an old prospector's shack, Max Huber mulled over the touchy situation with his wife. Estranged wife, if you wanted to quibble. Max hated that term although he and Nina hadn't spoken for over a year, not since he was sent to the joint for that botched armed robbery. Bad decision to get all hopped up on booze and dust off the old man's antique revolver to hold up a gas station. But who would have expected a scrawny, pimple-faced gas jockey to take on a guy twice his size?

The judge gave Max four years but he was out in less than a year and a half – time off for good behaviour was how Max saw it. It wasn't easy, but he'd kept his head down and worked out whenever he could. You'd think a bodybuilder with an Austrian name and a passing resemblance to Arnold Schwarzenegger would get some respect. But today everyone's a stand-up comic. Like the screw that never missed a chance to bawl, "Make my day!" or "I eat Green Berets for breakfast!" Asshole couldn't even get the accent right. Max was no Schwarzenegger but he was a hell of a lot fitter and stronger than that dickhead.

Max had done his stint at Matsqui, a medium-security prison down in the Fraser Valley, close to Vancouver. His parole order called for "confirmed accommodation arrangements" and lucky for him an old buddy in Abbotsford let him crash on a mouldy basement couch while he jumped through the parole board's hoops. When it seemed safe to slip away, he bought a ticket on the Greyhound to Creston. He sure as hell wouldn't have stepped off a bus in Nelson where he might have been recognized. After he got off at Creston all he had to do was hitch back to where Nina worked for that hoity-toity lawyer on the East Shore of Kootenay Lake. Slaved for, more like. For years that uppity bitch had run Nina off her feet. Enough was enough.

Max had known exactly where to leave the road to bushwhack up to the abandoned miner's shack on a slope above the lawyer's cottage. He'd discovered that little hidey-hole a couple years back when he and Nina were on a break, a fancy way to say she threw him out without a pot to piss in. The break Max blamed on steroids, which, okay, might have made him yell at times, maybe smash a couple plates. But even when she drove him up the frigging wall, he never laid a finger on her – give him credit for that.

Max hadn't told a soul about the shack, which had been smart. And now he was back. Settled in nicely, if he said so himself: sleeping bag, hatchet, pack full of canned food, fresh water from the creek. He'd even rigged up a nice little gizmo to spread out the smoke from his campfire. He didn't need some dumbass across the lake to report a forest fire.

No slip-ups, so far. Nina was as good as back in his arms. He could almost feel the press of her body, smell the Ivory soap she liked to use until the bars got so thin you could snap them in half. Man, just to look into eyes he could trust. Max could drown in those baby blues.

4

TO CATCH UP WITH Lawrence Ho, Stella cycled to Lakeside Park where if Patrick was right, she would find the retired RCMP Ident Officer at the rowing club boathouse. It was 9:15 a.m. The park was just waking up, the more serious sun worshippers staking out places on the beach, bacon sizzling at the concession stand. Children careened around the playground as their mothers fiddled with their phones. At a picnic table, two tattooed men hunched over a chessboard.

At the boathouse, barn-size wooden doors stood wide open and inside a tall, trim man of Asian descent leaned over a white shell, tightening nuts and bolts in the rigging with the concentration of a surgeon. Lawrence Ho, retired or not, had crime investigator written all over him: square, clean-shaven jaw, close-trimmed salt-and-pepper hair; a toolbox that looked like something out of CSI. Stella introduced herself and explained what she was after.

Lawrence slotted his wrench into the toolbox and studied her card. "About time for my morning coffee," he said, with a trace of an accent she didn't recognize. "Want to meet up at Oso? Best I can do is to tell you what I saw on the police float and speculate a little. You good with that?"

"Definitely. Great." Stella swung a leg over her bike saddle and headed to Oso Negro Café, a hip converted house in the centre of town, named after the black bear common to the area.

At Oso, Feist was singing her heart out in quadrophonic sound as the baker pulled an oversize tray of yeasty, sweet-smelling cinnamon buns from the oven. Stella and the retired cop placed their orders. A bearded man at a table full of seniors called, "G'day, Lawrence. Going to introduce us?" Lawrence smiled and waved as he led Stella outside to a curved bench nestled among trees and shrubs in a far corner of the garden.

"My favourite spot," Lawrence said. "No one will get close enough to eavesdrop unless they read lips." Australian – that was the accent, and hence the "g'day" from his buddies. You have to be a Canadian citizen or have permanent resident status to join the RCMP, but Lawrence Ho must have lived Down Under at some point, possibly as a child. An Aussie of Chinese origin – interesting background for a career member of the Royal Canadian Mounted Police.

He tore off a strip of his pecan-studded bun and popped it into his mouth before he got down to business. "I'm thinking suspected homicide," he said, meeting Stella's eyes.

"That doesn't make sense," she said, automatically. But as his words sank in, she took a moment to compose herself. "Everyone loved Lillian. No one would want to hurt her."

"Think I've heard that one." Lawrence flashed a rueful smile. "It might not have been personal. Your mate could have been in the wrong place at the wrong time. Got in somebody's way."

"In her rowboat? Let's back up a little. Who's to say Lillian didn't have a heart attack or some sort of accident. Why homicide?"

"Local cops must have been suspicious. I saw they'd called out an Ident guy and a SOCO from a nearby RCMP detachment."

"Wait a sec. SOCO?"

"Scene-Of-Crime Officer. Doubt if they got any fingerprints though – boat looked too rough. I'm watching all this from out on the water. Yeah, they smelled a crime all right. Photographer fired off multiple rounds then they spread a sheet over the whole boat – body's still in there, right? An unmarked SUV with a trailer towed it away. The examination would have continued at the police garage."

"So this is where you guys are hiding." A server had brought out their cappuccinos. After she moved away, Stella said, "I still don't get it. Why would they suspect foul play?"

Lawrence shrugged. "Any number of reasons – maybe just the circumstances, or a suspicious wound." He took a sip of coffee. "Or evidence the body had been moved. When the heart stops beating, blood seeps into the tissue in the lower parts making the skin look bruised. Here's the take home: if a body is shifted soon after death, the discolouration shifts too. But later on, you flip that body over – move it any which way – and the discolouration doesn't budge."

"Could you see that sort of thing from your boat?"

Lawrence shook his head. "Too far away to see the body."

The body. What was once a woman – a friend – was now a body. It was tough enough coming to grips with the fact Lillian was gone. But homicide? "You said the search would continue in the police garage," Stella said. "What would happen there?"

"Officers would go over everything again with bright lights, looking for fibres and hair, body fluids. Cameras in the garage recording it all. Samples would be sent to the RCMP Crime Detection Lab in Vancouver."

Stella cleared her throat. "And Lillian?"

"Wrapped in a clean sheet and put in a body bag," Lawrence said. "Unusual death like this, there's always an autopsy. Staff at the hospital morgue will keep the body secure until a forensic pathologist arrives, probably from Kelowna or Kamloops. Vancouver, maybe."

"How much time does all this take? I mean – a body sits for only so long before…"

"Let's assume the path turns up within in a day or two of the death. An autopsy can be done in a couple of hours. Afterward the body is released to the funeral home. Start to finish, you're looking at a few days. Weekend can slow things up, which might happen in this case."

"Now the results of the forensics tests – that's going to take a while," Lawrence continued, "depending on the backlog at the lab in Vancouver. Don't expect the instant results you see on crime shows." He drained his coffee cup. "You have my number. Any more questions, give me a shout. I'm home most evenings."

Stella thanked him and went inside to the restroom to splash cold water on her face. She came out to find the manager wiping her hands on a tea towel. "I have a few minutes before the lunch crowd comes in," she said. "You want to talk about Art Walk?"

Art Walk, right. Opening receptions were scheduled all over town for the upcoming weekend yet the whole event didn't seem to matter so much anymore . "You bet," Stella said, forcing her attention to the neon-bright abstract paintings that occupied every bit of free wall space in the café. "Tell me about the artist." She clicked on her recorder. But as the manager rhymed off highlights from the artist's statement, Stella's mind hummed with thoughts of Lillian. Why would anyone hurt Lillian?

* * *

Outside the coffee shop, a poster from the Women's Centre showed a harried mother and tearful child over the caption, "Need a break?" Lillian had been a staunch supporter of the Women's Centre. Stella helped out a little too, occasionally stopping by to sort donations for the free store or read to a group of children. But Lillian was the real champion – Lillian made things happen.

Stella moved her bike so a city worker could water the flower basket on a Victorian lamppost. Soon all along Baker Street the moss-lined containers would overflow with scarlet geraniums, variegated ivy, purple lobelia. And for two glorious months the people of Nelson would shift outdoors. The sidewalks in front of cafés would be choked with tables and chairs, the middle block roped off for a farmers' market. Lillian loved – had loved – the whole folksy scene.

Stella mounted her bike – and hit the brakes as a huge black SUV cut her off to glide into a parking spot.

Danger – everywhere she turned.

* * *

On a bench outside the offices of the *Nelson Times*, Carli DeLuca crossed one long tan leg over the other and greeted Stella with a wave of her cigarette. Not a good sign. Carli made it a rule never to smoke on the street.

Stella was glad to see her. Shortly after her return to Nelson, she'd bumped into Carli at the farmers' market and they had basically picked up where they left off as schoolgirls. "I think you were the best friend I ever had," Stella said. "How did we lose touch?"

"We moved on," Carli had said. "It happens. But you're back

and still ripping around on a bike. Hey, you still into reading? Want to join a good book club?"

Now she tilted her chin to expel a puff of smoke. "Lillian found dead – in her rowboat. Christ."

Stella flopped down on the bench. "I meant to call you last night. Sorry."

"Not a problem. I'm sure you were shattered after the day you had. Nina and Vanessa stopped by the office after the morgue. A lot of people in this town will miss Lillian, but those two are going to be lost without her." Carli uncapped a water bottle and took a big gulp that made her cough. "Okay, so tell me," she rasped. "What have you found out?"

"Not much. Nelson's finest aren't talking. This morning I spoke to a retired RCMP member who seemed to have a few insights."

"Such as?"

Stella hesitated. Lawrence Ho's theory about homicide seemed too far-fetched to repeat. "Just a bunch of forensics stuff, all hypothetical really."

Carli seemed to ponder that. She pulled the lid off a Tupperware container and held it out to Stella. "Want some? I have an extra fork."

Stella glanced at the mushy concoction of veggies and grains speckled with flax seeds. "Not just now, thanks," she said. "I have fruit mouldering on my desk."

"Have you talked to Henry?"

"Henry Sutton, our compassionate investor? No. Is he still around?" Some months ago, Sutton had turned up at Lillian's house for a book club meeting. Stocky, ruddy-faced, sixtyish, he'd stood by the fireplace with one elbow on the mantle like the lord of the manor. He was a self-described retired life coach from Idaho, in Lillian's eyes a wunderkind with an insider's take on *Your Money and Your Heart*, their book of the month.

Carli shrugged. "Not a clue. You never know with him, do you? Lillian was the go-between where Henry was concerned. Now..." They sat in silence a while. At the coffee wagon across the street, a woman in a wide-brimmed straw hat complained to the barista about her iced Frappuccino. Carli spoke again. "Listen, I have to get something off my chest. Day before yesterday Lillian called the house and asked to talk to Tim. I said – and I'm not proud of it – take a number." Tim was Carli's husband, a financial advisor to half the people in town. Carli managed the office for him.

"Why did she want to talk to Tim?" Stella said.

"Guess we'll never know. I forgot to pass on the message." Carli fiddled with her cigarette pack then flipped it shut and dropped it into her bag. "Could have been about any number of things Lillian's involved in – *was* involved in. Lillian and Tim both have been on the hospital board forever. I'm telling you, Stell, these community boards suck the life out of him. If there's a finance committee, Tim has to chair it."

Stella sat up straighter. "Lillian called me too. She left a message on my office phone at 5:30, probably just before she took off in her rowboat."

"Coincidence, I guess."

"But if there is a connection, it might be important. A clue to what happened the night she died."

"You think? I don't know – sounds kind of cloak and dagger." Carli put away her lunch things. "Incidentally, Zoe loves taking care of your boys after school. Seems the babysitting job is the only thing we can talk about without her throwing a hissy fit."

"Are you all right with her staying a little later again today?" Stella said. "My editor will have a stroke if I don't get caught up."

"I don't need that on my conscience too. I'll call Zoe on her cell. It'll be a good excuse to check in."

Stella stood up. "What was I going to do? Oh yeah, contact Henry Sutton. I'll email him tonight to arrange a time to talk about Lillian."

Back at her desk, she updated community events on the paper's website, but it was difficult to stay focused. Next to her screen, Matt mugged for the camera in his fourth-grade school photo. Second-grader Nicky's gap-toothed grin tugged at her heart. Lillian had been good to the boys; they were going to miss her too.

Stella pulled her thoughts back to the job and rang the main proponent of the skate park expansion for clarification on the drawings he had sent over. She called a spokesperson for the opposing side, noting his responses for a story to run in the next print edition. Then she interviewed two more Art Walk sponsors by telephone to flesh out the information she'd picked up at Oso that morning. But she had been so preoccupied by Lawrence Ho's bombshell, she'd forgotten to snap a picture at the coffee shop. Patrick lost sleep over slips like that. A story needs a photo, he liked to say; nobody reads gray.

It was two o'clock. Enough time to dash up to Oso, take a few shots (paintings in sharp focus, server a blur in the foreground) then return to finish the Art Walk piece. Afterward she would shoot the skate park. By then, school would be out for the day and the boarders would be happy to oblige her by risking their necks on the concrete half-pipes.

She grabbed her camera but before she could get away her desk phone rang. "Ms. Mosconi?" said a clear, melodic voice. "Beth Young from the school. I'm afraid there's been an incident."

5

AT THE END OF the workday, Stella unlocked her bicycle and pedalled up Baker Street, past the organic baker and the doll-house-like sushi café, the gift shop where a statue of the Hindu elephant god Ganesh reclined among jewel-tone pillows. She fell in line behind a dozen other cyclists and reflected on her day as she crossed the bridge for home.

The call from the principal at Matt and Nicky's school still nagged at her. The lunch monitor had noticed an older man with a small brown dog watching children from the other side of the fence. He had seemed to show a particular interest in Matt, moving along as he kicked a soccer ball around the field. "Our monitor Ms. Yablonski started to approach the guy but he took off before she could talk to him," Beth Young said. "Perhaps it was nothing, but I felt I should phone you. One can't be too careful these days."

Due diligence, thought Stella. There must be lots of grandfather-ly types who walk their dogs in that leafy neighbourhood. Still, like anywhere else, Nelson had its share of bad actors.

Exiting the bridge, she proceeded along the shaded lakeshore road. The wind was brisk and from the west. She shifted the bike's chain onto the big front sprocket and let the tailwind push her along like a skiff in full sail. Forty minutes later she stopped at the community mailbox, stuffed two bills and a flyer into her back pocket, and coasted down the driveway.

A familiar bronze Range Rover signalled she had visitors.

On the front porch, the normally effervescent Vanessa Levitt paced and fidgeted, patting her short, hennaed curls, twisting a gold-filigreed pendant that usually nestled in her generous cleav-age. In contrast, Lillian's housekeeper Nina Huber stood motion-less, expression flat, limp chin-length brown hair tucked behind her ears, arms folded across her thin chest as if to ward off evil.

Vanessa brightened at Stella's approach. "Sweetie, hi. I told Nina you must have taken the bike. I see Carli's girl out there with the boys. She's growing up fast."

A small commotion erupted on the lakeshore. "Eww!" "Yuck!" The phrase "dead fish" found its way to the porch. Stella looked longingly at her high-spirited sons. After the call from their principal, she wanted nothing more than to join them, not necessarily to ask about the man with the brown dog but just to be with them. The babysitter caught her eye and waved.

Vanessa continued. "Did you hear about our trip to the morgue? Good grief. It gave me the willies. A Sergeant McKean said you identified Lillian's body but you were upset – well, of course you were. How awful to be at the wharf when... well, you know." She shivered. "Anyhow, I guess he needed us to confirm Lillian's identity. He asked about next of kin but there's no one to speak of."

"There is a niece in Calgary," Nina said, dully. "Colette I think her name is. Colette Fenniwick. Lillian sends her a Christmas card."

"A niece on her late husband's side," Vanessa put in. "That's not technically kin, is it? I'm not sure Lillian ever met the girl."

Nina took up the story. "We told the policeman Lillian is the only child of dead parents, a widow with no children. I do not like him, this McKean. All these questions."

"Interrogating us in our time of grief," Vanessa added. "And he wasn't the only one. A couple of other officers came out to Nina's earlier, and when I got back from the morgue, they were snooping around my place too. Talk about a waste of time. You'd think the Nelson Police Department would have more important things to do."

"I'm sorry you both had to go through all that," Stella said. "But a death on the lake must be rare. My guess is Lillian had a heart attack. She was what – sixty-four? It's not unusual in a woman her age. But imagine having a heart attack in a rowboat, alone and at night?"

"Makes me shudder," Vanessa said.

Nina pressed the heels of her hands against her eyes and muttered something about the full moon.

Vanessa exhaled. "Superstition, Nina. Don't go there."

"But they will not release Lillian's body," Nina said, plaintively. "How can we go ahead with the funeral?"

Stella chose her words carefully. "I think there might be an autopsy. I guess we could go ahead and hold a memorial without her body, but..."

"An autopsy," Vanessa said. "Are you serious? They must know what happened."

Stella let it go at that. Without more solid information she wasn't about to bring up the possibility of murder. And the more she thought about it, the more implausible Lawrence Ho's theory seemed. She cleared the wicker chairs of Lego pieces and gnarly bits of apple core for her friends to sit down and offered tea, but both declined. Once her guests were settled, Stella said, "Minor point, but I'm curious about something. When the police brought in Lillian's boat she wasn't wearing those big wrap-around sunglasses. I don't think I've ever seen her outside without them. Was it still bright enough for them when she left the house, Nina?"

"Ya, ya. She wore them as usual," Nina said. "But I warned her the days are still quite short. She would soon have to take off those glasses."

"I guess she *did* take them off. Unless they fell off when..." Stella paused again. "She tried to get in touch with me that day."

"What?" Vanessa said. "She did? When?"

"Five-thirty," Stella said. "I assume she left the message shortly before she set out."

Nina frowned. "I must have been in the kitchen, washing up after our early dinner. Lillian likes to use her bedroom phone with the big numbers."

Stella said, "I wonder why she wanted to talk to me?"

Vanessa sighed. "I guess it doesn't matter now. Poor Lillian. I still can't believe she's gone."

"Please, Stella," Nina said bleakly. "You talk to the police. Lillian should not be in a cold, ugly morgue. She should be with her flowers. To rest in peace."

"Let's not jump the gun," Stella said. "We don't even know whether Lillian wanted to be buried or cremated. I tried to reach her lawyer but he was in court all day."

Nina shrugged sheepishly. "Ya, well, I have seen the will."

"The will?" Vanessa turned to look at her. "Why on earth did Lillian show you her will?"

"This was months ago." Nina waved her hand dismissively. "I

drove Lillian to her lawyer's office and later she brought out a copy. The will said when she dies she will be cremated, her ashes scattered on the lake and in the garden. That is her wish."

Vanessa pointedly made eye contact with Stella. "Was Lillian drinking when she brought out her will?"

"Lillian drinks wine with dinner. That is normal."

Stella stepped in. "Listen, ladies, I don't have any special influence with the police. But even if there is an autopsy, the pathologist will probably release Lillian's body within a few days. We can set the date for the funeral when we know more. But in the meantime, let's rally the book club and make tentative plans for the service. I'll get in touch with the others."

The visitors walked single file to Lillian's Range Rover and as Nina climbed behind the wheel, Vanessa glanced back and raised her finely plucked brows. The meaning of the gesture wasn't lost on Stella. *That business about the will did seem strange,* she thought. *Why show your will to your housekeeper?*

* * *

Zoe humoured Matt and Nicky down by the lake while their mom talked to her friends up at the house. The guys had found a dead fish and, boys being boys, made a big deal about it. After the guests left, Stella jogged down to the beach, still in her cycling clothes, ponytail swinging, and told Zoe to scoot or she might miss the bus to town. Stella was as old as Zoe's mother but way cooler. For one thing, she treated Zoe more like an equal than a child.

On the bus, Zoe chose a place and dropped her book bag on the next seat to discourage any lowlifes from sitting down. After a quick glance in the window at her longish blond hair, the bangs almost grown out, thank you God, she leaned her cheek against the cool glass and thought about Kieran Corcoran. Tall, totally hot Kieran, his dark wavy hair long enough to pull back and fasten with an elastic band. Incredible to think she hadn't known he existed until that very afternoon when he walked along the beach in front of the Mosconis' cabin.

Matt and Nicky had been messing around, trying to skip stones in the lake, and Kieran looked right at her and said, "Hey." All she could think to say back was "hey," but the boys stopped what they were doing and Nicky asked his name and how old he was and where he lived. He said he was sixteen and had transferred from a school in Toronto to move in with his musician uncle on the east side of the lake. "She's thirteen," Matt said, pointing at her. "My brother's only seven so he still needs a babysitter."

After that brilliant remark, Zoe expected Kieran to move on, but he hung around and talked to her, and not as if she was a lowly eighth-grader but a regular person with a brain in her head. He seemed to relate to her having an after-school job, which made her feel mature. He told her his first priority when he got to Nelson was to make some bread, which she guessed meant money. He did chores for people on the lake, including her mom's book club friends Vanessa and Lillian. "Too bad she died," he said, meaning Lillian. "She was a good customer."

He was probably just showing off, so Zoe overlooked the crude remark and gave him a straight answer. "Lillian may have had a heart attack," she said. "That's what my mom said."

"Does that make it true? Because your *mom* said it?"

Zoe felt her face get hot – she hated being put down. But then he smiled at her in a way that made her stomach feel kind of funny. "Whatever," she said, with a flip of her hair. She knew she hadn't seen the last of Kieran Corcoran.

6

STELLA ALLOWED THE BOYS to wade up to their knees but when it was time to go up and start dinner she made them get out of the lake. She always had to walk a fine line between keeping them safe and not passing on her anxiety about deep water. On the Coast, it had been easier to keep her phobia under wraps; not that many people there actually swam or paddled in the ocean. In Nelson, on the other hand, the rhythm of daily life seemed to shift with the rise and fall of the lake – a large, cold lake rumoured to be bottomless in places. Stella felt a familiar constriction in her chest. Reminding herself Kootenay Lake was not the enemy, she closed her eyes and counted ten deep cleansing breaths. She opened her eyes to the beauty around her, including the lake and the green, green trees reflected on the opposite side.

Even the family cabin looked like something out of *Grimm's Fairy Tales*. Definitely more charming than the brick and stucco box left behind in Vancouver. With two bedrooms, one bath, a combination laundry/mudroom, and a kitchen/sitting room, the new place was cozy, at least that was how the previous owner Will Irwin had pitched it. Will had lived in the area for years before he decided to ditch the responsibilities of home ownership and shift to a seniors' residence in town. The shiplap siding on the house, painted forest green back when Will could still go up a ladder, reminded Stella of childhood trips to a place on the Sechelt Peninsula, in happier times, before her parents gave up on their marriage.

She was halfway up the porch steps when her phone dinged with a text from Joe. He wouldn't be home for supper, late department heads meeting at the high school. Afterward, a few of them would go out for a drink to celebrate the upcoming final day of term.

With enough leftover lasagne in the fridge to feed the boys and herself, Stella could add a handful of raw carrots and call it dinner.

While the pasta heated, she went through Matt and Nicky's closet for outgrown clothes to donate to the Women's Centre, piled all the shirts and pants on the dining table, and checked for tears and missing buttons. When the oven timer went off, they ate on stools at the kitchen counter. Nicky almost fell asleep over his plate but nine-year-old Matt was wired. He talked so much about Zoe, Stella wondered if he had a crush on her, although he was equally voluble about a high school boy who had appeared on the beach that afternoon. She would find out who the kid was and where he had come from. There was unlikely to be any connection between him and the older man the school had reported, but two strangers in one day… She told herself not to be paranoid.

Stella put her seven-year-old to bed and told Matt he could watch thirty minutes of TV, something not too wild, a program conducive to sleep. Then she reached for her tablet and composed a short note to Henry Sutton, the investment dealer Lillian had introduced at book club. Seemed Henry had left town around the time of Lillian's death and Stella was uncertain of his whereabouts. In her email, she asked him to call her cell, anytime day or night, and provided the number. The note bounced back. She reached for her phone and scrolled down her contacts for Vanessa Levitt's number. Vanessa had a soft spot for Henry Sutton.

"Hey, Vanessa," Stella said. "Do you have a current email address for Henry Sutton? And maybe a phone number?"

A pause. "Possibly. Why do you ask?"

"I figured we should get in touch with him before news about Lillian's death travels beyond Nelson."

"I wouldn't tell him about Lillian in an email, Stella."

"I didn't plan to." Why were they having this prickly conversation? Stella steeled herself to cut them both some slack in their time of grief. She softened her tone. "I just want to set up a call with him, Van. So, *do* you have recent contact info for him?"

"Possibly," she said, again. "Look, sweetie, why don't you leave this to me? You're probably busy with the boys and all."

Stella thanked her and ended the call.

Eyes glued to the television, Matt slumped against her arm, and it struck Stella this was a moment to be cherished. In no time at all he would be a gangly, secretive teenager likely to stiffen when she tried to hug him. She didn't want to mention Lillian again but wondered how her death had affected him. He had never lost anyone close, and while it would have been a stretch to call Lillian a grand-mother figure, she had shown an interest in the boys, supported school fundraisers, bought them books. There were no real grand-parents on the scene, Joe's parents having retired to a village in Italy and Stella's mother and stepdad in a condo in Florida, about as far away as they could get and still be on the same continent.

The smell of burnt lasagne brought Stella to her feet; she had left the oven on and the near-empty baking dish inside it. The clock on the stove read 8:42 p.m. "Bedtime, Matt," she said, pulling on an oven mitt to transfer the dish to the sink. "No groans, okay? I don't want you to fall asleep at your desk tomorrow."

When the phone rang she expected it to be Joe, but the call display read Nelson Police Department.

"Hi, Sergeant Ben McKean here," the caller said. "Wonder if you could come into the station tomorrow? We want to try to piece to-gether what happened to Lillian Fenniwick on the night she died."

The night she died – not the night someone killed her. That was hopeful.

"Name a time and I'll be there," Stella said. "I want to talk to you too. I was over at the station this morning but –"

"Eight-thirty?"

"Done!" She was sweating when she hung up the phone. She told herself to grow up.

7

AT THE NPD, STACKS of papers and file folders blanketed every flat surface in Ben McKean's spartan office. Bare walls. No personal touches. Not so much as a family snapshot. He directed Stella to a worn oak armchair. "Sorry about the heat," he said, shirt-sleeves rolled up. "Furnace tripped on during the night – malfunction in the climate control. Normally we'd use the interview room but it's even hotter in there." His sinewy forearms made her think of the way he held a basketball just before he made a jump shot. A top-scoring player at school, Ben rarely turned up at post-game parties and when he did, he more or less held up a wall while Stella chatted animatedly with anyone willing to give her the time of day. Now he sat across from her and cut to the chase. "Let's talk about the victim," he said.

"Victim," Stella repeated. "Does that mean you suspect foul play?" As she crossed her legs, she felt self-conscious in her spandex bike shorts. Why hadn't she thought to wear something more business-like for the meeting?

"Well, not necessarily, but we can't rule it out." Ben clicked on a recorder, stated the date and time. "Give your full name, please, and describe your relationship with the deceased."

She leaned forward in her chair and tucked a curtain of hair behind an ear. "Stella Mosconi," she said, possibly a little louder than necessary. "Lillian Fenniwick was a friend. I met her almost a year ago at a benefit for the Women's Centre."

"Ms. Fenniwick a long-time resident?"

"I gather she first started coming here to spend the summers with her late husband, Clark. His family built the cottage over on the East Shore. He and Lillian lived most of the year in Vancouver and worked at the same law firm. Clark was older, a senior partner. When he died – about ten years ago, I think – Lillian upped and quit

33

the practice, sold the house in Vancouver, and moved to the cottage permanently." Stella winced. "Not permanently, obviously."

"Sudden move?"

"To hear Lillian tell it, yes. We compared moving stories once and she almost bragged about how quickly she'd wrapped up her affairs in Vancouver. Considering up to that point she'd lived on the Coast most of her life... Well, I guess she didn't want to be constantly reminded of Clark."

"Yet she took up residence at his family cottage?"

Stella sat back in her chair. "I suppose grief and logic don't always go hand-in-hand."

Ben nodded. "When was the last time you saw Ms. Fenniwick alive?"

"Saturday afternoon. I bumped into her at the library and we talked about our book club."

"This is the book-slash-investing club? Where did the group meet?"

"Lillian liked to host. And Nina – well, you've met Lillian's housekeeper. Nina spoils us with her homemade sausage rolls. I guess you've met Vanessa Levitt too. Then there's Carli DeLuca." Had he asked for names? He was watching her so closely she had to fight an impulse to look away. "Two other women are regulars, both from the East Shore. But I should correct one thing you said. The group is primarily a book club. The investing part is secondary. Minor, really."

He looked down at his notebook. "Was that where the American came in? Henry Sutton?" He met her eyes again.

"Oh, Henry. He wasn't a regular member. Henry turned up at a meeting when our book of the month was about investing. I shouldn't say he turned up – Lillian invited him. In any case, he seemed reasonably knowledgeable and trustworthy and we ended up doing a bit of investing with him."

"What do you call a bit?"

"At this point I'm in for about six hundred." Stella laughed weakly. "I suspect some of the others are high rollers compared to me."

"When was the last time you saw Mr. Sutton?"

"He hasn't been at a meeting for about two months. Spends most of his time in the States. I know he was in town last week because Lillian planned to have dinner with him." Now Stella recalled something odd during their conversation at the library. When Nina walked in, Lillian abruptly changed the subject. No more mention of Sutton or their dinner date. Had she intended to follow up and offer some sort of explanation? Maybe that was why she'd left the phone message.

"Was Ms. Fenniwick closer to Mr. Sutton than other members were?"

Stella snapped back to attention. "I'd say so, although Vanessa Levitt might take exception to that." *Whoops – just the facts, ma'am.*

"What was the nature of Sutton's relationship with Ms. Levitt?"

"Um, friends?" It was obvious Vanessa was smitten with Henry. On his first visit to book club he had offered his arm just to walk her across the room. Vanessa had almost spilled her wine cozying up to him, her cheeks a deep shade of pink.

Ben glanced down at his notes. "I understand Ms. Fenniwick's vision was impaired. How did she manage to read the books for your club?"

"Reading was tricky for her. She had a condition called macular degeneration that left her with only some peripheral vision. Mainly she listened to books on CDs. That day in the library she was picking up her latest stack of 'talking books,' as she called them. But she could read a little with a bright light and a special magnifier. She wrote cheques, signed greeting cards. Kept her magnifier handy at book club in case she wanted to look up something."

"I'm surprised she could see well enough to row a boat. Did she normally take the boat out alone? And at night?"

Stella had already thought that through. "She couldn't see well enough to drive a car but she could handle her rowboat. She'd stay close to shore and motorboats are usually respectful of boats not under power. And yes, I've known Lillian to row on a summer evening when there was plenty of light. This time of year, though, she wouldn't have had much time to get to Vanessa's and back before it got dark. Still, the trip doesn't strike me as too unusual."

Ben looked at his notes again. "The sun set that day at 8:34 p.m."

"Presumably she took along a flashlight. I guess if she had, it would have been in the boat. You guys would have noticed."

Ben didn't respond so Stella rambled on. "A trail connects her place to Vanessa's. The path is steep though, and it would have been even darker in the woods than on the lake. You can take a roundabout route by car but, as I said, Lillian didn't drive . I guess Nina could have driven her but…" She paused for a second to come up for air.

"Let's talk about Nina Huber," Ben said. "She identified herself to me as the housekeeper, but she seems to have done more than clean the house."

"That's true. She shops for groceries and cooks the meals, looks after the garden. She drove Lillian everywhere. But I guess we all think of her as 'the housekeeper.' I'm embarrassed to admit it, but even at book club, Nina is just… well, there. She serves the refreshments but otherwise pretty much stays in the background. The food is fantastic, by the way."

"She doesn't read the books and join in the discussion?"

"She skims, I think, but she doesn't have a lot to say and no one presses her to participate. There's this unspoken understanding Nina wants it that way." *Is that what Nina wants, though?* Stella wondered. She for one had never asked.

Ben McKean was quiet for a moment before he resumed questioning. "Let's get back to Ms. Fenniwick and the rowboat. You've seen her handle the boat alone. How long would it have taken her to get to Ms. Levitt's place? The distance is, what – about a kilometre along the shore?"

"Sounds about right. Let's see – half an hour if the lake is calm? One hour tops, I'd say. Longer in stormy weather, but Lillian wouldn't have rowed in a storm. That afternoon there were white-caps on the lake but the wind must have died down before she set out. When I looked out at the full moon, the lake was like glass but that was at two in the morning."

"You were still up at two? Sorry, but I have to ask where you were that evening from six o'clock on."

She should have seen that coming. "At home, with my family. I didn't leave the house until I cycled to work the next morning, which is when I saw you on the lakeshore road." She plunged on. "I was thinking… most of the other cottages on Lillian's side of the lake are summer places still closed up for winter. But a few boats pass that way. I wonder if anyone saw her rowboat that night."

"I had the same question," he said, tossing her a crumb. "The Chief of Police put out a news release today at zero-eight-hundred to ask anyone who might have seen Ms. Fenniwick that evening, in her boat or elsewhere, to come forward."

"Can I get a copy of the release?"

"I think you'll find it in your inbox." He clicked off the recorder. "Thanks for your help."

"I'd like to ask you a couple of questions if I may."

"Sorry." He got to his feet.

"I'll be quick. I just need to get a clearer picture –"

"Have to let you go." Before she could squeeze in another word, Ben McKean was on his feet, swinging open his office door then closing it firmly behind her.

In the entranceway, a young woman shushed a baby in a stroller. "You can go in now, Mrs. McKean," the receptionist told her, as Stella exited the building.

Mrs. McKean? Seriously? Dark hair swept to one side, multiple earrings, pierced eyebrow, dangerous curves. She didn't look a day past twenty.

8

FRIDAY, HIGH NOON, AND despite the usual chaos at the *Times*, Stella took a break to dash to the drugstore. The family was out of everything but she would have to limit purchases to items that fit into the handlebar bag of her bike: toothpaste, tampons, the only no-tears kids' shampoo Nicky would tolerate – and what? She was forgetting something.

Nelson was served by two chain drugstores, but Stella liked to support local business. Vanessa Levitt was the second-generation owner of an independent on Baker Street called Levitt Drugs, established by her pharmacist father, now deceased. Vanessa kept tabs on every aspect of the business but her pet project was the cosmetics counter, as her personal grooming showed.

In the shampoo and bath products aisle of Levitt's, Stella bumped into Carli DeLuca. Sergeant McKean had called her too; she was slated to speak to him later that day.

"He's curious about Henry," Stella said.

"Well, Henry's a wildcard, isn't he?"

From the next aisle, Vanessa's impeccably coiffed, disembodied head appeared above a display of Epsom salts. "I don't think Lillian would have wanted you to impugn Henry. She thought very highly of him."

"Impugn?" Carli said. "You sound just like him."

"I like to think the best of people, Carli," Vanessa said, "so I'll assume that being even more flippant than usual is your way of grieving." With that, she vanished to the back of the store.

"That was a bit harsh, Carl," Stella murmured.

Carli lowered her voice too. "Vanessa can take care of herself. Listen – let me know when you get in touch with Sutton. I need to talk to that man."

* * *

Henry Sutton was still on her mind as Stella hurried back to the newsroom. From the start, his entry to the book club had changed the dynamics of their little group. In Sutton's presence, each woman seemed herself only more so. Carli upped her daily cigarette ration from one to two and puffed them by an open window on the porch. Nina, skittish at the best of times, was wary as a deer when Henry was around. Vanessa chattered and preened even more than usual, and Amelie and Nathalie, the club's French-speaking members, played their hippy shtick to the hilt. For her part, Stella always had to fight a journalistic urge to uncover the *real* Henry Sutton. There was something about him that set her reporter antennae twitching. "Are you writing this down?" he once asked, unpleasantly, when she had pressed him on an issue related to foreclosures in his home state of Idaho.

Stella had laughed and held up her hands in surrender. But she *had* wondered what Henry Sutton had to hide.

Lillian's relationship with Henry had been more complicated. Ever the gracious hostess, she had introduced him at book club as if he were a VIP. Yet at times, Stella caught her watching him with bemusement. They had met at church. "I looked across the aisle one Sunday and there he was smiling back at me," Lillian had reported at one of the book club get-togethers. "That morning the minister talked about the fishes and loaves parable, and later at coffee I found out Henry had helped several parishioners multiply their savings. I just loved the synchronicity of that. We got to talking about a new book he found inspiring, *Your Money and Your Heart.* The author's emphasis on ethics was what appealed most to me. I had to invite Henry to book club. I thought: the girls won't forgive me if I don't."

Along with a collection of down-home life lessons, *Your Money and Your Heart* made a case for socially responsible investing: no to tobacco companies, weapons makers, and major polluters; thumbs up to anything eco-friendly or ethically sourced. Sutton claimed he knew the author personally. "The man briefly attended my church in Coeur d'Alene," he had told the group. "The Board of Deacons embraced his approach as a matter of principle, despite the possibility of a lower-than-average return on investment. But quite the opposite happened. Virtue may be its own reward, but our church's small surplus grew enough to expand our holdings. A most profoundful blessing."

Profoundful. A stickler for good grammar, Lillian had never remarked on Henry's way with words, not to Stella at least, not even in private.

That first night from her place on the porch, Carli had stubbed out her cigarette and suggested they put some money on the table. Why not give socially responsible investing a shot? Throw in a grand apiece.

After an uncomfortable silence Henry spoke up. "I wouldn't want to disencourage you, my dear, but perhaps that's a little rich – this being an impromptu idea and all."

"I agree, Henry," Lillian had said. "Let's start with a more modest sum. A hundred dollars, say. Or whatever amount each of us feels comfortable with."

Carli had already stepped through the open window to grab her purse. "I'm in," she said. "I don't mind writing a cheque for a hundred bucks. Who should I make it out to?"

"The club would need a banker," Henry said.

Lillian must have sensed him smiling in her direction. "I could do that," she said. "If everyone agrees, we'll start a kitty and I'll set up an account for it at the Royal Bank."

"Well then, dear ladies, perhaps you would permit me to feed the kitty too?" Henry had reached for his wallet and pulled out two new fifty-dollar bills and so a small investing club was born. Amelie and Nathalie kicked in twenty dollars apiece and even Stella allowed herself to be swept along in the tide. Of the seven book club members, only Nina had been a holdout.

Back at her office, Stella put aside thoughts of Henry Sutton and tied up some loose ends. If she could get away early, she wanted to interview the canoe makers across the lake for a novelty piece she'd pitched to Patrick. "Why You Need a Canoe" would be fun to write, a little light for Patrick's tastes but vintage Nelson.

At the end of the day, Stella cycled across the bridge, made a sharp left instead of veering right, and headed for the canoe shop. After the interview, she snapped photos as the two craftsmen – father and son – carried a bright yellow canoe overhead from the showroom down to the beach. On the opposite side of the lake, the small city of Nelson looked like a watercolour painting of itself, trees in full leaf softening the hard edges of old stone buildings, clusters of houses scattered against a backdrop of purple-green mountains. The threesome stopped talking for a moment as the afternoon train entered city limits and screeched to a crawl, whistled at the first crossing then again at the second. The elder boat builder said, "I never get tired of that view. Or the whistle of that old freight train."

"I can see why," Stella said. But she was thinking about her family's recent purchase of the red canoe and flirty Jade Visser posturing in a wet T-shirt. Now that was an image that would sell newspapers.

9

SATURDAY MORNING STELLA ROLLED over in bed and snuggled deeper under the covers. Nicky and Matt were laughing at a cartoon video in the next room. Joe was banging around in the kitchen. A wave of gratitude washed over her. Two healthy sons and a husband good enough to let her sleep in – did it get any better? Lillian would have been thankful just to be alive. Seven days ago, they had chatted in the library and now she was gone. How to make sense of a friend's death by any cause, much less murder? Of course, no one other than Lawrence Ho had said anything about homicide. Yet late in the day Friday, the retired crime investigator had called the newsroom to say he hadn't seen any follow-up in the *Times* about the Fenniwick death. He asked if Stella had been riding McKean's tail.

"Why would I do that?" she'd replied, immediately on the defensive. "He seems to know what he's doing."

"I hope so," Lawrence said. "He's in charge of the investigation. But like most small-town cops, he has competing priorities. Isn't it your job to ask the tough questions? With the possibility of a killer on the loose, public safety is compromised. Even if your friend's death turns out to be accidental, perceived public safety is always an issue."

Stella told herself to consider the source. Lawrence Ho must have seen a lot of bad things go down during his long career in the RCMP, things that made a phrase like "killer on the loose" trip off his tongue. Still, serious crimes could occur anywhere, even in places where people knew their neighbours. What's more, cool methodical Lawrence Ho hadn't struck Stella as alarmist.

She threw off the covers and let the smell of fresh coffee draw her into the comfort and safety of her kitchen. The cartoons on TV continued full bore. Joe's hair stuck out in all directions under his

43

headset as he flipped pancakes and hummed along to something on his phone. Adorable. But then Joe always looked good, and both boys were miniature versions of him: wavy brown hair, slate blue eyes, medium height and stocky build, a talent for sports. Stella squeezed the back of Joe's neck and said, "This is a treat. I'll make blueberry sauce." She looked out at the smooth-as-a-mirror lake and felt brave. "Maybe I should go for a paddle after breakfast."

He lifted one earphone and a faint lament from Leonard Cohen trickled out.

Stella repeated herself, this time with less conviction.

"By yourself? You sure? What about soccer – I thought you were taking them today."

"Yeah, I know. I hate to miss the boys' games. But the lake is perfectly calm. I think I could handle the canoe alone. Be interesting to recreate Lillian's route the night she died."

He pulled off the headset. "Leave it to the police, babe. They're trained for that sort of thing."

"True, but I might get a good story for the paper." She poured a cup of frozen blueberries into a saucepan, added a little cornstarch mixed with cold water and a dollop of sugar, set the table as the sauce bubbled on the stove. But she kept glancing out the window at the lake. "I should give it a shot," she said, finally. "I have to make peace with the lake at some point. It might as well be for a good cause."

In the end Joe helped carry the red canoe to the shore, grumbling that the rising lake was covering up what little beach they had. "Not even space for a bonfire anymore," he griped.

"Patience, honey," she said. "What goes up will come down."

"Sure. When the summer's half over." He nosed the canoe into the water.

Stella waded in to position her bag and paddles. She took some comfort in the generous width of the mid-section, good for stability. For her that had been a deciding factor in the purchase. She got in and scuttled to the stern. "And maybe after soccer you could take the guys for haircuts," she said.

"You're pushing it, woman."

"Love you."

"Uh-huh."

"I mean it." She splashed him lightly with her paddle. "I owe you."

"How about I collect on that tomorrow? Few of the guys want to hike up to the glacier, adults only."

"I could make that work. We're planning the funeral tomorrow but Matt and Nicky can come to Nina's with me."

"Right on." He lifted the bow and launched her on her way.

Stella eased the boat into a wide arc and aimed for the opposite shore. When she stopped to cinch the straps on her lifejacket she could still see the bottom of the lake. But after a few more strokes of her paddle it disappeared into blackness.

Okay, now she was a bit nervous, her euphemism for scared witless. As a child, she had let her dad try to teach her to swim, clinging to him like a barnacle, but only in the community pool where the depths were clearly marked and bright underwater lights made the experience less terrifying. By age ten she could thrash across the shallow end of the pool but that had remained the extent of her water skills even now.

Behind her, the cabin slowly receded.

Shortly after the family had moved in last summer, Joe had given her paddling lessons in the previous owner's classic green Chestnut. Twice they had gotten out on the lake before Will Irwin's daughter came by to pick up the canoe. Now, first time on the water this season, Stella began to feel the effort in her arms and shoulders. She rested the paddle across her knees and let the canoe drift a bit. The air was cooler out there but she didn't want to take off her lifejacket to put on the sweater she'd brought along. For one insane moment, she considered stretching her cardigan over the bulky, so-called lifejacket. *Idiot.*

Strange that Lillian hadn't worn a sweater when she set out in her rowboat that fateful evening. The image came back of Lillian bruised and broken with her sundress hiked up above her knees. She had died out there, taken her last breath not far from where Stella now sat in her canoe.

The hum of a motor in the distance slammed her back into the present. She had to get to the other side before the speedboat caught up. Paddling like a wild woman, she tried to calm her nerves by focussing on her goal. Around the first bend she would come to the yellow cottage where Nina would be puttering, a little lost without Lillian. A short distance beyond, Give Out Creek would be on the rampage. And now Stella realized how risky it was going to be to cross the confluence of creek and lake. Yet there was no other way to get to Vanessa's place, Lillian's destination on the last night of her life. *Damn.* For someone who overthought every petty detail of her life, she had clearly dropped the ball on this one.

With a blast of heavy metal, the speedboat caught up and whizzed past leaving the red canoe rocking dangerously from side to side. *Oh, God.* She struggled to hold the paddle perpendicular to the hull the way Joe had shown her, but on her own the manoeuvre wasn't pretty – she nearly capsized, and then nearly tipped over a second time, her pulse thrumming in her ears. By the time she had steadied the canoe she was in the middle of the lake with the bow pointed in the direction she'd come from, no closer to the cottages on the opposite shore than to her own cabin.

"I surrender," she shouted, her voice echoing off the blank, lonely hills, not a soul around to hear. Even the speedboat had vanished into silence.

Home. *Please God,* home. From that vantage point her cabin looked like a child's playhouse.

A breeze rippled the surface of the lake, causing the boat to balk as she dipped and pulled. And now with barely contained panic clenching every major muscle, her arms didn't work right. She had to switch sides every few strokes just to keep moving. Joe had told her to use her core strength to save her arms, but her core was abysmal – when did she have time to go to the gym?

At last she glimpsed a few rocks – the bottom was becoming visible. *A little farther,* she urged herself, *just a few more strokes.* In the shallows at last, she climbed out of the canoe clumsily, losing her balance and getting soaked to the waist. She dragged the wretched thing well beyond the water's edge and dropped to the beach like a gutted fish.

But the pity party didn't last long. With Joe and the boys not due back for hours, Stella rethought her plan. If she hustled she could make the next ferry, check in on Nina, then explore the shoreline between Lillian's property and Give Out Creek by foot. Joe had taken his beloved Subaru to town; she went inside for keys to their aging Pathfinder.

* * *

Max Huber liked to do twenty-five push-ups before breakfast back in the joint, and now he could add chin-ups to his routine. He'd stripped the lower limbs from two pine trees and fastened a sturdy branch between them with leather straps he found in the rafters of the shack. Flexing his biceps, Max smiled at the effect – not bad for an old guy of fifty-three, not bad at all. At first he'd been afraid someone might sneak up on him as he worked out. But what were the odds? The prospector who built the shack must have cleared trails to work his claims a hundred years back, but now the whole area was overgrown.

Still, Max was edgy as hell, what with the creek threatening to jump its banks and all the creepy noises that kept him awake at night. When he did manage to get a bit of shut-eye, the frigging train blew by at four in the morning then the birds started up. But it was Nina who really messed with his mind, day and night.

In prison, he never stopped thinking about her, and being this close nearly drove him crazy. He was still a tad uneasy about a re-union though. Their parting had been a disaster. Him hauled off to prison, her shacking up with the lawyer.

Max did five more chin-ups then paced around the camp until he decided to make a move. If he slipped partway down the mountain he might catch a glimpse of her. Get a sense of which way the wind blew. He hitched up his pants and hiked down the hill until the yellow cottage came into view.

The backdoor opened and from his cover in the brush, Max sucked in his breath. Nina came outside dressed in skimpy shorts and a tight undershirt. The sight of those skinny legs, her little tits moving under the shirt... He had to push his fist into his mouth to keep from crying out. And then damned if an old white Pathfinder didn't come crunching down the drive, behind the wheel a woman with long brown hair, no one he recognized. But Nina must have heard the car. She dropped the compost pail she'd been carrying and tore back inside.

The entire scene was a bit of a wake-up call. There was no use surprising Nina until Max knew for sure she was alone. Timing was everything if he didn't want to end up back in the can. He crept up the hill to his still-smouldering campfire and reheated a pot of gritty coffee.

10

HAVING GIVEN UP ON the canoe, Stella caught a ferry to the East Shore of Kootenay Lake and proceeded to Lillian's cottage. A hand-carved wooden nameplate marked the top of her driveway. *Le Chalet Jaune*, it read, the yellow cottage – Lillian's nod to a francophone background on her mother's side. Despite having lived in Vancouver most of her adult life, Lillian had never lost affection for the language of her Montreal childhood.

As Stella proceeded down the gravel drive, she half-expected to see her late friend tending to a perennial bed, a trowel raised in greeting. As usual the cottage was worthy of the cover of a home and garden magazine. Lustrous pale-yellow siding, spotless white shutters, window boxes ablaze with colour, manicured lawn, sparkling lake out front and velvety mountains behind. Now that Lillian was gone, what would happen to *Le Chalet Jaune?*

Stella parked the car and crossed the lawn.

A front-room curtain twitched, and after a series of clicks and slides, Nina opened the door wearing a bathrobe turned inside out. With her feet bare, hair loose around startled blue eyes, she seemed younger than her forty-one years – a defenceless girl. "I didn't think you locked your doors over here," Stella said as she stepped inside.

"Ya, well, that was before." Nina slid a deadbolt into place. "Now I am frightened. I see in the newspaper the police asking the public for information. Why ask for information if Lillian died of a heart attack?"

"They don't seem to know what caused her death yet, Nina. Should you go stay with someone for a while?"

"No, I will stay here. This is my home."

Stella didn't know how to respond to that.

After an awkward pause, Nina forged on. "Ya, this is still my home, Stella. That day when Vanessa and I came to your cabin, I did not want to say. But the will, Lillian's will – it is written that I can stay here. The cottage is mine now. Lillian explained some months ago. At the time, her death seemed a long way off. Who could have known –" Nina's voice caught but she lifted her chin. "I will make tea, Stella. Then I will show you the will."

So Lillian left the cottage to Nina. Well, that was Lillian, thoughtful and generous – to a fault, some might say. This development would not go unremarked in Nelson. Lillian's lakefront property, which bordered Give Out Creek and extended halfway up the mountain, had to be worth a bundle. But Lillian had often said she'd be lost without Nina, and she must have imagined Nina would be lost without her.

As the tea steeped, Nina slipped away and returned with a copy of *The Last Will and Testament of Lillian Margaret Fenniwick of the City of Nelson in the Province of British Columbia.* The official-looking document had been signed, witnessed, and dated four months back. The format was similar to that of the wills Stella and Joe had asked a lawyer to draw up for them.

In Lillian's will, her lawyer Arthur Nugent was named as executor. The document directed him to pay all just debts, expenses, duties, taxes, and so forth. Next came the legacies. Topping the list was a legal description of the property next to Give Out Creek, including the yellow cottage. The real estate along with the late-model Range Rover were to go to Nina Katrin Huber, assuming she survived Lillian by a period of fifteen days, a reasonably standard survivorship clause. Stella and Joe had been advised to include such a clause in their wills to avoid legal complications should both partners die within a short time of one another, in an accident, say.

Along with Nina's boon, the will included a number of charitable bequests, large and small.

Stella wondered how long Nina had served as Lillian's housekeeper but it seemed indelicate to ask. She had the impression the job had grown over several years. Originally, Nina had worked days, driving out to the cottage to do the housework and heavy gardening, leaving a meal in the fridge for Lillian's dinner. At some point Nina had moved in, probably not much more than a year ago, because when Stella first met the women they seemed to be still adjusting to the arrangement. Lillian would grumble about where Nina had put away a garden tool or seldom-used pot. At times Nina slipped quietly into her room and closed the door, as if to signal she was off-duty.

Stella handed the document back to Nina. "I'm happy the place will be in good hands," she said, as she looked with fresh eyes at the immaculate kitchen, Nina's kitchen now. "So tomorrow we'll plan Lillian's funeral. I emailed the book club members and didn't receive any regrets. Everyone should be here by one o'clock if the ferry is on time."

"Ya, good," Nina said. She folded the will and slid it back into its envelope.

"I started to paddle over in the canoe this morning" Stella said, "but I turned back. I'd wanted to follow Lillian's route to see if I could find any clues as to what happened to her." She ran her hands along the smooth arms of a bentwood chair that smelled of wood soap. "I was wondering, Nina... It's often cool on the water, especially in the evening. Do you know whether Lillian took along a sweater that night?"

Nina frowned, then walked to the entranceway where several items of outerwear hung on pegs. "I think the brown cardigan. Otherwise it would be here," she said. "Ya, I remember now. She tied it around her waist in the garden before she picked the flowers."

"Speaking of flowers," Stella said, "did you see the actual bouquet? There were flowers scattered all over the rowboat when I saw it. Lillian usually tied her bouquets with raffia, didn't she?"

"Always. The spools of raffia are in the shed. For spring her favourite was deep purple." Nina paused. "But this time how could I know for sure? I was in the house when Lillian left in the boat."

"I'll look around outside before I go home," Stella said.

With the lake rising, the beach was already narrow in places. Soon the water would reach a sheer cliff edge and parts of the shoreline would be impassable. Stella scrambled over a boulder field to get close to the creek but saw no sign of the brown cardigan. On the way to her car, she snapped pictures on her phone of the shoreline and garden areas, the shed in the background.

By now Joe and the boys would be back from town and primed to pull her back into the vortex of family life. She felt uneasy leaving the somber scene at the yellow cottage, doors bolted, blank empty windows that gave away nothing. She had to shake off the troubling sense of being watched as she opened her car door.

* * *

In a neighbourhood in uphill Nelson, Sergeant Ben McKean climbed the back steps of his two-story, wood-frame house. From a top floor window came the sound of a baby's cries. His son Aiden needed attention. McKean didn't have to guess what his wife was up to. Miranda rolled her eyes at him as he crossed the threshold into a sixties-style kitchen with knotty pine cabinets and a turquoise wall oven. "You're crazy, Ma," she said into the phone.

Her mother, then – it was always her mother or sister. She spoke to them for hours at a time. What did they find to talk about day in, day out? Nelson for one, that was a popular topic. Miranda hated the way the mountains made her feel hemmed in and depressed. She missed the big sky up North. She missed everything up North.

McKean went upstairs to Aiden's crib and scooped him into his arms. The little guy stopped fussing and broke into a big smile, two tiny teeth on top and two on the bottom. Ben changed Aiden's wet diaper and tickled his tummy. Aidan grabbed his small rubber giraffe that squeaked when he bit on it. Father and son laughed together as downstairs Miranda's voice droned on. Ben carried Aiden to the kitchen, settled him in his highchair, and poured a handful of Cheerios onto the tray. He looked at Miranda and noisily exhaled; she turned her back and kept on talking, probably still mad at him for not taking her for coffee when she turned up unexpectedly at the station. She had no idea of the pressures he was under, the suspicious death that had half the town talking, and then this break-and-enter at a hotel bar on Baker Street last night that had taken up half his day.

After a few more minutes of inane chatter Miranda put down the phone and gave him a dirty look. "Aren't we in a sweet mood," she said. "Sorry, but it's not my fault you had to work today. Why do you have to work on Saturday when you have a family?" She nudged him aside and began to pull small jars of food out of the fridge.

"Look, there's nothing I can do. If this case turns out to be a homicide, the first few days are crucial – you know that."

"You think it's fun looking after Aiden all day by myself? I'm whacked. How about ordering some food? Thai, Chinese, whatever. I'm sick of pizza."

"I'll pick up something after I shower," he said.

"Yeah, well, hurry up already."

He stopped to catch her eye but she had already turned her back to tend to the baby. Hurry up already. The words she used to whisper when he crept into bed after the late shift, a phrase he hadn't heard in a long time.

Under the shower, McKean dialed the hot water as high as he could bear and thought about Stella. It was hard to picture her at home with a family. In his head, she was always alone, cycling on the highway in her spandex shorts and red jersey. He wondered if she was happy, wondered if her husband treated her right.

11

JOE WHISTLED AS HE packed a lunch for his Sunday hike up to the glacier with his buddies. Matt laboured underfoot on a Lego space station. He asked if he could go along on the hike.

"Not this time, bud," his dad said. "I think your mom is going to take you guys for a ferry ride. Listen, could you scooch over a bit?"

"Boring," Matt said, stretching out the word as he moved aside. "It's always boring around here. We should get a dog. Like the one we saw at soccer."

Stella switched off the vacuum cleaner. "What dog is that?"

"A guy at the soccer field had this dog," Joe said. "He let the boys play with it while I gathered up their gear after the game."

"What kind of dog?" Stella asked. "Had you guys ever seen it before?"

Joe reached for something in the fridge. "I hadn't."

"It was really smart, Mommy. It could do tricks," Nicky said. "When are we going on the ferry?"

"A little later," Stella said. "We're going to Nina's. So, *have* you boys seen that dog before yesterday?"

"Yay. Nina gives us treats," Nicky said. He asked Matt if he could play space station. His brother ignored him.

"Ferry rides are for babies," Matt said. "I'd rather go on a hike."

"I'll tell you what," Stella said, giving up on the dog question. "On our way to the ferry slip we'll stop at Kokanee Park and walk up to the waterfall. You can be the leader on the way up and Nicky can go first on the way down."

Matt begrudgingly agreed; Nicky wanted to leave immediately.

The hike to and from the waterfall turned out to be a sprint in both directions, each boy trying to outdo the other. Mother and sons easily made it to the ferry terminal in time for the noon sailing.

Carli DeLuca waved from the upper deck as Stella drove on board in Joe's Subaru. He had warned the boys not to eat or drink anything in his car before he hopped into the old Pathfinder to drive up the rough road to the glacier trailhead.

On the ferry Stella gave Matt and Nicky change for hot chocolate. While the boys lined up at the coffee bar, she found Carli at a nearby table. "Who would have imagined we'd have a funeral to plan today," she said.

"Not me. Not any of us," Stella said. "Hey Carl, that day in front of the *Times* – was there something else you wanted to tell me? Something about Lillian's attempt to get in touch with Tim?"

Carli shrugged. "That day's a total blur to be honest."

At the landing on the east side of the lake, Stella followed Carli's Lexus off the ferry and along the twisting gravel road to the yellow cottage.

Nina had nothing of the girlish appearance from the previous day when she met them at the door. Her slight body was camouflaged by a shapeless blue denim shirt that might have been Lillian's, paired with relaxed-fit cargo pants that made her look about twenty pounds heavier. Her lifeless brown hair had been scraped into a sparse ponytail so tight it almost hurt to look at her. Yet her face softened at the sight of the boys. A lifelong diabetic, Nina tended to avoid refined sugar but she had dug out a packet of glucose-free biscuits and glammed them up with frosting and coloured sprinkles kept on hand for visiting children. Matt and Nicky sprawled on the porch steps to eat their treats.

Vanessa arrived and sat down next to the boys to unlace her boots, complaining that the footbridge over Give Out Creek was even wetter and slipperier than usual. Inside, she stepped into a pair of blue silk mules, a perfect match for the twin set she wore with form-fitting jeans.

With a crunch of tires on gravel, a bumper sticker-bedecked Toyota Corolla pulled up carrying Amelie and Nathalie, both longtime residents of the East Shore and back-to-the-landers. Amelie also ran a home-based accounting business. Nathalie painted and wrote poetry.

As if by tacit agreement, the book club members put off any talk of Lillian's death while Matt and Nicky were within earshot. After the boys finished their snacks, Stella sent them to play on the beach with a stern reminder to stay out of the water. "We can skip rocks, right?" Matt said. "There's nothing else to do."

Vanessa suggested they collect smooth stones in pinks and grays for her new planters. "Grab a couple of those pails outside the shed," she said. "If you fill them up there might be a little reward in it for you." The boys took off for the shed, arguing about which one of them would get to use the largest bucket.

While Nina served coffee in the kitchen the women gathered around Stella to hear her account of the discovery of Lillian's body. Amelie and Nathalie knew only what they had read in the paper and even Carli seemed eager for details. Stella was just setting the scene of her place on the bridge as the rowboat was about to pass under when someone hammered on the door. She groaned, got up, and opened the door to Nicky. "What now?"

"We found something, Mommy. Matty said we shouldn't even touch it. It might be drugs."

Stella winked at the other women and promised to be right back.

Matt was down on his haunches, peering at something on the beach. When Stella got close enough she recognized a clear plastic syringe with maybe a 30-gauge needle. Living in Vancouver, she had seen her share of syringes while on assignment in the city's Downtown Eastside. She'd also visited a safe-injection site. "You did the right thing, Matt," she told her son. "We won't touch it. Run up and ask Nina for a garbage bag, a strong, clear baggie if she has one."

Matt took off like a shot and returned with a freezer bag, the women trailing behind him. "Is it drugs, Mom?" he said, full of self-importance. "Are you going to call the police?"

"*C'est dangereux*, Matt." Amelie switched to French when things got serious. "*C'est bizarre!* Where does such a thing come from?"

"Good question," Stella said. "The guys were digging around in the rocks so it could have been there a while." She pulled out her phone and snapped a picture of the syringe where it lay then eased it into the bag without touching it.

"Could it be yours, Nina?" Vanessa said. "Do you use needles like that to inject your insulin?"

Nina shook her head. "No more needles. I have an insulin pump now – you have seen it?" She pulled from her pocket a device the size of a pager with a length of narrow tubing attached. The opposite end of the tube disappeared under her bulky shirt.

"No old syringes lying around?" Vanessa pressed.

Nina shrugged. "Likely a teenager threw this one off a boat. Young people and drugs are a big problem around here."

"I'll call..." Stella caught herself before she said his name. Best not to mention Ben McKean around this group and put ideas in their heads. "I'll call the police and turn this over to them. Maybe it has no bearing on Lillian's death, but I agree with Amelie. A syringe is a strange thing to find on her beach."

Her beach: Lillian's. The beach was Nina's now but Stella didn't correct herself. Nina likely hadn't told the others yet about the inheritance.

"That seems wise, Stella," Vanessa said. To Matt and Nicky, she added, "Back to work, boys. Those pails aren't going to fill themselves."

The women trudged back up to the cottage to refill their coffee cups and sit on the porch. But Stella decided not to pick up the thread of her story. Instead, the group segued to their usual favourite topic – the weather. Unseasonably high temperatures meant the lake level might peak sooner than usual. Vanessa mentioned she would pay a local boy, Kieran Corcoran, to do a major clean-up of the beach once the lake level peaked and receded. She'd have him clean up the driftwood left on the shore and chop down a rotting birch tree next to the house. Stella pricked up her ears. Kieran was the name of the boy who had appeared on her own beach one day when Zoe DeLuca was babysitting. She wondered if Carli knew anything about him.

But now Nathalie brought them back to the task at hand, to plan Lillian's funeral. "So, where will the funeral be held? Her church, n'est pas?"

"Bien sûr," said Amelie.

The obvious choice was the United Church in Nelson where Lillian had served as an elder. They settled on the Saturday after next as a tentative date. Vanessa offered to host a wake for book club members after the formal service. Everyone except Carli and Stella lived on the East Shore, and what better place to scatter Lillian's ashes than on a stretch of water close to her own much-loved home.

Nobody mentioned the syringe again. At four o'clock the women dispersed, each with a to-do list for the upcoming memorial.

* * *

Nina hand-washed the six blue coffee mugs and put them away, handles aligned with the others in the cupboard. Now what? Perhaps she should change into some old clothes and go out to the garden. Take a shovel to that fallow vegetable plot.

But first she went to the medicine cabinet and removed a packet of syringes identical to the one found on the beach. Nina hated to be wasteful and throw them out, but Stella was sure to show Sergeant McKean the used syringe. If he were to search the cottage again, the fresh pack of needles would raise suspicion. Nina slipped the packet into a plastic grocery bag, bound it with several layers of duct tape, and put it in the bottom of her handbag. Tomorrow she would drive to the mall in Nelson and drop the parcel into a dumpster out back.

Fretting over the syringes ended any thought of work in the garden. Nina was too anxious and tired now even to change into gardening clothes. The vegetable garden had always been her project. If Lillian had her way, every square inch of soil would have been planted with flowers. Nina's mother would never have approved of such a thing. A passion for flowers would have seemed frivolous, an affectation. Lillian probably would have considered her mother a drudge, not that she ever asked much about Nina's family. It was just as well. Nina preferred to stay quiet about her past.

She loosened the waistband of her pants and massaged her abdomen to relieve the tightness in her belly. From the look Vanessa had given her on the beach, she seemed to think the used syringe was Nina's. Perhaps the others did too . Her mother's reedy voice came unbidden. *Who else to suspect but the foreigner? With your luck, what do you expect?*

12

FIRST THING MONDAY MORNING, Stella called Ben McKean from her desk at the *Times* and told him about the syringe the boys had found in front of the yellow cottage.

"The pathologist should see it ASAP," he said. "I'll come get it."

Stella glanced over at Patrick, pecking away on his keyboard. "How about I deliver it myself?" she said, hoping for a chance to rub shoulders with the pathologist. "I could cycle up to the hospital on my lunch break."

"This can't wait." He paused. "I'll swing by and pick you up."

Pick you up – not pick it up. Stella grabbed her bag and waved at Patrick on the way out.

Dr. Ralph Antoniak, a forensic pathologist who had flown in from Vancouver to work the case, sat hunched over a tiny desk in the hospital basement. He'd arrived on Friday afternoon to perform the autopsy on Lillian Fenniwick's body and had already sent toxicology samples to the RCMP lab in Vancouver for analysis. He was writing up his final notes for the coroner before leaving to catch his flight back to the Coast when Stella and Ben arrived at his office.

Stella was quick to introduce herself as a friend of Lillian and hand over the new evidence. "My sons found this on Lillian's beach yesterday," she said, holding up the clear plastic bag that contained the syringe. "Looks like it's been used. We were careful not to touch it. Sergeant McKean thought you should see it right away."

The doctor lifted the bag up to the light. "A trace of clear liquid inside. With luck, there'll be enough to identify the substance. Be nice to know what to look for – makes for quicker test results."

Stella cleared her throat. No sense hedging. "Lillian's housekeeper has Type 1 Diabetes."

Dr. Antoniak's eyebrows shot up. "So it could be insulin."

"Would that be consistent with your other findings?" Stella said. She glanced at Ben. He was frowning, probably starting to regret bringing her along.

"Hard to say," Antoniak said. "The victim's blood sugar was low but then her stomach was empty. Anything she might have eaten that evening was fairly well digested by the time of death."

"And that was…" Stella resisted a powerful urge to turn on her recorder.

Antoniak smiled indulgently. "I put the time of death between eight p.m. and midnight."

"And she set out in her rowboat around sixish," Stella said. "What do you think might have happened, Dr. Antoniak, between then and the period you mentioned?"

Ben spoke up. "Sorry to interrupt, but I should get Ms. Mosconi back to the newspaper office."

Ralph Antoniak laughed. "A reporter, eh? Well, Ms. Mosconi, I trust I can depend on your discretion."

"Absolutely," Stella said. "One thing though – as a friend, I wonder about the state of Lillian's clothing when they brought in the rowboat. Her sundress was hiked up way above her knees…"

Antoniak shook his head. "I saw no sign of sexual interference, if that's what's worrying you."

Ben was by the door now, his hand on the knob. Stella blundered on. "How about other kinds of interference? Like was there any sign she'd been moved after, uh, after she died?"

Dr. Antoniak closed the file folder in front of him. "I think Sergeant McKean is anxious to take you back, Ms. Mosconi," he said. "It's been good to meet you. Oh, and Sergeant – in light of the new evidence, I'll reschedule my flight. Wife won't be pleased but that can't be helped." He looked almost cheerful. "You and I will talk again soon."

Back in the police cruiser, Stella turned to Ben. "How long before he gets back to you, do you think?"

Ben pulled out of the hospital parking lot before he replied. "Likely be a day or two."

"Then we'll know whether the syringe has any significance to the case," she said.

He pulled over to the side of the road. "Look Stella, there is no 'we' here. You're not part of the investigation and there's a good reason for that. If you were to leak anything you heard this morning – however insignificant it might seem – you could seriously compromise this case."

"Ben, please. Trust me. I wouldn't do anything to interfere. I'm sorry if I spoke out of turn in there."

Ben pulled out into the traffic and proceeded downtown, eyes firmly on the road ahead.

Stella was a minefield of conflicting emotions. Even as she grieved for Lillian, she was perversely intrigued about the manner of her friend's death. She had relished that encounter with Dr. Antoniak, a small window into the investigation that left her hungering for more. Yet if he found insulin in that syringe, the implications for Nina would be bad. Stella spoke again to fill the silence. "Interesting Dr. Antoniak didn't have much to say beyond the approximate time of Lillian's death. Yet he was wrapping up, ready to go home. If the syringe turns out to be a red herring, no one might ever know the truth. This could be one of those cases that never gets solved."

Ben refused to engage as he pulled up in front of the newspaper office.

"I am sorry if I overstepped," Stella continued. "No, let me re-phrase that. I'm sorry I did overstep. It won't happen again."

"I don't believe you," he said. But the scowl was gone. "You're too good a reporter to make a claim like that."

She grinned a little sheepishly. "Strange, isn't it? Both of us leav-ing Nelson after high school then returning within months of each other – meeting again under these circumstances."

"How long you been back?" he said.

"Less than a year."

"You like it here?"

"Getting used to it," Stella said. "You?"

There was that fleeting smile. "Have to get back to you on that."

* * *

Max Huber carefully unfolded a yellowed newspaper clipping, torn along the creases from frequent handling. Gym for sale, it read. The asking price included a one-bedroom apartment on the top floor of the building. The location: Fruitvale, a village sixty-seven clicks from Nelson. Property values were lower there, which made the gym a steal – well within Nina's budget. He knew she'd been put-ting away money for years. Back when they lived together, she'd crossed the lake every frigging weekday to work for that lawyer.

Half her pay cheque covered the rent for a dump downtown and a few bucks went to her parents in Germany until they passed on. Most of the rest Nina squirrelled away.

Her shacking up with that frigging lawyer had sickened Max. But what could he do? They put him away. On the bright side, with Nina's living expenses covered, she must have saved a lot of dough while he was in the slammer.

From the moment Max had picked up a week-old paper in the prison chow hall and read that ad, the idea of owning his own gym had kept him going. And the place was still for sale. From a pay phone at the Greyhound station in Creston he'd called a realtor and the guy confirmed it. Hell, the owner had dropped the price. Max pictured himself in the gym – Max's Gym, he would call it – hob-nobbing with the clientele, coaching the real bodybuilders. He'd order up some mugs and T-shirts with the gym's name on them. First class all the way.

Max folded the clipping and put it away. He was ready to face Nina. More than ready. He straightened his shoulders and headed down the mountain.

People today hooked up on the Internet but he and Nina had been ahead of the curve. He'd advertised for a wife all over Austria and Germany and finally got a letter with a photo from a slim, good-looking girl of nineteen. Nina had been born and raised in some one-horse town in East Germany. When the Berlin Wall came down in '89 her old man lost his job as a farm worker for the Commies and the family moved west. Poor beggar couldn't get work and turned to the bottle. The mother wasn't much; she didn't take to the flashiness of the West and made a religion of her misery. No wonder Nina grabbed at a chance to escape. More than twenty years had gone by since she stepped off that plane in Vancouver. She was over forty now but she was still the girl for him. Max had never strayed and he swore he never would.

From his lookout above the cottage, he watched Nina water the planters on the back porch dressed in a short, flimsy night shift, hair falling over her face. He ran his hand over his own springy, rust-coloured hair, tucked his T-shirt into his jeans, and strode toward his woman.

* * *

Stella cycled home reflecting on the meeting with the pathologist that morning. He had seemed willing to open up to her until Ben got all twitchy and practically dragged her out of his office. What she would have given to spend just a few more minutes with Dr. Ralph Antoniak. Well, she'd handed over the syringe and Antoniak would take it from there – not that the needle was necessarily relevant to the case. Injection drug use in Nelson was likely as common as in other places these days. The syringe could have been dropped anywhere near the water's edge then been deposited on Lillian's beach with changes in the lake level. And that was just one possible explanation.

As she pumped along the highway Stella indulged in a brief fantasy of solving the case, her astute probing (ha-ha) bringing honour to Lillian while yielding a landslide of hits on the paper's website. Of course the *Times* was too small to support a full-time investigative reporter, but a girl could dream. Meanwhile, it was her turn to attend the school board meeting that evening and God only knew what time it would be over. The present chair tended to draw things out.

Once home, she tossed together a spaghetti dinner for her ravenous boys – all three of them – and was out the door and heading back to town in the Pathfinder within forty minutes.

The meeting was long but it didn't drag. Someone had leaked the agenda and the public came out in droves. With the threat of school closures in the coming year, the discussion was heated.

At 11:15 p.m. Stella arrived home to a sink full of dirty dishes, kids in bed, thankfully, and Joe sprawled in front of the tube watching a *Law & Order* rerun. "I'll clean up later," he said, from his reclined position on the couch. "Just need to unwind a bit. How was the Board meeting?"

"Long." Stella made a pot of Earl Grey tea and took it out to the porch. She wondered if it was too late to call Ben to find out if he'd heard back from Dr. Antoniak. If she worked for a big-city paper she might not have hesitated. But in Nelson it didn't seem right to disturb an over-worked cop at home with his family – the curvy, raven-haired wife she had glimpsed at the station, the sweet baby boy.

13

TUESDAY, ONE WEEK AFTER Lillian Fenniwick was found dead in her rowboat, McKean took a call from Dr. Ralph Antoniak. The syringe found on Fenniwick's beach had indeed contained traces of insulin.

Once McKean was seated in the cramped little office in the hospital basement, Antoniak elaborated on the new findings. "Insulin has some history as a murder weapon, you know. A substance normally present in the bloodstream doesn't tend to raise suspicion. But a sudden big hit of insulin can cause a sharp drop in blood sugar, effectively cutting off the brain's supply of glucose. A victim could remain unconscious for some time before it killed her. But it's not unheard of for a hefty dose to kill a person in minutes."

The presence of insulin in the syringe had prompted the pathologist to re-examine the body for needle marks. He found a small injection site on the victim's left buttock. Analysis of the tissue around the site confirmed the presence of insulin. "Had to change my initial conclusions," Antoniak said. "Up until your visit with Ms. Mosconi yesterday, I was leaning toward accidental death as a cause." He interrupted himself to pour each of them a cup of strong black coffee then settled into his chair again, ready to resume his story. "You see the victim had a high level of blood alcohol. Alive she would have failed a Breathalyzer test. Before I started looking for injection sites, I hadn't noticed any evidence of foul play. My best guess was that with all that booze in her, she'd become disoriented, rowed in the wrong direction, got lost in the dark, and succumbed to exposure. She was frail, and her vision was limited. All in all, the proverbial perfect storm."

"But now – with the new evidence?" McKean prompted.

"I'd say the likely cause of death was an insulin overdose," Antoniak said. "With the excess insulin administered by injection."

McKean's pulse quickened. The chance discovery of a used syringe had turned this case on its head. He tried to speak but found his mouth had gone dry. The words came out in a whisper. "Murder?"

"I doubt she injected herself in the ass."

McKean leaned back in his chair, his mind racing. "What about the boat? Any sign the body was moved after death?"

"None, although we can't rule it out."

McKean struggled to consider the possibilities. "Could she have died from a combination of circumstances? Say she was injected but later died of exposure?"

"Could be. But the insulin piece suggests someone intentionally harmed her."

Murder, or homicide at any rate. McKean collected his thoughts as he walked out to his car, squelching a reckless impulse to immediately call Stella and share the doctor's findings. He couldn't take a chance on her tipping off the diabetic housekeeper before he could get to her. Or worse, talking to her editor. No, he had to re-interview Nina Huber and the sooner the better. He could call her in to the station but she would likely be more forthcoming in a non-threatening environment. Even before this new evidence came to light, the woman appeared to be afraid of her own shadow.

McKean drove straight to the ferry and once on board reviewed the facts of the case. Antoniak had estimated the time of Lillian Fenniwick's death at between eight and midnight, roughly two to six hours after she supposedly took off in her rowboat to visit Vanessa Levitt. That was assuming Fenniwick actually left home at around 6:00 p.m. There was no one to back up the housekeeper's story. By Stella's estimate, it would have taken Fenniwick an hour at most to row the one-kilometre distance to her friend's place. That is if she made it that far – Vanessa Levitt insisted Fenniwick had never arrived.

So, what the hell happened? The alcohol factor could be important. At the time of death, Fenniwick had been drunk. Nina Huber, possibly the last person to see her alive, had likely cooked her final meal and poured her a drink or two. Or had she plied her employer with enough booze to incapacitate her before poking her with a needle? Huber was a diabetic and had easy access to insulin. It seemed very tidy – but where was the motive? Why would Nina Huber have wanted Lillian Fenniwick dead?

McKean glanced up as two school-age boys raced by, darting among the parked vehicles on the car deck. Directly in front of him, a woman horsed around in the back of her pick up with a couple of noisy hounds. He closed his eyes to concentrate.

Huber. The name had niggled at him since he had first spoken to the housekeeper. He did a search on the car's computer using CPIC, the Canadian Police Information Centre database, and bingo. Three weeks back a Max Huber, age fifty-three, had been released from Matsqui Institution after serving one third of a four-year sentence for attempted armed robbery. That would have been about two weeks before Lillian Fenniwick was killed. Huber wasn't a very common name. Odds seemed to favour a connection between the convicted felon and the housekeeper.

McKean disembarked and followed a rough, winding road on the east side of the lake, crossed the bridge over Give Out Creek, and knocked on the door of the yellow cottage. Nina Huber didn't seem surprised to see him; maybe she'd realized it was only a matter of time before he caught up with her. She looked shaky, as if a sudden puff of wind could knock her down. Her eyes were dull and red-rimmed. He wondered how much Stella really knew about this woman.

Stella. He couldn't forget her look of surprise and almost betrayal when he had asked her whereabouts on the night of Fenniwick's death. Even in retrospect it did something to his gut – the way her eyes had widened, the hint of a wobble in her voice. He had tried to keep things professional but that was quickly slipping away. A big mistake. Yet he couldn't stop thinking about Stella and didn't want to. He sat on a wooden chair across the table from Nina Huber and added a teaspoon of sugar to the cup of tea she had put in front of him. "All right, Ms. Huber," he said. "Let's go over this again."

* * *

After his failed attempt to get Nina back, Max just wasn't himself. His own wife had refused to let him in the frigging door. Unbelievable. But then he'd shown up out of the blue and come on like gangbusters. He probably looked like hell to boot, after roughing it in the bush.

Well, if at first you don't succeed, spruce up. He brushed his teeth, wetted down his hair, and put on a shirt with a collar. This time would be different. He had a good feeling about it – and why not? Nina would be expecting him now, and didn't she need him as much as he needed her?

But when he stopped at his lookout halfway down the mountain, he almost crapped himself. Outside the yellow cottage, a police cruiser had come to a stop in the driveway. A cop in uniform got out, rubber-necked around the yard then went to the front of the house, out of Max's view. He would have given his right arm to see Nina's reaction when she opened the door.

Had the cop come to warn her about Max's release? Did they do that – notify the next of kin? Even if the next of kin had not once gotten her skinny ass in gear to visit him in prison? What the hell – he wasn't a sex offender, a danger to the public. If he'd been guilty of anything it was poor judgement. And he'd served his time, goddamn it!

Bad enough that Nina had shunned him last time he'd come around. Just stood there clutching a watering can to her chest like he might jump her on the spot. Over and over, she'd told him to go away and nothing he said made any difference. And now a cop shows up to badmouth him – or worse. Why else would a uniform come all the way out there? Max hoped to hell the frigging parole board wasn't looking for him.

For the first time since he'd gone off steroids, he wanted to smash something. *Don't do anything stupid*, he told himself. Even without the 'roids he had a temper on him. If he lost it now in front of a cop all his plans would go up in smoke.

No, he'd have to regroup, that's all. He hadn't come this far to let some two-bit plod screw everything up.

* * *

Tuesday, the hottest day of the season so far, the newsroom was an oven. Stella opened three windows and turned on a fan near her desk, causing a heap of papers to flutter to the floor. The fan had two speeds: on and off. She moved it closer to a window and sorted her papers. At least the place was quiet. Patrick had left a message to say he'd be back after lunch. Jade Visser was on assignment.

Almost twenty-four hours had passed since Stella and Ben had delivered the syringe to Dr. Antoniak and she was getting antsy about the test results. She rang Ben's office but the receptionist couldn't connect her. She tried his cell and had to settle for voicemail.

Stella wrote up her piece on the school board meeting and posted it on the paper's website, but she couldn't stop thinking about the investigation. She wondered if Vanessa had been able to reach Henry Sutton – that was a loose end. She tried her cell but Vanessa wasn't picking up; a pharmacist at the drugstore said she was at the pool.

At noon Stella cycled to the recreation centre and pounded up a flight of stairs to the observation deck. Sure enough, in the far lap lane, a familiar bright blue cap cut through the water. Could she, Stella, ever learn to do that? To glide gracefully through deep water without her muscles seizing up, without flailing to the apron of the pool, gasping for breath? Doubtful.

Time all but stood still as Vanessa churned back and forth in her lane. Stella was about to give up and return to the office when the swimmer slipped out of the pool like a seal and pulled off her blue cap. Stella tapped on the window of the observation deck; Vanessa looked up and pointed toward the change room.

Vanessa peeled off her swimsuit and stood under the open shower for what seemed like an eternity, finally moseying over to the lockers where Stella waited.

"So – any news from Henry?" Stella said.

"That poor man." Vanessa smiled tenderly. "He must have tried three times to return my call before he finally got through. He sounded exhausted. I said, 'Henry, I hope you're not working yourself to the bone. Financial matters can be so stressful.' Well, he just melted. Grateful for the sympathy, I guess." Vanessa towelled off and smoothed a sweet-smelling lotion on her arms and legs, over her shoulders, under her breasts. You had to hand it to her – at fifty she was in good shape.

"Did you tell him about Lillian?" Stella glanced at her watch.

"I broke it to him gently. Naturally it was a shock." Vanessa sat down and eased her pantyhose up one perfectly waxed leg. "I invited him to the funeral. I said it would mean so much to us if he came. 'I'll try, my dear,' he said. Who says 'my dear' anymore?" She chuckled fondly.

"Can you forward me his new email address?" Stella said. "And maybe attach one of those group shots we took on your phone the night we set up the investing fund."

Vanessa slipped into a lacy blouse. "Hmm. Not sure if I kept those photos."

"Have a good look, okay? What about our investments – he hasn't sent a report in ages. Lillian was going to follow up when she met him last week."

Vanessa stopped mid-way through buttoning her blouse. "Stella, sweetie. Listen to yourself. How could I tell him about Lillian in one breath then question him about money in the next?"

"Okay, okay. You're right, but –"

"Why don't you leave Henry to me? I'd be more than happy to take over Lillian's role as liaison with him." Vanessa moved to the mirror and emptied a bagful of cosmetics onto the counter. "You know, we haven't had a good gab in ages. Why don't we get to-gether for a coffee or a glass of wine? Cheer ourselves up – what do you say?"

"Let's do it. I'll call you." Stella hesitated at the exit to the change room. "You looked impressive in the pool, by the way. Guess you've been a good swimmer all your life."

"Well, I grew up on the lake." Vanessa dabbed foundation on her nose and under her eyes.

"I should take lessons," Stella said. "Never did get the breathing right." Colossal understatement.

"Breathing's not that big a deal," Vanessa said. "Come to the pool some lunch hour. I'll give you pointers." Now she turned to look directly at Stella. "I wonder if the police are still investigating Lillian's death. Have you heard anything?"

"Not a word." Stella felt herself flush but was saved by the ring-tone on her phone. "I better take this, Van," she said, with a little wave. "Let's talk soon."

It took Stella a second or two to recognize Nina's voice on the line. "The police," Nina said, between sobs. "McKean. He thinks I am a murderer."

14

AFTER NINA'S DISTRAUGHT CALL about Ben McKean, Stella looked for any excuse to get out to the East Shore that afternoon. Tomorrow's front page still had holes and a rumour had come into the newsroom about a break-in at the gas station next to the ferry terminal. The owner had been evasive when Stella called that morning but it would be harder to brush her off in person. Patrick didn't bat an eye when she asked to borrow his car to follow up. He simply tossed her the keys and alerted her to a new Chris Botti album in the vehicle's CD stack.

At the ferry slip, Stella parked and entered the store at the gas station. The owner wasn't there. The teenager behind the counter claimed not to know anything about a break-in.

"Who reported it?" Stella said.

"Dunno," the kid said. "Think it was a mistake."

"Anything missing – money, cigarettes, lottery tickets?"

"Not sure. You'd have to ask the owner."

They went around in circles a few more times before Stella gave up and drove onto the ferry. On board, she called Patrick. "No one's talking at the gas station."

"You on your way back?"

"Um, no, I'm on the ferry. Following up on another story. Maybe you could fill the hole on page one with a piece from page two and I'll pull together something for page two."

"Shit."

"Yeah, I know. Sorry."

Stella opened the windows to let the wind rip through Patrick's older silver 4Runner, and as the rich tones of Botti's trumpet spilled out over Kootenay Lake, she tried to come up with an idea for page two.

A brisk rap on the roof and a face appeared on the passenger side. "You that reporter?" The man looked to be in his late fifties with thinning hair and a pocked complexion, tobacco-stained teeth.

"Stella Mosconi. What can I do for you?"

"D'ya hear about the upcoming ferry repairs? They're gonna put this one in dry dock and run that old tub that holds about ten cars. How are people like me supposed to get to work in Nelson on time?"

"Good question," Stella said, but she was thinking, *Beggars can't be choosers.* She pulled out her recorder, interviewed the concerned citizen, and for confirmation, spoke to one of the crew. After disembarking, she pulled over and snapped a nice shot of the ferry. On the return crossing she would churn out an article on vessel repairs for page two. The piece would almost write itself.

The chain was still on when Nina opened the front door. Through the narrow gap, she said, "He thinks I killed Lillian."

"McKean?" Stella said. "What did he say?"

Nina closed the door, undid the chain, and opened the door again. "He toyed with me. First he drinks my tea, then all the questions. Are you diabetic? Do you inject yourself? I showed him the pump and my prescription. I told him I have no more syringes. What use would needles be anymore?"

Stella tried to keep her expression neutral as Nina spoke. But Ben's questions about diabetes could have meant only one thing: the test results must have come back identifying the substance in the syringe as insulin.

Was that enough to pin a murder charge on someone? Nina certainly had the opportunity and the means to kill Lillian – that's how Ben must see it. But if the syringe was the murder weapon, why ditch it on the property where she and Lillian both lived?

Stella's mind raced as Nina ranted about Ben grilling her. "Then he asked about Max," Nina said. "I have a husband, Stella. I never talk about him. He went away and after that I came to live with Lillian. Among our friends, only Lillian knew he was in prison. I never visited him. I never wanted to see him again. He was sentenced to four years but McKean says he only served one third of the sentence. Apparently that is normal. I had no idea. So now he is out."

Stella dropped her bag on the dining table and sat down. "Your husband – has he tried to contact you since his release?"

Nina took her time pulling out a chair to sit opposite Stella. "I have nothing to say to Max."

That didn't answer the question, thought Stella. "What did he do, Nina?" she said, gently. "Why was your husband sent to prison?"

Nina puffed up her cheeks then slowly exhaled. "He was a thief. Because of the drugs he used to work out. Steroids. They made him insane."

"Did he inject the steroids? If he did, he knew how to use a syringe. Nina, did you tell any of this to McKean?"

Nina shook her head vigorously. "That part of my life is over. Police, Stella – the less you tell them the better."

"But what if Max..." Stella leaned in closer to Nina. "What if Max had something to do with Lillian's death?"

Nina put her hand over her mouth. One round tear rolled down her pale cheek.

"Oh Nina, I'm so sorry to talk to you like this," Stella said. "But Lillian's death is like a puzzle and McKean has to figure out where each piece fits. Tell him what you know, okay? But try not to worry – I can't believe he thinks you killed Lillian."

Nina's eyes flooded. "How could I kill Lillian? I loved her."

"Poor Nina, of course you did." Stella got up and walked around the table, leaned down to put her arm across Nina's shoulders. "We all loved Lillian. Everyone loved Lillian."

"No, no," Nina cried, "not like that." She covered her eyes with both hands.

"Well, your friendship with Lillian was special. She was obviously very fond of you." Stella rifled through her bag for a tissue and handed it to Nina.

Through gasping sobs Nina tried to speak. "Lillian and I ... different... our ... secret."

"I know," Stella said. Clearly Nina had been completely invested in caring for Lillian. Moving to that isolated cottage had probably cut her off from her previous life – particularly with her husband in prison – and now she didn't know which way to turn. Maybe being stuck with the cottage was a bit of a curse. Nina probably would rather have inherited some money to put toward a fresh start.

Nina accepted another tissue before she found her voice. "Lillian and I were more than friends Stella," she blurted with heart-rending clarity. "We were a couple. Like married people. We did not need men. You understand?"

15

MCKEAN KNEW SOMETHING WAS wrong the instant he stepped onto his back porch. The door opened to silence. The phone was on its charger, the message light off. No sound from Aiden. No sign of Miranda.

A note on the kitchen table read, "I need a break. I really hate this town. Everyone's a snob and you're always busy. You don't know what it's like to be alone with a baby 24/7. I'm taking Aiden to Ma's. Two days to get to Fort St. John – ugh. Not sure how long we'll stay. Not sure about anything, to be honnest."

Honnest. This from a woman who had dropped out of college three courses short of a diploma because she had more important things to do.

"Like what – paint your nails?" he'd said, meanly.

"Like have a baby. Now. While I'm still young."

Ben reread the note. 24/7. Hadn't he rushed home every bloody day to be with them?

He called her cell. Out of range, the phone probably turned off. He went upstairs to change out of his uniform and nearly stepped on Aiden's rubber giraffe on the bathroom floor. His eyes smarted as he picked up the little giraffe and ran it under the hot-water tap, patted it dry with a fresh washcloth. What kind of mother forgets her baby's favourite toy?

The fridge was bare, except for a bottle of ketchup, two limp carrots, half a carton of milk, and a six-pack of Heineken. He popped the tab on a beer and slumped on the living room sofa, flicked through the channels. No basketball. No hockey. A college football game with cheerleaders so young it seemed indecent to watch them. He opened the *Times* and found Stella's by-line; at least he could read the newspaper without having to listen to Miranda yap on the phone.

At seven o'clock, he crumpled his beer can and got himself a refill. Miranda would be – where? It was so like her to run off with-out even telling him where she was staying for the night. He tried to remember if the tank was full. She would run it to empty before she stopped for gas. He called her cell again but couldn't connect. A female alone with a baby, on an isolated road in the North where numerous women had disappeared – had she taken leave of her senses? No thought of him going out of his mind with worry.

Ben was halfway through his third Heineken when he remem-bered he had to get up at 4:30 a.m. to drive to Kelowna. The Chief, stupid bugger, had ordered him to take a three-day course on com-munity relations – in the middle of a goddamn murder investiga-tion.

* * *

On Wednesday, Stella felt uneasy as she cycled to work. Two days had passed since the meeting with the forensic pathologist and she still hadn't heard from Ben. Judging by what Nina told her about his questions, the syringe on the beach must have contained insu-lin. And Nina seemed convinced Ben suspected her of killing Lil-lian. Her startling admission that she and Lillian had lived together as a couple further muddied the waters.

Stella's mind reeled with possible scenarios. Had Nina killed Lil-lian in a lovers' quarrel? Had jealousy prompted Nina's estranged husband to kill Lillian? An ex-con with a history of injection drug use, Max Huber seemed a likelier suspect than his wife.

Stella didn't rule out the possibility that Nina had overreacted to Ben's enquiries. But one thing she knew for sure: there could be no backing away from the investigation now. Like it or not, she was neck deep in the whole sorry affair. And not just because she'd been close to Lillian, close enough to want justice for a woman who had spent her career seeking justice for others. No, handing over the suspicious syringe to the police had helped to put the spotlight on Nina as a prime suspect. For better or worse, Stella couldn't turn her back on her now.

She arrived at the *Times* early and flipped on the lights in the empty newsroom. A crazed, happy-face balloon floated above Jade's desk, a gift from her feckless boyfriend in honour of her kick-ass piece (his words) about a tanker that slid off a rural road and into a creek. A spill of jet fuel had contaminated the water supply of a rural community, home to several of the region's most ardent environmentalists – Christmas morning for Jade.

While her computer booted up, Stella tried again to reach Ben. The message box on his cell was full; reception at the station said he'd be out of town on a course for the rest of the week. Great timing.

Stella called the hospital and asked to speak to Dr. Antoniak but no one seemed to know where he was. The switchboard operator thought he might have gone back to Vancouver. Stella asked to be connected to the morgue. The person who answered wouldn't say whether or not Lillian Fenniwick's body had been released to the funeral home. At the funeral home, no one wanted to talk to a reporter from the *Times*, not even someone whose older boy played on the same soccer team as the undertaker's son. "How are we supposed to plan the funeral?" Stella fumed. She leaned on the receptionist until she put her through to the funeral director, who verified that Lillian's body had been released to their care and was slated for cremation the following day.

"We'd be pleased to help with the arrangements, Ms. – uh – Mosconi," he said in a flat tone. Probably checking his Facebook page as he spoke.

"Lillian's friends will take care of the arrangements," Stella said, with more confidence than she felt. At least now she knew the service could go ahead one week from Saturday, a date she had already cleared with the church. And today was the first Wednesday of the month, the usual date for book club. Why not see who was available that evening? They could check in on the funeral plans and maybe even discuss their assigned book. Inject a little normality into their lives. It might even prove a good distraction for Nina after Ben's upsetting visit. Stella called her first then emailed Vanessa, Carli, Amelie, and Nathalie to confirm the date for Lillian's funeral and suggest they meet at the yellow cottage after dinner that evening.

For the benefit of Lillian's friends and former colleagues outside of Nelson, Stella placed death notices in the *Vancouver Sun* and the *Globe and Mail*. She would write and post an obituary for Lillian in the *Times* on the following Monday.

Back to doing what she was paid for, Stella was about to ring the next contact person on her story list when Jade pulled up a chair. "Busy?" she said. "I'm swamped – a tonne of chatter on the tanker story. Just wanted to say we missed you up on the glacier last Sunday."

"The glacier?"

"You know, the big hike. Your husband's so sweet. My boyfriend talked me into going then took off with the guy in the lead. Typical. And me, I'm wearing these klutzy boots that kept breaking through the snow crust. But Joe kept me company. He was like patience incarnate."

"Well, that's Joe," Stella said.

"Yeah. Anyway, see you later." Jade tripped back to her workstation where the happy-face balloon still bobbed menacingly under a ceiling fan.

16

STELLA STEPPED OUT OF the car to find the plum tree next to Nina's cottage alive with crows, the racket, unholy. A murder of crows – the term said it all. She slammed the door but the birds stayed put.

It was Joe she was mad at. He'd known it was their regular book club night but assumed that with Lillian gone the group had folded. Then he got all bent out of shape because he wanted to go to a buddy's place after supper to change the oil in the Subaru. Stella couldn't find a sitter so he grudgingly stayed home, but his surliness rubbed off on the boys. Had it been too much to ask for five minutes alone to get ready? Matt and Nicky banged on the bathroom door, whined, and fussed, and when she let them in, jabbed at each other with toothbrushes. She nearly put out an eye with her mascara wand.

Down on the lake a houseboat blasted its horn, which sent the crows off en masse. On the porch, the tantalizing aroma of fresh-baked sausage rolls hung in the air. Sausage rolls handmade by Nina, the pastry so flaky and buttery they usually had to wipe their hands with Lillian's linen napkins to turn the pages of their books. Carli appeared in the doorway holding out a glass of wine, a generous Carli-pour of a deep, rich red. Stella took the first sip right there on the porch. "Life support," she said.

"Bad day?"

"Had a little set-to with Joe."

"Men," said Carli, rolling her eyes. A little disingenuously, Stella thought. Carli and Tim had married right out of school and still held hands in public, Nelson's favourite sweethearts. Carli's only complaint about Tim was that he was too generous with his time.

In the dining room Vanessa peeled back the plastic wrap from a tray of antipasto Nina would have put out earlier: artichoke hearts, olives, grape tomatoes, pickled asparagus, fresh mozzarella with basil. An extra-bright bullet lamp cast a circle of light over the far end of the polished oak table where a large magnifying glass lay at Lillian's empty place.

Outside Amelie and Nathalie pulled up in the Corolla.

The near perfect first moments of book club – marred by the absence of the grand dame of the group. Stella took a swipe at her eyes. "Come join us, Nina," she called toward the swing door of the kitchen.

"I wait for the sausage rolls in the oven," came the muted reply.

Vanessa gestured toward the bright lamp and magnifier and lowered her voice. "We could have done without the altar."

"*Ce n'est pas un problème,*" Nathalie said. "It's OK if Nina needs this, yes?"

"You're absolutely right, Nathalie," Vanessa said quietly. "As long as she doesn't turn the whole cottage into a shrine. No one misses Lillian more than I do. But this sort of thing isn't healthy."

Carli picked up the bottle of Merlot. "Who's for a top-up?"

While they waited for Nina, Stella did a quick check-in related to the upcoming funeral. Everyone seemed to be on task. "Nina?" she called again.

"Ya, coming."

The women began to pull out copies of *Bury Your Dead* by Louise Penny. Mysteries were a book-club tradition in the summer, but this month's title – chosen the month before Lillian's death – seemed too close to home.

"I loved this book," Nathalie said. "Right to the last page. *Un dénouement parfait.*" A perfect ending.

"You finished it?" Carli said. "My bookmark is at page seventeen."

"You started it?" Stella said.

Carli snorted at the playful jibe.

Vanessa patted Stella's arm. "You look a bit worn out, sweetie. Why don't you treat yourself to a mini-makeover? I have a new concealer at the store that would make all those little lines around your eyes disappear like magic."

"Give it a rest, Vanessa," Carli said. "Just drink your wine."

Vanessa huffed. "You're out of line, Carli. I was only trying to help one of my favourite people."

Stella resisted saying that if she'd wanted to hear people bicker, she could have stayed home. It was a relief when Nina backed through the swing door with a tray of steaming sausage rolls.

Both Nathalie and Amelie had read the book cover-to-cover. Nathalie, a history buff, led off with a vivid overview of the setting. Amelie, bless her, had brought a list of study questions. But most of the discussion centred on the main character, Chief Inspector Armand Gamache. Tall. Elegant. Kind. Selfless. Utterly devoted to his wife. Nathalie admitted to being in love with him, seriously in love, mainly due to Gamache's exceptional capacity for compassion, not only for family and close friends, and not just for likeable, appealing people either.

Amelie said, "*Alors, Nathalie. Une bonne lecture* but not your usual read, *oui?* I know you as a fantasy girl."

Carli said, "Face it. We're all fantasy girls. Gamache is too good to be true."

With that the evening came to a close, having at least provided Stella with a brief respite from a real-life murder mystery.

* * *

Despite her frustrations with Joe, Stella was happy to get home after what turned out to be a surprisingly tense book club meeting. After she'd put away her coat, Joe showed her an old photograph that had fluttered to the floor when he was rummaging through his climbing gear on the uppermost shelf of their bedroom closet. It was a black-and-white snapshot of four men at a golf course. Snow-capped peaks in the background made it pretty clear the setting was the local course in uphill Nelson.

They sat together at the kitchen table and tried to figure out which of the four was Will Irwin, the original owner of their cabin – Stella was certain he was one of them. They had met Will only briefly, first when he showed them the place and then on moving day. But Stella had taken an instant liking to him. The shortest man in the photo, second from the left, had the same warm smile as Will. Joe thought he would have been taller, even taking into account the aging process. He had Will pegged as the fourth man. Stella tacked the snapshot up on the fridge with a magnet that read *Kiss the Cook*. It occurred to her it might be fun to drop by Will's retirement home some time and surprise him with the old picture.

After their earlier argument, the photo had been a good ice-breaker. Fighting with her husband reminded Stella too much of her parents' battles, not that she considered herself anything like her temperamental mother, and Joe certainly wasn't passive like her dad. Later that night she almost turned to Joe, but something held her back. The thing was, she wanted to want him, wanted to feel wild with desire, but she didn't want to pretend. She blamed her mood on her period being overdue, which made her feel bloated and frumpy. The upheaval of the past week had likely messed with her hormones.

* * *

On the way out the next morning, Stella impulsively popped the photo of the golfers into her bag. At work, she found herself thinking about Will Irwin more than once. By the time her lunch break rolled around she couldn't resist taking a quick ride up the hill to Will's new home at Mountain Lake Centre. He greeted her like an old friend.

Will was still quite independent; his unit in the assisted living wing included a bed-sitting room, private bathroom, and kitchenette. He insisted on making Stella a cheese and bologna sandwich and a cup of orange pekoe tea.

A humungous mounted rainbow trout shared a wall with framed photos of Will's family members at various ages and stages. Before Stella brought out the snapshot of the golfers, she asked Will to tell her who was who in his photo gallery. There was a daughter and son-in-law and two married grandsons, all based in Kelowna. His wife, now deceased, had been photographed as a young nurse with a bouquet of roses and later as a beaming grandmother cradling a small toothless bundle. "I have boxes and boxes of pictures," Will said. "Couldn't begin to hang them all in this little place."

"Well I have another photo that must have slipped out of one of your boxes. I'm sure I recognize you in this one."

He reached for his glasses. "Yep, that's me all right, second from the left." Stella wouldn't tell Joe, but she was pleased her guess had been right. "Now who's that first fellow?" Will continued. "Doesn't look familiar. Could've been someone we pulled in to make a foursome. Next to me that's Vern Levitt. And beside him, that's his brother John."

"Levitt. Are Vern and John related to Vanessa? Do you know Vanessa, from the drugstore downtown?"

"Sure I do – I've known Vanessa since she was a little girl. I still go into Levitt's once in a while to say hello. Vern was her father, John her uncle. Both gone now." Will shook his head. "What about your parents, Stella? Are they still around? Would I have known your father?"

"I lost touch with my dad a long time ago," Stella said. "He'd be seventy now. My mom and her current husband live in Florida. Mine isn't one of those old Nelson families. We moved here from Vancouver when I was three. I guess I had a decent childhood compared to some. My parents' divorce was another matter."

"Tough on kids when the parents split up."

"You lose your mooring," Stella said. Interesting choice of words – had she ever felt secure? "Anyway, I hate to eat and run but I better get back to work. Thanks for lunch. I just wanted to make sure you got that photo back. It was good to see you again."

"Good to see you too, Stella. Don't be a stranger now. Come by again."

* * *

Friday after babysitting, Zoe DeLuca cashed her first pay cheque and headed down Baker Street toward La Belle Femme, the town's only lingerie shop. Now that she had a real job she could afford to replace the lame bras her mom bought her at Walmart, plain white with cups that puckered – the sort of thing a nun probably wore under her habit. The lingerie shop was the last place she would have expected to find Kieran Corcoran, but there he was, hanging out with two girls from high school just outside the store.

"Oh, hey, Zoe," he said.

"Hey, Kieran" was all she could manage before she went inside, her face all hot.

As the door closed behind her, she heard one of the high school girls simper, "Hey, Kieran."

The two girls followed her into the store but Kieran, thank you God, stayed outside. Through the window Zoe could see him sitting on the edge of a planter in front of the shop. She put on a bored expression and began to browse. When the older girls drifted to the back of the store, Zoe asked the saleswoman if she could try on a bra.

The carpeted area at the back featured a pink velvet lounge, a three-way mirror, and two curtained change rooms, side-by-side. The high school girls opted to share one. Zoe made sure her change-room curtain was fully drawn before she took off any clothes. The bra she had chosen was made of pale green silky fabric with cream-coloured lace trim and a butterfly-shaped clasp in front. But no matter how she adjusted the straps there was room to spare in the firm, underwired cups. "Knock, knock." The clerk had come to check the fit. Zoe opened the curtain about one centimetre. "Oh-oh," said the clerk. "Don't think I have that in an A cup. Let me bring you something with more shaping."

She could hear the high school girls mocking each other about who had bigger boobs and now one of them said something about training bras and the other spluttered and snickered.

The clerk returned with three choices. One of them fit Zoe perfectly although it was plain white without a scrap of lace and cost forty-five dollars plus tax. She made her purchase and slunk out of the store ahead of the others, relieved that Kieran had left his post out front.

* * *

Carli DeLuca didn't say a word when her daughter flounced into the house with a glossy pink La Belle Femme bag and disappeared into her bedroom. Carli had a more serious concern, namely that Henry Sutton seemed to have dropped off the face of the earth. Stella hadn't been able to reach him and Vanessa was maddeningly vague about his present locale. The bigger issue was the simultaneous disappearance of a whole whack of money that belonged to Carli. She made herself a cup of lemon tea and took it to her little office. But even gazing at the restful watercolours by her favourite local artist didn't help. She carried her tea to the daybed, put up her feet, and tried to figure out what to do about Henry Sutton.

A few months back when the self-described life coach crashed their book club, she and her friends had lined up to throw money at him. Normally Carli was shrewder than that; she routinely followed reports on the *Financial Times* website – watched the stock market, checked out the DOW Jones, read all the boring little numbers. How else to maintain common ground with her genius husband? She had told Tim all about Sutton's scheme to invest in home foreclosures in the States, including his claim to know a way people could stay in their homes after the sale. Tim had been sceptical from the outset – what rational person wouldn't be? But he saw no harm in dabbling. If things went pear-shaped it would be a lesson learned. They wouldn't miss a few hundred bucks. All fine and good had Carli left it at that, but she hadn't.

One night she and Lillian had gone out for a meal, and after a couple of vodka tonics and a good bottle of Pinot Grigio they decided to help Henry Sutton save a few more householders from themselves, pledging to cash in some mutual funds and raise a hundred grand between them. After all, the original five-hundred-dollar fund from the book club had doubled in no time, and on Sutton's advice, several people from Lillian's church seemed to be making money hand over fist.

Compassionate *bloody* investing – how could she have let herself get sucked in? It wasn't long before Sutton's reports stopped showing up in her inbox. Carli searched the Internet for information and came up empty. When he breezed back to Nelson a couple of weeks back, Lillian suggested a dinner date to find out, in her words, what the heck he'd been up to. But Lillian had insisted on handling the situation herself. She didn't think it was wise for the two of them – her and Carli – to gang up on Henry and possibly frighten him off.

Carli still kicked herself for letting Lillian meet with him alone. The so-called showdown with Sutton didn't yield any answers on the money and only made him harder to reach. To top it off, when Lillian called the house to try to get Tim's advice, Carli screwed that up too. Her nerves were totally shot. She couldn't help wondering if the whole thing had been too much for Lillian, maybe bad enough to bring on a heart attack. Carli needed to know what happened. She was tempted to launch a complaint with Ben McKean but cops are typically so tight-lipped. Stella seemed to have an in with their old classmate, even though she kept quiet about it. Maybe Stella would be the best person to approach Ben.

17

IT WAS ANOTHER SATURDAY morning at the Mosconi cabin. Stella and Joe, still in pyjamas, lingered over a second cup of coffee while the boys watched cartoons. "No soccer today," Stella said. "What should we do for fun?"

Joe said, "Count me out. I have to go to the school to mark assignments and get the results into the system. The seniors need their projects back to study for finals."

"Poor you. How long will it take?"

Joe shrugged. "Hard to say. If I get done in time, I wouldn't mind hiking up Elephant Mountain, shake out the cobwebs."

"I guess we could meet you at the trailhead," Stella said. "Matt's been hounding me to go on a proper hike."

"Like I say, I'm not sure when I'll be finished. Wouldn't want to keep you and the boys waiting."

Stella let Matt and Nicky watch one more TV show then bundled them into the Pathfinder to go visit Nina again. Nina needed her friends after all that business with the needle on the beach and cops crawling around the house .

On the ferry Stella bought the boys cups of hot chocolate and amused them with a made-up story about a mother bear and her two cubs. One of the cubs was a bit of a daredevil, the other small and timid. Matt and Nicky drank their hot chocolate and laughed at the antics of the mischievous bear cubs and their frazzled mother.

At the yellow cottage, the Range Rover wasn't in its usual place and Nina didn't answer the door. Stella didn't want to turn around after dragging the boys across the lake yet again. She looked for an opening in the woods and suggested the three of them hike up the hill behind the cottage while they waited for Nina to return. "Maybe we'll see a bear," Matt said hopefully, prompting Nicky to reach for his mom's hand.

She continued the bear story as the three of them bushwhacked through the forest. "One day a little girl got lost on a walk like this," she said. "The mother bear and cubs noticed her from a branch high up on a tree. The larger, braver bear cub wanted to show the girl the way back to the beach. But the mother bear said he was too noisy and rambunctious – he might frighten the little girl."

Matt chuckled knowingly. "She might run the wrong way and get even more lost," he said.

In the end, the quiet little bear saved the day. Taking care to stay hidden, he picked flowers and scattered them along the path. The little girl followed the trail of flowers back to the beach and was reunited with her family.

"I have to pee," Matt said.

"Go for it," Stella said, pointing to the bush.

"You can't watch. I need privacy," he said. Stella told him to walk a distance away counting backwards from ten loud enough for her and Nicky to hear. When he got to number one he was to stop and do his business. While Matt was doing his thing, Stella and Nicky sat down on a large moss-covered rock to wait. They were trying to figure out where a bird song was coming from when Matt bellowed.

Stella grabbed Nicky's hand and sprinted in the direction of her older son's voice. In front of a rough shack, Matt lay squirming in an ash-filled fire pit. He was covered in soot and howling his lungs out. One leg was tangled in a chain connected to a fine-mesh screen suspended over the pit.

"It's okay, Matt," Stella said. "We'll get you out of there. What kind of crazy contraption –?" She quickly scanned the strange tumble-down shack. It had to be about a hundred years old but it was clear from the fire pit that someone had recently been using it. For starters, the pit contained charred tin cans, none of them rusty. A new-looking hatchet was embedded in a chopping block and fresh kindling was scattered on the ground. A reasonably clean towel hung over a pole suspended between two trees.

Stella knew right away who had been there. Max Huber, Nina's husband – it had to be him. Who else would be squatting in a rotten old shack so close to the yellow cottage? Now Nina's evasiveness made sense. Max must have confronted her. And Stella had blundered into his camp with her two sons. "Come on, Matt," she said, her voice remarkably steady. "I'll give you a hand."

"I can't move," he moaned. "I think my leg's broken."

Nicky started to cry.

"Your leg's likely not broken, honey," Stella said. "Where does it hurt?"

"All over." He clutched his left ankle. "Maybe you should call for a helicopter – or cut down branches and drag me through the woods." Stella mentally calculated how long it would take to get an ambulance from either Nelson or Creston, for paramedics to work their way up the hill. A quick glance at her phone showed sketchy reception. She felt Matt's left foot and ankle and worked her hands up his calf and shin and upper leg without eliciting any shrieks of pain. She helped him stand up, put his arm around her neck, encouraged him to try to put some weight on the sore leg. "I can't – it hurts too much," he whimpered. "You might have to leave me here and go for help."

"No," sobbed Nicky. "Don't leave him, Mommy. Phone the ambulance."

Cold sweat trickled from Stella's armpits and down the small of her back. "Matt's going to be okay, honey," she crooned.

And then a loud thrashing in the woods almost stopped her heart. An unrecognizable sound escaped her throat.

"Mommy!" Nicky clutched at her arm.

A stag with a massive rack of antlers zigzagged through the clearing.

In a single bound, Matt cleared the fire pit as the stag disappeared into the forest.

Almost faint with relief, Stella said, "Let's go, boys." She looked around to get her bearings, knowing how easy it would be to take a wrong turn in her addled state of mind.

"Are we lost?" Nicky asked, his voice still shaky.

"Can you hear the creek?" Stella said. "As long as we can hear the creek, we're not lost. We'll keep that sound to our right and follow it all the way to the bottom." After his miraculous recovery, Matt found a long pole to whack brush out of their way, and the three of them hiked down the hill with the roar of Give Out Creek as their compass.

Back at the cottage, there was still no sign of the Range Rover. Nina hadn't returned and Stella wasn't inclined to stick around and wait for her. "Aw," Matt whinged, "Nina would give us treats."

"Get in the car," Stella barked, and both boys meekly complied. She climbed behind the wheel, locked the doors, and started her engine. With a three-bar signal on her phone now, she texted Ben McKean: *Found evidence Nina's ex-con husband Max Huber is in the area. Call me.*

That should get his attention.

* * *

"Hey."

Nina started at the voice of Kieran Corcoran. He had come up behind her as she unloaded groceries from the back of the Range Rover, her Range Rover. It still felt strange to think of the car as hers.

The boy stood waiting for her to speak but she saw no need to respond to "Hey." Young people in Canada do not greet their elders with respect – or even say hello. And this one, his eyes darted here and there. Drugs. She knew the signs. And she knew why he had come. He wanted money. Lillian always paid him too much.

Finally, he spoke again. "So, you want any help? I could cut the grass maybe?"

"No, thank you," Nina said. "I manage fine."

"But see, I owe you. The other lady overpaid last time. Two twenties stuck together. She didn't see too well, did she?"

Nina wanted him gone. She hated the way he loomed over her, big hands and feet, those shifty eyes. But he insisted. He said he felt bad about the extra money. If he felt so bad, why not return it? He had probably already spent it. His guilty conscience had brought him back. What else did this boy have to feel guilty about?

Nina relented and told him he could burn the trash. There was still a pile of dry branches from when she and Lillian pruned the red osier dogwoods. The boy could burn them in the metal drum behind the shed. Then they would be done with each other. Nina went inside with the groceries and left him to it.

* * *

Max hiked back up to his shack weighed down with several tins of Campbell's Pork and Beans, a couple loaves of bread, a nice little mickey of Canadian Club and – *what the hell*? His fire pit looked like a herd of elk had run through it. Ash everywhere. Grill kicked over. Campfire screen off-kilter. Max went inside to take off his pack and poured a healthy glass of rye.

Only an animal would make a mess like that. A bear? Max had been careful not to cook meat right on the grill but a bear had a good sniffer, and shitty eyesight. Bears were known to stumble into things.

Max refilled his glass. He'd meant to go easy on the rye, but hell…

Could be a deer had done it – or two deer chasing each other through his camp. There were deer everywhere in these woods. No sign of people around. Teenagers would have pinched the hatchet and trashed the place. He grabbed the mickey and sat on a stump to pour himself another snort. Too bad he didn't still have the old man's revolver.

18

WHEN STELLA'S PHONE RANG Sunday evening the call display read Nelson Police Department. Ben McKean had seen her text about Max Huber and wanted to meet as early as possible the next morning. He suggested Lakeside Park, at a bench up behind the float.

Ben was leaning against a fender of his cruiser when Stella arrived the next morning. The proposed bench was occupied by two overly affectionate teens so they crossed the park to find another place to sit. Perspiring from her bike ride, Stella pulled on the sky-blue vest she carried in her handlebar bag. The weather was crisp and clear. A doubles scull cut through the surface of the still lake. Carli's husband Tim DeLuca jogged past and grunted a greeting. Stella called good morning to his back.

Ben got straight to the point. "The syringe found on the beach contained insulin. Not only that, Antoniak found an injection spot on the body with traces of the drug in the surrounding tissue. Lillian likely died from an insulin overdose, which puts her diabetic maid Nina squarely in the frame for murder."

"Wait wait wait," said Stella. "I'm not surprised to hear about the insulin. Nina already told me about your visit. But I don't believe she would have hurt Lillian. You saw my text. Someone is living up behind Lillian's place and I'd bet money it's Max Huber. He's just out of jail and Nina told me he was a a drug-user. I think he's already confronted her, although she wouldn't tell me about it."

Ben's shoulder grazed hers as he shifted on the bench. His after-shave smelled like the forest. "She wouldn't talk to me about him either." At Stella's look of surprise, he said, "Yeah, I knew about Huber. Popped up on our database. He was released from Matsqui about two weeks before the murder. As I said, your friend Nina was evasive when I asked about him. Who knows, they might have acted together, the housekeeper and her ex-con husband."

Stella shook her head. "I can't see it. First of all, they're estranged. I think she's afraid of him."

"Doesn't mean she wouldn't collude with him, or follow his orders. For now, let's put aside her feelings for her husband and talk about motive. Did either of them stand to gain by Lillian Fenniwick's death?"

"Oh, man." Stella ran her hands over her face. "Nina stood to gain, all right."

Ben leaned back on the bench. "I'm listening."

"Nina inherited the cottage and the car, a newish Range Rover. She showed me a copy of Lillian's will."

Ben whistled. "We'll have to confirm that the will is legit. Does Fenniwick have a lawyer in town?"

"Arthur Nugent. His office is on Baker Street. But there's more." Stella took a breath. "Look, I'm about to betray a major confidence, which I wouldn't do if it wasn't relevant."

Ben waited.

"Nina and Lillian lived together as a couple. Nina was in love with Lillian."

"Hold on," Ben said as he shifted upright. "Huber was her maid. Who says they were involved?"

"Nina. She told me last week. I was as shocked as you – I never picked up on that vibe between them. But if they were together, the inheritance makes a lot more sense."

"By that reasoning, she might have claimed they were a couple so no one would look too closely at the will. If she and Fenniwick really were an item, why would they have kept it under wraps?"

"Because it was no one's business but their own? I don't know. I mean Lillian had gay friends. I can't see why she would have been secretive about her sexual orientation. Thing is, Nina seems truly miserable without her. More like she's lost a partner than an employer."

"Partners are often the prime suspects. But I still need to talk to Max, the estranged husband. A big inheritance might be all the incentive he needed. Get rid of Fenniwick and he gets back his wife along with a valuable lakefront property. We're talking about a guy convicted for attempted armed robbery. Who knows what he's capable of?"

"True, but did he know about the inheritance? The will Nina showed me was recent, signed only a few months ago when he was still at Matsqui. I got the sense she had nothing to do with him while he was in prison."

"He was convicted only a little more than a year ago though," Ben said. "That's a blink of an eye in the context of a marriage of any significant length. You say Fenniwick's will is recent? That alone is suspicious. Apart from his being locked up, what else did Nina tell you about Max?"

"Not much, except the part about the drugs. The syringe on the beach could have been his."

"Any reason to suspect he used insulin? "

"Nina said he took steroids, supposedly for bodybuilding. But insulin can help build and maintain muscle. I read about it on a couple of bodybuilder sites. Sounds dicey, but insulin is legal and it's easy to come by."

"Particularly when your wife is diabetic. So, we've come full circle. Anyhow, thanks – you've done good work. I'll check out the shack."

"I could take you there."

Ben shook his head. "Stay clear of the area – that's an order." His smile softened the command. "Seriously though, I don't want you to risk crossing paths with Max Huber." He pulled out a notebook. "Okay, ma'am, let's have the directions to the alleged hideout." Stella closed her eyes and called to mind each landmark she and the boys had passed; it was surprising how many details she could summon under questioning. But then she had paid attention to avoid getting lost. When she opened her eyes, Ben was getting to his feet. After a quick farewell, he cut across the park to his car. She remained on the bench for a moment, wondering, *what just happened?* Police officers were usually cagey around reporters. Things had started out that way with Ben. But something seemed to have shifted, and Stella wasn't sure why.

* * *

McKean's boss gazed out his office window while he received an update on the murder investigation. Was he keeping an eye on traffic? Watching planes take off on the airstrip down by the lake? He was always staring out that window. But then again talking at the Chief's back was no worse than speaking to his face.

Without warning, he swung around and cut off McKean mid-sentence. "I want a result, dammit. I don't need to remind you we're a small department. Your colleagues have been covering for you while you're off on this job. It's not sustainable. The town is talking too. You can have Eberly for a day or two to wrap this up, but that's it. We've got a drug bust about to go down out near Ymir. I can't spare any more resources. Let's do it. Clean this up."

Corporal Ray Eberly, a mouth with a badge, was not McKean's favourite person. But he would take any help he could get. He would need backup to flush out Max Huber, if Huber really was the squatter in the shack above the yellow cottage.

* * *

The Osprey's captain held the ferry for McKean, a courtesy he acknowledged with a wave toward the wheelhouse as he drove aboard. Other passengers got out of their cars to photograph the scenery – the real ospreys squawking on their twiggy nests, pleasure boats criss-crossing the lake, in the background the highest peaks still capped with snow. McKean stayed put in his car and used the time to return phone calls. Eberly was to meet him near the bridge at Give Out Creek, as close to Nina Huber's cottage as they could get without announcing their presence. The plan was to hike up the mountainside and surprise whoever had set up shop in that backwoods shack.

McKean got there first and reviewed Stella's directions. He looked around at the rhododendron bushes growing all over the place and found the one she'd noted on the edge of the property, deep pink in colour and the size of a single-car garage. Next to it, a narrow opening led into the forest, the brush underfoot slightly trampled. Stella had an eye for detail all right – the reporter in her.

Eberly would be on his way from the nearby town of Creston where he represented the department on a high school grad committee. McKean looked at his watch, checked his gun. From the distance came a faint drone.

The siren got louder.

McKean wanted to punch something. He got on the radio and ordered the moron to go silent. But no doubt the damage had been done.

* * *

At the faint wail of a siren, Nina turned down the volume on the radio. The ambulance or cop car, whatever it was, was getting closer. Was there a fire? Then, as Lillian might have said, the penny dropped. A police car: Sergeant McKean was on his way to arrest her.

Heart racing, Nina pulled back the curtains. She wondered if McKean would give her time to collect a few things and put the house in order. Or would he just shove her into the patrol car, pushing down her head the way they did on television.

Nina reached up and touched the framed photo of Lillian on the mantle. If only the smiling face that stared back could tell her what to do.

The noise stopped.

Could she be mistaken? The thump, thump, thump of her heart made it hard to hear anything else. She left the photo and slipped out to the porch.

Nothing.

On the lake, a motorboat zoomed past. Then, silence.

* * *

After that fouled-up robbery landed him in prison, Max Huber vowed to lay off the sauce. But now only a few weeks after being sprung he'd already polished off a whole mickey of rye in one go. He knew he should eat, but he didn't feel like fixing the mesh gizmo over the fire pit just to heat a lousy can of beans. That frigging bear or deer or whatever it was sure had made a mess of his camp.

Max stepped into the woods to take a leak and heard a whining noise in the distance. His alcohol-soaked brain took a few seconds to register the sound. A siren. *Son of a bitch* – they were coming to get him.

That sobered him up fast. Max tossed his gear into a pack then crashed through the brush to the road to thumb a ride to anywhere.

A bus ticket to his buddy's place in Abbotsford would almost bank-rupt him. Better to stay around here, close to Nina. The sooner he was back with her, the sooner his cash-flow problems would be history.

His ride dropped him outside a run-down motel and RV park where a woman was hanging laundry on a clothesline. Blousy fig-ure. Shapeless clothing. Three inches of grey roots showed in her lank, black hair. Max wandered over. "Hi there," he said. "I hope you won't think I'm too forward, but you remind me of an old girl-friend. Not old. I shoulda said ex-girlfriend. You're not Betty, are you?"

Through a mouthful of clothespins, the woman snorted. "I'm not Betty."

"Well, it was a long shot. Sorry to bother you. Have a good one... It's just – damn but you remind me of Betty. Pardon my French."

"Oh, yeah?" She picked up a sheet and wrestled it onto the line.

"Betty was a fine woman." Max slipped off his backpack and set it on the ground. "A real sweetheart. The one that got away."

The woman looked him up and down. "I have a pot of coffee on," she said. "If you want to sit at the picnic table, I'll bring you a cup. I'm Wanda. And you are –?"

"Max. Pleased to make your acquaintance, Wanda. A cup of cof-fee would sure hit the spot."

* * *

Eberly was full of excuses when he pulled up at the bridge over Give Out Creek. "Not my fault," he said. "I was running late in Creston. Had to light'em up to get here in time."

McKean told him to shut up and stay close as he struck off past the rhododendron. Staying within earshot of the creek, they climbed over a branched windfall and jumped a minor stream to follow the rough directions Stella had passed on. McKean pictured Stella and her sons scampering along, chattering happily.

Behind him, Eberly sounded breathless as they climbed the steep path. McKean quickened his pace.

Thirty minutes later Eberly was panting when they reached the moss-covered rock shaped like a Volkswagen Beetle. McKean gestured for him to angle off to the left while he proceeded around a cluster of pine trees. He came out at the windowless back wall of a shack and slipped around to one side. Eberly stood directly opposite, partly shielded by brush. At McKean's signal, he charged forward, his gun drawn, then flattened himself next to the front door.

McKean shouted, "Police. Come out with your hands up."

No sound from inside the shack.

He ducked under a front window and nodded to Eberly, who immediately rushed forward and kicked open the shack door holding his gun at shoulder height. After a beat, he said, "Nobody home."

McKean picked up an empty rye bottle. "Your siren gave him a nice head start."

They checked the shelves. A few tins of food, a frying pan with a skim of fat. Before McKean could stop him, Eberly stuck a finger into the grease and licked it. "Not rancid," he said.

"Yo, Sherlock," McKean said. "Keep your hands to yourself. This could be a crime scene."

"Doesn't look like it," Eberly said. "And if our squatter used a pack to carry his supplies, it's gone now. He must have split."

McKean shook his head in disgust. "And if he has half a brain he won't be back."

19

ZOE HADN'T SEEN KIERAN Corcoran since Friday when he was outside the lingerie shop with those two slutty high school girls. Boys were attracted to girls like that – they couldn't help it. Zoe had tormented herself for days with the image of Kieran dating some skank, while she was totally forgotten. So when he appeared on the beach outside the Mosconis' cabin on Wednesday, she felt a little flutter. And the flutter pulsed through her entire body when he said he needed to talk.

In Zoe's experience, if someone needs to talk, you need privacy. Matt and Nicky were fooling around on the upside-down canoe, so after reminding them to stay out of the lake – strict orders from their mom – she invited Kieran inside for a glass of lemonade.

He drank it in about two gulps. "Thing is I need to tell someone about what happened on Sunday and I wasn't sure who else to tell," he said. "I was over at Fenniwick's house to see if her house-keeper had any work for me." Zoe lifted the pitcher of lemonade and poured a refill while she waited for him to go on. "Last time Ms. Fenniwick overpaid me and I never said anything. She could afford it, no sweat. But now she's dead and I figured ripping off a dead person has to be bad karma. Anyway, on Sunday when I go over to try and help out, the housekeeper gets all wigged out, acts like she wants rid of me. I keep on asking, so finally she says I can burn the trash. Like she's doing me a freaking favour. I don't know why I'm telling you this. It's stupid."

"No no, it's cool. Then what happened?"

"There's this metal drum for burning shit? I look inside it and there's a sweater in the bottom – a brown sweater." He looked at Zoe as if he expected her to gasp or something but she didn't know what to say.

"Did someone drop it there or –"

"Zoe. The sweater was Ms. Fenniwick's. Why would anyone want to burn it? Who burns a sweater?"

"I don't know, maybe someone just accidentally –"

A woman screamed.

Zoe and Kieran raced outside.

The red canoe was out on the lake a few metres from shore. Matt and Nicky were both in it. No paddles. Stella's bike lay on its side in the middle of the driveway and she was down at the beach screeching at the boys to sit still. Matt kept shouting some garbled explanation. Nicky was crying. When Zoe and Kieran got to the beach, Stella yelled at them too. "What the hell is going on? Where were you?"

Cool as can be, Kieran kicked off his shoes and waded into the water. He swam out to the canoe, put his shoulder to the stern, and kicked. As the canoe inched toward shore Matt yelled, "Faster." Stella told him to keep quiet. Still in her bike shoes, she waded toward the canoe saying, "Be careful, be careful," maybe to Kieran, maybe to everyone. Zoe waded in too and steadied the bow when Kieran was close enough to stand up in the shallows. He helped Matt get out and Stella grabbed Nicky, who was still crying. She cried too.

Zoe wanted to die right then and there.

* * *

Carli poured herself a glass of Chardonnay and stepped onto her capacious deck cantilevered over Kootenay Lake. A breeze put a chop on the water and riffled the surrounding trees. The *whoosh, whoosh* of the trembling aspens soothed her. Carli pulled her yoga jacket tighter across her chest and stretched out on her favourite lounge chair. With her almost-perfect life about to unravel, she felt it important to look after herself.

That afternoon she had endured a frustrating conversation with Vanessa, who seemed hell-bent on running interference for Henry Sutton. Vanessa claimed he had closed his email account and had yet to replace his Canadian phone. *Quel surprise*. No doubt his new phone would be a throwaway, not easily traced. Vanessa was gaga over the man, but if she believed the feeling was mutual she was dreaming in Technicolor. Money was the only thing that gave Henry Sutton a hard-on.

After the call to Vanessa, Carli gave in and told her husband about the fifty grand she had dropped on Sutton's harebrained investment scheme. Naturally they had their worst fight ever. In the end she knew she had to suck it up – what else could she do? She'd screwed up big-time.

And just when it seemed her world couldn't get any blacker, Stella called. She was very disappointed in Zoe – that was how she phrased it. Stella went on and on and Carli didn't interrupt, but she kept thinking: *Zoe? My Zoe?*

By strange coincidence, a short time earlier, Carli had left a message on Stella's voicemail. She must have rung while the whole debacle at the beach was in full swing.

Tim would soon be back with their wayward daughter and Carli craved a smoke. But she didn't want to have a cigarette in her hand when she read Zoe the riot act. She went inside and topped up her wine.

* * *

Stella's feelings ran the gamut from humiliated to downright silly. When she found the boys floating away in the canoe, no babysitter in sight, she'd lost it. Even when Matt and Nicky were safely on shore, she bawled out Zoe then raved over the phone at Carli, a friend kind enough to remain calm and reasonable throughout the tirade. When Tim arrived to pick up his apologetic daughter he took the high road too. She wished Joe were home. Why did he have so many meetings? He had never been that busy with work when they lived on the Coast.

But why blame Joe? He was adapting. Throwing himself into his job, tuning in to every opportunity Nelson had to offer. She would do well to follow his example. Not to make excuses, but her period was still overdue, most likely because of stress. A pregnancy was out of the question. Stella was careful. She'd always been careful.

And denial is not just a river in Egypt.

It wasn't until after the boys were in bed that she checked her phone and discovered Carli's earlier message. Taking a deep breath, she punched in the number for the DeLuca residence.

"You okay?" Carli never bothered to say hello.

"I'm okay. Except for embarrassing myself this afternoon. Sorry, Carl. I lost my mind for a while there."

"Yeah, well, don't worry about it. I'm not going to make things any better. You'd better sit down." Stella could hear the click of a lighter through the receiver. "I think I might be responsible for Lillian's death."

"*What?*"

A monumental crash brought Stella to her feet. "Carli, just a sec." In the boys' room, a four-drawer oak dresser lay on its side. "You guys are so in trouble," Stella said, yelling at them for the second time that day. "Leave it and get back to bed – I said *leave it.*" She left them shouting blame at each other and carried the phone back to the front room.

Carli continued as if uninterrupted. "Remember when we met on the bench in front of your office just after Lillian died? A few days later on the ferry, you asked if I'd had something else to tell you that day. I lied. I guess you'd call it a lie of omission. I didn't give you the backstory behind Lillian's attempt to contact Tim." She paused, probably to exhale a puff of smoke. "Lillian and I had a side investment from the rest of the book club with Henry Sutton. The deal went south. Stell, we lost about a hundred grand."

"A hundred grand."

"Thank you for your restraint," Carli said. "Look, the whole point of the dinner with Sutton was for Lillian to pin him down about our losses. When she tried to reach Tim, it must have been to discuss what went down at that meeting. I put off giving him the message because I hadn't told him about the small fortune I'd squandered. By the next day it was too late. Lillian was dead."

"And remember she also tried to contact me that day," Stella said. "Left a message on my work phone. I don't know why she didn't try my cell."

"Lillian hated cell phones – didn't you notice? Old school, I guess. If someone's not home sitting by the landline, don't intrude. Whatever, the point is she tried to reach both you and Tim. I assume the rowboat fiasco started out as a plan to give Vanessa a heads up – we all know how Vanessa feels about Sutton. Lillian probably wanted to soften the blow, bring her flowers, yada, yada. Tim would have talked her out of going – that's why I feel so bad now about not telling him. Lillian ended up dead and the whole thing could have been prevented. And another thing Stell, I can't help wondering – what if she didn't have a heart attack? What if Sutton killed her? Lillian knew more about his operations than anyone in town. In the end, she might have found out stuff we'll never know."

Stella let the comment about the heart attack go. Clearly, the fewer people who knew about the insulin connection the better. "God, Carli," she said. "That's a leap. Henry Sutton, a killer? I don't know what to say except don't blame yourself. Lillian always did what she wanted to, right?"

"Do you think I should call McKean?"

"Yes. Tell him everything you told me. Call him right now. I'll give you his cell number."

"You have his cell number?"

"Never mind. Long story," Stella said. "Just call him."

After she hung up, Stella trundled into the bathroom and stripped down for a soak in the tub. The slight swell of her belly she put down to bloating. But when she towelled off, her breasts felt slightly tender. Where on earth would they put another baby?

* * *

It was Thursday morning, twelve hours after Carli's call. Stella hadn't let her phone out of sight all night. She'd slept with it. Propped it on the soap dispenser in the shower. Carried it in the back pocket of her bike shirt when she rode to work. But so far, no further word from Carli. Well, maybe she hadn't been able to connect with Ben – he wasn't the easiest guy in the world to reach by phone.

Halfway through a meeting with Patrick at the paper, Stella received a text from Carli: *McK's a good listener. Call u in 1 min.*

The morning had begun as a slow news day and Stella had just pitched a series of interviews with Nelson pioneers, starting with Will Irwin, the previous owner of her cabin. Patrick was in a testy mood. Probably sleep deprived again. "Pioneers? You kidding me? Definitely not a grabber." he said.

"Fine," Stella said. "If a knife fight breaks out at City Hall I'll cover that first. Patrick, c'mon. Readers like good-news stories too."

"So they say, but they actually read stuff about crime and misfortune. Even reports on fender benders and out-of-control house parties boost our ratings. Human nature."

She threw up her hands. "You're the boss, but there's no harm in me taking my lunch break up at Mountain Lake. At the very least, Will Irwin will make me a sandwich." Her phone vibrated. Carli. "Sorry, I got to take this call."

Stella darted to the restroom. "What'd he say?"

"He'll follow up with Sutton. I feel better now. McKean is so, I don't know, sincere. I don't really remember him from school. Do you?"

"A bit. He strikes me as a good cop."

"He seems to like you too."

Stella resisted asking what Ben had said about her. "Well, we're colleagues. We respect each other."

"I'm teasing, Stell. Don't get all prissy on me."

At noon Stella cycled up to Mountain Lake Centre. It was only her second visit to Will Irwin's retirement home but again he made her feel right at home. She settled comfortably at his small table while he brought out the fixings for cheese and bologna sandwiches. With Lillian's upcoming memorial top of mind, Stella asked if he had known her.

"Never met the lady," he said. "Although I was sorry to hear she passed. I read in the paper the police found her in her rowboat. Do they know what happened?"

Stella hesitated. "Still investigating."

Will sat with that a moment. "I knew her late husband, Clark," he said. "I should say I knew of him, met him once or twice. His father golfed up at the club when he was in town. The Fenniwicks were summer people. Built the cottage out by Give Out Creek. Well, you'd know that."

"I met Lillian long after Clark died," Stella said, "so I don't know much about him. Even less about his parents."

"Clark was a bit of a playboy in his early years. Kootenay Lake's answer to *The Great Gatsby*." Will grinned. "As I said, the Fenniwicks were strictly summer people. Came up from Vancouver on the first of July, left at the end of August. At some point, the parents stopped coming, but Clark remained a fixture on the summer scene. Threw lots of parties – talk of the town. This is all hearsay, Stella. What do I know?"

"Clark must have put all that behind him when he married Lillian. I can't see her with a playboy. She wasn't the partying type."

"Well, you knew your friend. And you know what they say about the love of a good woman."

Back at work Stella was gripped by abdominal cramps all afternoon. Either the bologna Will served had been off, or her overdue period was finally about to start. She said a little prayer for the latter. At the end of the day though, still too uncomfortable to ride, she moved her bike into the newsroom. On the bus-ride home she reflected on Carli's speculation about Henry Sutton. Ben had told Carli that he'd follow up on the slippery investor but maybe Stella could find a way to help.

20

IT WAS THE DAY before the funeral, and Stella woke to the sound of gushing water; Joe was in the shower. In the kitchen, the boys squabbled over a breakfast cereal. She was tired, having stayed up late to comb the Internet for info on Henry Sutton, which had been a complete waste of time. Nothing, zilch – the man didn't even have a Facebook page.

Stella dragged herself out of bed and put on the only clean clothes she owned, including last summer's cropped pants, the ones that made her feel fat even when she wasn't bloated. She made the boys settle their argument and sent them to school in yesterday's T-shirts turned inside out.

Still no trace of her period; she was two weeks late. Having left her bike at the office, she took the Pathfinder to work. On the drive to town she allowed herself a short daydream about having a baby girl.

At the end of the day Stella slipped into the drugstore at the mall to purchase a pregnancy test. Having checked to make sure she was alone, she tucked the small box under some tissues in her shopping basket. A dose of big-city anonymity would have gone down well about then.

"Busted." Carli's husband Tim had come up behind her. "What would Vanessa say if she knew you shopped at the competition?"

Stella felt herself flush. "Tim, hi! Well, normally I go to Levitt's. I usually do, but today…"

"Stella," he laughed. "I'm yanking your chain. I come here all the time. Parking's easier than on Baker Street. All right, nice to see you. I've got to grab my paper and run. Bye!"

Later that evening Joe walked in on her in the bathroom as she brushed her teeth. The pregnancy test kit was on the counter. "Is that what I think it is?" he said.

"My period's late."

He was struck dumb. Dazed expression, gaping mouth – she half expected him to keel over.

"Relax," she said. "No reason my diaphragm would have failed. I just wanted to reassure myself."

"Where would we even put another kid? In the laundry room?"

"Why not? That would work." Stella rinsed off her toothbrush. "Joe. I'm kidding. Let's not get ahead of ourselves. I haven't even opened the package. The directions say to take the sample in the morning."

"You don't even seem upset," he said. "Is this what you want – another kid?"

"No. God. Come on." They'd been looking at each other in the mirror and now she turned to face him. "It wouldn't be the end of the world though, would it? I mean the boys are the best part of our lives, right?"

He pointed a finger at her, nearly jabbed her in the chest. "Don't make this about the boys," he said in a barely recognizable voice. He smacked the doorframe hard with the flat of his hand and strode away. A second later the screen door slammed.

"Mommy, what was that noise?" Nicky.

She poked her head into the boys' room. "Nothing, honey. Go back to sleep."

In the linen closet she found a blanket, tossed it along with Joe's pillow into the hall outside the master bedroom, and closed the door. She was angry with him on so many levels she didn't know where to begin. What hurt most was his snap reaction, like it would be entirely her fault if she were pregnant. She worked hard at their relationship. If you worked hard to please someone, shouldn't that someone want to please you too? As opposed to coasting along, saying whatever the hell popped into his head?

Halfway through the night she woke up wet and sticky, the sheets stained red. The physical release was familiar but the sense of loss – the emptiness – almost overwhelmed her. Instead of the relief she'd expected, even hoped for, she felt hollowed out. Getting up to soak the bloody sheets in cold water and change the bed doomed her to sleeplessness. She was still awake when the early morning train chugged by across the lake.

* * *

On the day of Lillian's funeral, the United Church in uphill Nelson was filled to capacity, as if it were Christmas Eve or Easter Sunday. Rows of blush pink candles flickered on wrought iron stands, perfume from pink lilies and cream roses wafted over the altar. To Stella the overall effect was more suited to a wedding than a funeral, but presumably the decorating committee of Vanessa, Amelie, and Nathalie knew Lillian's tastes best.

Carli stayed outside to watch for Zoe while Stella ushered Nina up the carpeted centre aisle to a front pew. Behind them in the second row, Joe sat between Matt and Nicky. When she reached back to pat each of her sons on the knee, he offered Stella a weak smile, which she didn't return. She felt like hell and looked worse. Good day for a funeral. If she broke down who would be any the wiser?

From a side aisle Vanessa scanned the crowd, probably on the lookout for Henry Sutton. At the back, Ben McKean almost blended in with the other men in suits.

Among the lavish floral arrangements on the altar, stood a simple mixed bouquet Nina had picked from the garden, next to it a framed studio portrait of Lillian. Stella let her gaze rest on the portrait, trying to put aside her disappointment in Joe and think about Lillian, conjure up happy memories of their all too brief friendship.

Carli's husband Tim delivered the eulogy. The mayor of Nelson said a few words, as did the chairman of the hospital board. The choir sang "Amazing Grace," which was another surprise. It was difficult to imagine Lillian petitioning God "to save a wretch like me."

Nina looked straight ahead through the entire service.

Stella had struggled with how to refer to her in Lillian's obituary. If the two women truly had lived together as a couple, the arrangement had been neither public nor obvious to anyone. Maybe Lillian's feelings for Nina hadn't run as deep. Surely if Lillian had been gay, Stella would have known. Or was she kidding herself? Compared to most of the people seated around her, she had known Lillian about five minutes. For the obit, she'd settled on the term "companion" for Nina – let people read what they wanted into that. In the notices for the *Vancouver Sun* and *Globe and Mail*, Stella hadn't singled out anyone other than Lillian's late husband, Clark.

After the memorial, the ladies of the church put on a spread in the hall downstairs. They had brought along silver tea services and arranged dainty *petits fours* and crust-free sandwiches on their best platters and cake stands as a way to honour Lillian. The book club members mingled for a respectable period of time before they left for the wake at Vanessa's place on the East Shore.

* * *

In the lead-up to the funeral, Zoe had dodged her mother to keep an eye out for Kieran. At first, she'd chilled by a window in a corner of the lobby, then she'd climbed the stairway to the balcony to look down as people filed into the church. No Kieran anywhere. She hadn't seen him since the canoe disaster. Talk about unfair – Matt and Nicky had been left alone for about two seconds. And who would have expected their mom to totally lose it when they were only in a few feet of water? It wasn't as if they were about to drown. Stella had thanked Kieran for rescuing the boys but she had still banished him from visiting unless an adult was present.

Zoe had no idea where he lived. She didn't even know his cell number.

After the funeral, she continued to avoid her mother, which was easy because the book club members left early to go to Vanessa's. Zoe's dad had a squash game with the chair of the hospital board. He waved at her as he exited the church, already tugging at his tie.

Zoe left the churchyard and walked downtown. She felt her face heat up when she saw Kieran lying on his back on a ledge by City Hall, eyes half-closed. A lit joint dangled from one hand. "Hey, Zoe," he said, real casual, as if he'd been waiting for her to come along.

"Hey." She sat down on the ledge and stretched out her legs. "So, what's happening?"

"Nada."

"I was at Lillian's funeral. The church was packed."

"Yeah?" He swung his legs around and sat up beside her. "That was freaky last week. That lady going ballistic over her kids in a canoe."

"My mom thinks she might have a water phobia. Stella doesn't talk about it."

"Huh? Weird."

"I know." She stared straight ahead, conscious of his arm touching hers. "I was wondering… What happened to that sweater you found at Lillian's place? Did you burn it with the trash?"

"Nah. I stuck it in the garden shed. The housekeeper will know what to do with it. I still think it was kinda strange. Anyway, whatever. You want to get a coffee or something?"

Zoe's heart soared.

21

TO STELLA, VANESSA'S GARDEN had never looked love-lier. As planned she'd hired the infamous Kieran to help her get it ready for the wake. Two of the planters flanked the entrance to a series of rickety floats Vanessa liked to refer to as "the wharf." She suggested book club members file to the end and take turns scattering a scoop of Lillian's ashes over Kootenay Lake, holding back some for Nina to take home and spread on Lillian's treasured flowerbeds. Carli led the way, stepping gingerly in her strappy high-heeled sandals. Amelie and Nathalie followed. Nina came next, carrying the blue and white cremation urn.

"Is it safe enough to hold all of us?" Stella asked Vanessa. Several planks showed obvious signs of rot, a few were missing entirely.

"Of course," Vanessa said. Then she seemed to read something into Stella's expression. "Are you okay, sweetie? I think we're all a little off after that funeral. Want me to take your arm?"

"I'm fine. Thanks, though." Stella took a deep breath, stepped onto the first float, and willed herself to keep going right to the end. The so-called wharf swayed with every step. When her turn came, she spilled a ladle of ashes onto the surface of the water then tiptoed back to dry land as hastily as she dared.

Vanessa served her guests little cakes from the French bakery, courtesy of Nathalie, and pink sparkling wine from bottles chilled in a big tub of ice. Carli was into her third glass of bubbly when she said, "Too bad Henry Sutton didn't turn up to pay his respects, not that I expected him to show. Too many people would have tried to buttonhole him about the status of their life's savings."

"Trust me," Vanessa said. "Henry would have made it if he could. He's doing his best for his investors. You have to expect ups and downs in the financial world."

"As well as shysters who make off with their clients' money,"

Carli said.

"C'mon guys," Stella said. "Let's keep our attention on Lillian today."

"You're right, Stell," Carli said. "My apologies. Bad timing."

Stella raised her glass. "To Lillian," she said. "She brought us together, and I for one would like to keep up the book club, if for no other reason than to honour Lillian."

"Hear, hear," Vanessa said.

Nina appeared too choked to speak.

When the celebration began to wind down in the late afternoon, Amelie and Nathalie took off. Stella excused herself to use the washroom. One of the vanity drawers had been left ajar. She tried to close it but it was jammed. Stella couldn't help herself; she wiggled the handle and reached inside to pull out a small silver frame that contained a close-up of Vanessa with Henry Sutton, a cropped version of a group photo taken the first evening the old charmer had ambled into their lives. So the woman who couldn't recall keeping any of those photos had turned one into a framed portrait then hidden it. Bizarre.

At the sound of a car outside and raised voices, Stella dried her hands and left the bathroom. Maybe one of the East Shore ladies had forgotten something. Or had Henry Sutton come after all – a case of better late than never? But before she could ask, Vanessa brushed past her in the hallway and ducked into her bedroom. What was going on?

The sitting room was empty.

Carli and Nina were out on the porch. At the bottom of the steps stood a statuesque woman and a whippet-thin teen, in the background an older grey BMW with a touch of rust on the wheel wells.

Carli was saying, "And how is it you're related to Lillian?"

The woman ignored the question and smiled up at Stella. "Vanessa – is that you?"

Given that Vanessa was more than a decade older, Stella was slightly taken aback. "Vanessa is inside. I'm Stella Mosconi, a friend of –"

"Oh, well, okay." The visitor laughed. She was dressed entirely in black from her stiletto heels to a tiny fascinator on the side of her bottle-blond head. "Because you don't look anything like the way I remember Vanessa." She laughed again. "I'm Lillian's niece –

well, Clark's niece to be precise. Colette Fenniwick. And this is my son, C. I was so close to my uncle I named my boy after him." She beamed at her son, who briefly shrugged and looked away. With his fifties-style haircut and button-down shirt he looked nerdy enough to be hip.

Colette Fenniwick continued. "The minute I saw the notice in the *Globe* about poor Aunt Lillian we jumped into the Beamer and drove straight here from Calgary. We missed the funeral but people were still tidying up the church basement. I introduced myself to one of the ladies and she said Lillian's friends had gone out to scatter her ashes at Vanessa's. And I thought, Vanessa? I remember Vanessa. I had to get directions though – I haven't been out to the East Shore for years. I'm just dying to go over to Uncle Clark's cottage to show C around."

After a moment of stunned silence Stella spoke again. "That cottage hasn't belonged to Clark for a long time," she said. "Nina lives there now. This is Lillian's friend, Nina Huber. But I guess Lillian would have –"

"Oh now, I'm confused," said Colette. "A friend? Well, never mind. Right now, I would just kill for a glass of water. I'm sure Vanessa will want us to come in for a visit. Did you say she was inside?"

Carli took over. "Vanessa is a little, uh, indisposed. This has been a stressful day for her – for all of us, really. But if you'd like to sit down on the porch I'll get some glasses and a pitcher of ice water. Maybe tomorrow you could drop by to –"

The screen door creaked open and Vanessa appeared with a tray of fresh drinks. She had reapplied her lipstick and changed into snug white chinos and a V-neck knit top that showed her figure to advantage. "Hello, Colette," she said. "Long time no see."

* * *

McKean took off his suit and hung it up in the half-empty closet. Miranda had taken a lot of her clothes when she had left with the baby. Ten days they'd been gone. The house was a morgue.

During the two days Miranda had been on the road, he'd tried almost hourly to reach her. On the second evening, almost frantic with worry, he had rung her mother's place to see if she'd arrived. The old shrew answered the phone. "Miranda's resting," she bleated. "Poor thing's wiped out after driving all that way by herself." As if he should have quit his job to drive Miranda and Aiden to Fort St. John. Throughout the call Aiden cried in the background and McKean wanted to drop everything and fly up to be with his son. But just to get there would require two flights and take the better part of a day. Not feasible after he had lost half a week to a course in Kelowna then wasted more time going after the elusive squatter in the shack. Add to that the necessity to respond to thirty-seven tips from concerned citizens, including a call from Carli DeLuca about the American, Henry Sutton. Follow-up on Sutton would require cooperation with law enforcement south of the border. The Chief was going to shit a brick.

Meanwhile McKean had gone to Lillian Fenniwick's funeral. Murderers have been known to turn up at a victim's funeral, or so the theory went. In this case that narrowed the list of suspects to about two hundred and fifty. At the service Stella was front and centre with Nina Huber, whose grieving widow act seemed a bit much. Maybe she had been in love with Fenniwick but she still had a husband. And until McKean could apprehend and question Max Huber, Nina remained a key person of interest in the death of her employer, particularly after the incriminating syringe had turned up on the beach. You don't expect a killer to leave a murder weapon lying around, yet people do stupid things in the heat of the moment and some have killed for less than a lush lakefront cottage. Next time McKean would question Ms. Huber at the station. Turn up the heat. No more Mr. Nice Guy sipping tea at the kitchen table.

An empty Sunday loomed. He decided to drive out to the yellow cottage and bring her in.

He should also talk to Stella again. She was close to Huber, and possibly in possession of vital information without even realizing it. The truth was he wanted to talk to Stella, and he didn't trust his own motives for that.

22

NINA RETURNED FROM THE wake at Vanessa's to find the porch carpeted with flowers. A volunteer from the church must have dropped them off – the kindness of strangers. And strangers they were. Nina had never attended services with Lillian.

She found a place inside for each floral tribute and added water where needed. Bone-tired but still worked up, she swallowed two of Lillian's sleeping pills and went to bed.

The next morning as she sipped at a reheated cup of coffee, Nina looked at Lillian's portrait, now returned to its place on the mantle. "What should I do now, Lillian?" she asked the image in the photo. Lillian only smiled. The cottage smelled like a funeral home. The lilies nearly made her gag.

People spoke of the emptiness that follows the funeral of a loved one. Mourners fuss over the bereaved then go back to their usual routines. That was natural. And Nina had to get back to some sort of life herself. Make the best of the situation. Her lot was to be un-lucky, as her mother always said.

"With your luck, the bread will run out before you reach the front of the line."

"With your luck, you will fail the test by one point."

What would her mother have said about Max? The drugs, the armed robbery, and prison term – none of that would have sur-prised her mother. But Max had never lifted a hand to Nina. For that she must be grateful. And she had been fortunate to have Lillian in her life, even though their time together had passed too quickly. Still, she had a quiet, beautiful place to live and Lillian to thank for that.

She must keep busy, tire herself out so she could sleep at night Today she would scatter the rest of Lillian's ashes and dig them into the soil. She put on a pair of worn jeans and an old plaid shirt that had belonged to Lillian. Arms wrapped around herself, she inhaled Lillian's smell, a blend of deodorant and hair spray with a lingering hint of tobacco smoke. Lillian had been so proud when she had finally given up cigarettes for good; Nina had cooked a celebratory meal and opened an especially good bottle of wine. Now she lifted the decorative urn that contained the last cupful of Lillian's remains and held it to her heart. But she did not give in to tears; she had a purpose.

The phone rang. Nina was tempted to ignore it and go outside. No good ever came from wasting time on the telephone. Two more rings, three. She picked up.

"It's me," Vanessa said, with a sigh. "I feel dreary."

"Ya, me too," Nina said.

"Listen, has that Colette person been out to see you? I wouldn't be surprised if she came by today. Be careful, Nina. Don't let her be a nuisance. Give her a few minutes to trip down memory lane then tell her you're busy. You need to take care of yourself today."

"Ya, sure," Nina said. "I will go to the garden now."

"Ni-na," Vanessa drew out her name. She wanted something. "To change the subject – what do you know about the last time Lillian saw Henry? I think she might have said something to upset him."

Nina bristled. "I did not talk to Lillian about that man."

"Something was up," Vanessa pressed. "They went out to dinner and later that evening I couldn't reach either of them. I thought Lillian liked Henry, but I think she may have had a change of heart, what with Carli casting aspersions on the poor man. If Lillian said something to make Henry feel unwelcome it might explain why he stayed away from the funeral. Did she mention anything like that to you? I can't think of any other reason why he didn't come."

Nina's heart began to beat faster. She did not want to talk about Henry Sutton. She did not want to even think about him, certainly not about his being with Lillian. Of course, she remembered that dinner – Lillian all gussied up, Henry insisting on coming to call when Nina would have been more than happy to drive her to town and wait. "Lillian is gone now, Vanessa," she said. "And I will go to the garden and try to forget things that no longer matter."

While Vanessa nattered on, Nina closed her eyes and tried to conjure up the essence of Lillian, the music of her laughter, the warm grip of her hand on Nina's arm when she had stairs to negotiate. The spontaneous, rib-crushing hugs she bestowed in moments of great happiness. Rare though they were, Nina had lived for those embraces. With her and Lillian there had been no need for the groping and clutching and nakedness favoured by men.

If only Max had not returned to Nelson. The first time he came to her door, she had managed to rebuff him, refusing to let him in the cottage. But Max was not easily put off. He would be back. He was probably still nearby, spying on her. Nina held the phone lightly as she walked from window to window, straining to see if he lurked among the trees.

After the unsettling telephone call, Nina had to re-summon the strength to go outside. She opened the cottage door and glanced quickly around. No sign of Max. She darted toward the garden shed and was partway across the yard when the grey BMW came down the drive, Colette Fenniwick honking the horn and the thin boy slouched on the passenger side.

Colette stepped out of the car in beach attire: lime green short shorts and matching flip-flops, a black tank top with "Foxy Lady" embossed in sparkly silver letters across the front. Orange bra straps, which she had made no effort to conceal, dug into her shoulders, straining against the weight of her breasts. The boy remained in the car, his eyes cast down as if he were sad.

"Kids and their phones, eh?" Colette said, and it took Nina a moment to realize she was referring to her son's strange behaviour. The woman surveyed the grounds approvingly. "Look at the size of those rhododendrons now. Amazing. Rhodies look after themselves though, don't they? Uncle Clark was never one to putter in the garden. He liked the wildness of the place. The grounds certainly aren't wild anymore. Aunt Lillian must have had a green thumb." She marched over to the porch, parked a large canvas bag on the seat of an Adirondack chair and began to apply sunscreen to her arms and legs, shoulders and chest.

Nina said, "You did not meet Lillian often, I think."

"Not in later years, no. Not after Uncle Clark died. She was a second wife remember. Not part of the social group I grew up with. Vanessa was always around in those days. The Levitts have owned that cottage forever – I guess Vanessa inherited it. I hope you won't be offended if I say I expected to inherit this place. I mean, Uncle Clark never had any children and we were very close. I was like a daughter to him. Lillian was much younger than Clark so I guess it's no surprise she outlived him." Colette dropped the tube of sunscreen into the bag and pushed her dark glasses up onto her coarse, platinum hair. "It's Nina, isn't it? Did you ever meet Clark, Nina?"

"No, he passed before I came to work for Lillian."

Colette's eyes widened but the innocence was put on; her pupils shone like sharp black diamonds. "Work for Lillian?" she said. "What were you – a maid? She had eye trouble, right?" Without waiting for a reply, Colette forged on. "Well then, what makes you think the cottage is yours now?"

"Lillian and I were close," Nina said, her mind racing. "She wanted me to stay in our home."

"My goodness, that's unusual – for a maid to stay on," Colette said. "Do you mind if I take a look inside – for old times' sake?"

Nina thought about Vanessa's warning over the phone, but what could she do? Tell her to leave? She did not know how. There was no choice but to give the brash creature a tour of the cottage.

"The original fireplace!" Colette exclaimed, as she strode into the living room. "That brings back memories. All those summer parties, Uncle Clark tossing logs on the fire to make the sparks fly. It can get chilly on a summer evening on the lake. Something about cold air drainage flowing down the creek? I was a little kid – nine-ten years old – when my parents first brought me here. I'd find a place to watch all the fun. Clark had an eye for the ladies. They flocked out here on the ferry with their homemade pies. Dressed in their best flower-children garb – not a bra among them," Colette laughed, exposing two gold molars. "Vanessa came by all the time, usually without her parents. They were older than Clark's crowd and never stayed long. It's probably hard for you to picture Vanessa as a cute twenty-year-old, but she was very sweet. Uncle Clark always had time for Vanessa. Did she ever marry?"

Nina shook her head, wondering how someone could talk so much and barely take a breath. "It is not my business."

"Nina – my goodness, you're discreet! You must have been a perfect servant. Aunt Lillian was lucky to have found you." She yawned. "I think I'll see if I can persuade C to come down to the beach with me."

While Colette Fenniwick cavorted on the lakeshore, her son sat on a log engrossed with his phone. Nina waited inside and peeked through the drapes. It was not the time for a quiet moment in the garden with Lillian's remains. The phone rang and the call display read Vanessa Levitt. "Me, again" Vanessa said, unnecessarily.

"Ya, that woman Colette is here with the boy, down on the beach now."

"Ugh, I warned you, Nina. Even as a child, Colette was a drama queen with an overactive imagination. I hope she hasn't been telling stories."

"I do not listen to her gossip."

"So, she *has* been telling stories. Did she say anything about me?"

"Only rubbish about Lillian's husband Clark. Oh, they come up from the beach. I have to go." Nina put down the phone and stepped outside.

Colette waved and called, "It was so fun to be back at the family cottage. We'll see you again!" The pair got into their BMW. With a distressing familiarity, Colette reversed into the turn-around behind the shed, swung to the left, and sped up the drive. How Lillian would have disliked her. Common: that would have been her word for Colette Fenniwick.

But even worse, her drop-in visit must have been planned. All that talk of inheriting the cottage had left Nina sick to her stomach. With Lillian gone, what chance would she have to stand her ground against the likes of Colette Fenniwick?

The hubbub of the funeral and the arrival of distant relatives had left Nina out of sorts. With no appetite for lunch, she paced aimlessly around the cottage trying to muster the energy to go back outside. As was her habit now, she checked every window, ever on the lookout for Max. At last she picked up the cremation urn and carried it to the area designated for annuals. Here Nina felt easier. Soon the plot would abound with crimson seed geraniums and white salvia and three varieties of yellow marigolds – all nourished by Lillian's remains. Nina fought back tears as she poured the last of the grey ashes over the dark brown earth. Now she would dig them in around the seedlings so that nothing of Lillian would blow away when the wind came up. She bowed her head a moment. If only she could turn back the clock...

Nina walked to the shed to get a trowel and hoe. She also would take out a hose and wash down the wheelbarrow. That shifty-eyed boy Kieran had not cleaned it after burning the branches.

Inside the shed, Nina waited for her eyes to adjust to the relative darkness.

Seconds later, her blood ran cold. There, carelessly tossed onto the workbench, was Lillian's brown cardigan. Nina screamed so loud she thought her throat would bleed. She clamped a hand over her mouth – what if someone had heard?

Sweater in hand she stumbled back to the cottage, bolted the door, and frantically punched in Stella's number. When she picked up, Nina blurted, "I found it. The cardigan."

"That's good, Nina. Mystery solved." Stella sounded distracted. "How are you feeling today?"

"I am afraid, Stella. The sweater was in the shed. I –"

"But that's okay, isn't it? Lillian must have left it there. You know Nina, if you're feeling unsettled today, that's perfectly normal. Just a sec – Joe is calling me." The conversation with Joe was muffled; Stella must have put her hand over the mouthpiece.

Nina paced.

"Sorry about that," Stella said, breathlessly. "The guys are waiting for me in the car."

Nina's heart sank. "You go then."

"Are you sure? I'll call you back later. Take it easy today, okay? Don't worry about the cardigan."

Nina put down the phone and clasped her hands together to stop them from shaking. She tried to think what Lillian would have done in her place. Pour a stiff drink? Yes. Nina went to the liquor cabinet, settled on a bottle of cognac, and half-filled a crystal snifter. Lillian favoured cognac when she needed to think. Or relax. Or solve a problem. "Must be five o'clock somewhere," she often said.

Nina grimaced at the first sip but the second went down easier. She tried to concentrate. On the last day of her life, Lillian had tied the brown sweater around her waist in the garden. How had that gotten into the shed and how long had it been there? Nina knew she had not put it there. And she would not have failed to notice the sweater had she gone into the shed. Had she not once ventured inside there in the nineteen days since Lillian had passed away? Maybe Lillian had gone to the shed to cut raffia for the bouquet. But even so, she would not have left her sweater behind. Lillian was not forgetful.

No, someone else had put the sweater in the shed – but who?

Inside Nina's head, the voice of her dead mother shrieked, *Who else?*

Max.

Nina wondered if her new life with Lillian had pushed him over the edge. Max's drug habit had made him violent before – it was the reason he was in jail in the first place.

She refilled the snifter and scanned the lake at the front and the forest in back. Just when she was beginning to feel a little safer, there was a flash of movement in the woods.

Then a noise, as if the metal drum behind the shed had been bumped or knocked over.

Nina gulped the rest of the cognac and placed the crystal snifter in the sink. Not stopping to wash the glass – a first for her – she found the car keys. She opened the front door a crack and held out the key fob to unlock the Range Rover, ran to the car, got in, locked the doors, and started the engine. At the dock, the ferry was about to depart but Nina leaned on the horn – another first – and seconds later drove on board.

23

THE DAY THAT FOLLOWED Lillian's funeral passed without incident in the Mosconi household. Yet in the aftermath of what Joe termed the pregnancy scare, Stella fought back feelings of resentment toward her husband. She and Joe went through the motions of family life like casual acquaintances, treating one another too politely.

The lake – choppy and still rising – felt too cold for a dip, so in the afternoon, for want of anything better to do, the family drove to the indoor pool in town. Stella bluffed her way around the shallow end, racing Nicky on paddleboards, while Joe gave Matt a diving lesson. It never failed to amaze her that her own flesh and blood could fling himself into the deep end and trust he wouldn't die.

For dinner that evening, Joe grilled burgers and Stella made a salad no one except her ate.

Joe clicked on a crime show and Stella got ready for bed early. She still felt guilty about giving Nina the brush off on the phone that morning, but now she was too tired to get back to her. Promising herself she would get in touch the next day, she crawled gratefully under the covers and didn't stir when she heard the phone ring. Joe let it go to voicemail.

Monday morning, Stella checked the landline. The previous evening's call had come from the NPD but there was no message. She assumed the caller was Ben and made a mental note to call him back from the office. The phone was still in her hand when it rang. Patrick. It was layout day at the paper and his wife was in her first stage of labour; he had just dropped her at the hospital. Stella sent him back to his wife's side and phoned Jade Visser to come in early.

Twice weekly the *Times* produced hard-copy issues in addition to the website version. The layout of the print editions involved a back and forth dance between the production people who set the ads and the editorial staff that filled the remaining space with news. Everything was done on computer using relatively new software.

By rights, Jade should have helped Stella cover for Patrick. But she was still finishing a story that had been due the day before. "Late-breaking details," she said, importantly. "Patrick knew about this."

At various times Stella went to the production side to check on progress and was reminded of slip-ups. Once she had forgotten to put page numbers on the news stories; another time she'd entered two captions in wrong places on the computer. She overheard a production associate complain about a rookie editor at another paper who'd forced them to re-dummy multiple times and hoped she wouldn't mess up too badly.

It was standard practice at the *Times* for reporters to copy-edit each other's work. But that morning Jade only skimmed Stella's pieces and challenged Stella's corrections of her own. Stella wasn't entirely sorry when Jade took off to cover a soft-ball tournament. But by the time she'd finally put the paper to bed she had been at the office ten hours. A euphoric Patrick called to say he and his wife were the proud parents of a beautiful baby girl. Stella reassured him the layout had gone as smooth as silk.

She got home to find the boys already asleep and Joe watching a baseball game. At a little past nine, she realized she had forgotten to get back to Nina. But as she scrolled through her contacts for the number, Joe stuck his head out the door and asked her to come to bed. She put down the phone.

The lovemaking was over in a record four minutes. Which was fine; Stella was tired. But sleep eluded her. She listened to Joe snore a while then nudged him to roll over. He was a good man, basically, a good husband and father. Maybe it was up to her to rekindle the flame.

When the snoring resumed, Stella went to the kitchen for a glass of milk and considered calling Nina. But by then it was too late. No sense waking her up just to say hi.

* * *

In a windowless, cinder-block cell at the Nelson police station, Nina Huber sat on the edge of the stiff vinyl mattress that topped her concrete bunk. She assumed it was morning because the lights, which had been dimmed overnight, had been turned up. A camera mounted high in one corner of the lockup meant the guards would be watching. With the lights on full, Nina could not bring herself to use the toilet.

A slot in the door clanged open and breakfast was passed through: a Styrofoam bowl of sugary cereal with a small carton of milk and a sliced orange, a paper cup of strong black coffee. Nina drank the coffee, ate a little cereal then put aside the plastic spoon.

So this was what it was like to be in prison. She had heard stories about the GDR prisons when she was a kid in East Germany but had never seen the inside of a cell. For Max, it would have been rougher. No nice policewoman like the one who apologized for the thinness of the blanket when she brought Nina a cup and toilet paper. The policewoman had also allowed her to make a call and even provided a telephone book, but there had been no answer at Stella's home. Nina had not left a message – it would have been difficult enough to explain her situation in person.

Nina moved her tray to the floor and tucked in the blanket taut. How had it come to this? Arrested for dangerous driving while drunk. McKean said she could have killed someone. A more brazen person might have replied, "Oh, you mean besides Lillian?"

Nina had panicked when she found Lillian's sweater in the garden shed, afraid Max might have put it there. Afraid he might have killed Lillian and planned to kill her next. Almost blind with fear, she had sped along the highway with only a half-formed idea of going to Stella for help. She had not noticed her speed. A police car in the oncoming lane turned and gave chase, lights flashing, siren shrieking.

If Lillian were still alive, she would find her a good lawyer and have the driving charges dropped. Nina almost smiled at the irony. Perhaps Stella could help, but then again, why should she? Anyway, with Lillian gone, the worst was over. Whatever happened now, what did it matter?

Spineless fool! Nina heard the voice as clearly as if her dead mother was next to her in the cell. *Even insects on the ground scurry away when someone tries to stomp them.*

"Leave me alone." Nina looked up at the camera and wondered if she had spoken out loud.

If her mother *could* speak to her, she would not skirt the harsh truth that Lillian had forsaken her. It was so clear to Nina now. Lillian had risked their quiet, happy existence by trying to appease Vanessa Levitt. And why? Because some schemer had cheated the book club members and played them off against each other.

As if to staunch such ugly thoughts, Nina pressed her fists against her eyes. "Stop." Again, she had spoken aloud. Another mistake. She needed to keep quiet and stop drawing attention, especially with the evidence against her.

Still, whatever happened, Nina would survive. Even if they condemned her for Lillian's murder she would survive. In Canada, murderers are sent to prison but they are not put to death. And in prison, Max would not be able to get to her. If he tried to visit, she could refuse to see him. In this country, even prisoners have rights.

* * *

Nina Huber had McKean baffled. On his way to bring her in for questioning, he had met her almost head-on darting down the highway towards town. Even after he had turned around to give chase and activated his lights and siren, she'd continued to careen around curves, at times weaving across the double line into the oncoming lane. She damn near hit a pedestrian in front of a postal box and would have if the man hadn't lept out of the path of the Range Rover.

Huber had been more agitated than usual; her breath stunk of alcohol, her speech was slurred. She'd been drinking cognac, she admitted, two or three glassfuls. "How big was the glass?" he'd asked.

"Big," she admitted. "I do not drink normally. The cognac was Lillian's." When he cuffed her, she didn't resist. At the station, she walked alongside him like a lamb to slaughter to take a breathalyzer and be fingerprinted.

McKean had charged her. Her condition had warranted holding her in a cell overnight for her own protection but while he explained what was happening, Nina remained totally blank.

He wondered what had triggered the drinking and reckless driving. When he sat her down in an interview room she admitted she had panicked after she found a sweater Lillian Fenniwick had worn on the evening she died. Huber claimed no knowledge of how the sweater ended up in the garden shed, or how long it had been there. If the woman could be believed, she hadn't been inside the shed for weeks.

McKean asked if Fenniwick might have left the sweater behind before she took off in her rowboat. "Ya, ya." Huber had answered with surprising candour. "But why? It gets cool on the lake in the evening. No, the murderer – he must have put it there."

"Murderer? Why are you so certain she was murdered?" McKean asked. "There's been no statement on her cause of death."

"I am not stupid," Nina said. "You questioned me before and asked about needles. You must think someone killed her."

"Well, if that were the case, why would they leave the sweater in the shed?"

But Nina Huber couldn't, or wouldn't, explain. She wasn't any more forthcoming the following morning, but McKean saw no point in holding her longer. Off the road, Huber posed no real threat to the community. And if her husband was still in the vicinity, he was more likely to show his face if Nina Huber was back at the yellow cottage.

* * *

For days now, Stella had been too busy to cycle to work. Driving was faster, so taking the Pathfinder back and forth to town had become a habit, as had feeling crabby and out of shape. On Tuesday morning, Joe found her car keys dangling from the lock in the front door where she had left them the previous evening . He gave her a hard time about it.

Outside three large, gritty splotches of bird droppings blotted the windshield of the Pathfinder. Stella cursed the osprey still circling overhead and went back inside for a spray bottle of Windex and a roll of paper towel. On the lakeshore road, a paving crew held up traffic. She was late for work.

When she walked into the newsroom, Jade was leaning over Patrick in a pair of tight, ripped jeans, enumerating the many feature articles she wanted to write. Adding to Stella's growing list of irritations, she had no luck connecting with Ben McKean in response to the call from the NPD she'd missed the night before. She also wasn't able to reach Nina, despite several attempts over the course of the morning. They hadn't spoken since that hurried conversation the day after the wake. Stella kept wondering why Nina had been so worked up about the sweater she had found in the shed. Why would such a minor detail send her into a spin?

In the afternoon, Patrick left early to drive his wife and baby daughter home from the hospital. Stella polished his editorial and rounded up a few items for the next edition in case he had to be late the following morning. With the end in sight, she placed a telephone order for two large pizzas and at 6:25 p.m. locked the front door of the newspaper office and walked to the pizza parlour up the street.

The clerk at the counter said, "I'm sorry for your loss." She looked familiar: spiky red hair, sparkly nose stud, bracelet tattoos around both upper arms. "I work at Jigsaw's three nights a week," she explained. "I've seen you there with Ms. Fenniwick."

"The bistro, right. That's where I know you from," Stella said. "Thanks for your condolences. Lillian was a good friend." She pulled out her Visa card. "Hey, I have a question. Did Lillian ever come in with a dapper-looking man about her age? I assume they'd go to Jigsaws to eat. It would have been, when? – a little more than three weeks ago, I think."

"Three weeks ago?" The clerk frowned as she handed back the card and receipt. "Oh, you know what? I do remember. They came in one night when I was serving but they didn't stay. The Track and Field Association had a banquet and the room was too noisy for Ms. Fenniwick. She apologized to the hostess but said she and her friend needed a quiet place to talk. I think they went to the dining room at the Lakeview."

On her way home, Stella stopped at the Lakeview Hotel, wrapped the pizzas in a car rug to keep them hot and went inside. In the wood-panelled bar, Harold the catering manager was unpacking a case of red wine.

"Poor Lillian," he said. "What a way to go. I saw you up front at the funeral. Nice service, wasn't it?" Harold remembered seeing Lillian in the dining room with a well-dressed gentleman, not long before she passed away. "The two of them made quite a night of it. But you have to hand it to people that age – they know enough to stay off the road after having a few drinks. After they paid their tab at the restaurant they went straight to the front desk and checked-in."

24

MCKEAN MISSED HIS BOY, his burbling laugh and rubbery little body. The way his fair, damp hair curled on his neck after his bath, the smell of him when he fell asleep on his dad's chest. In a weak moment, he put fourteen hundred bucks on his credit card to book a flight to Fort St. John that coming weekend. Most of Saturday would be taken up just getting there and most of Sunday getting back. A hotel room would probably set him back another two hundred or so, but Miranda said the house was full to the rafters with her brother there now. The prodigal son had decided to crash for a while, his gear all over the place.

McKean massaged his neck and tried to focus on the Lillian Fenniwick murder; the Chief was riding him to make an arrest. He reviewed his case notes and decided it was time to call in Vanessa Levitt. There was no clear indication one way or the other if the victim had made it to Levitt's place on the night she died, but that had been her presumed destination. Levitt might have some information on the elusive Harry Sutton too. They were rumoured to be close.

From down the hall, McKean heard the staccato beat of Vanessa Levitt's footsteps on the tile floor. She was all a flutter as she entered the interview room, jumping right in before McKean could ask the first question or even close the door. "I'm not sure how I can help," she said, smiling up at him. "What do I know about police work? But I've lived in this town my whole life if that counts for anything."

McKean turned on the recorder and asked her to talk about Henry Sutton's involvement in the book club.

"Oh, dear," she said, the patient insider with a lesson or two for the naïve newcomer. "I don't think the business with Henry has anything to do with Lillian."

"That's what I'm trying to find out."

"Well, I should warn you, Sergeant, gossip and rumours abound in this town. Henry introduced the club to his principles of responsible investing. But he didn't twist anyone's arm to participate – we had to coax him to accept our money. At first our little investment doubled in value, but then when profits took a slight dip some people got upset. But financial ups and downs are to be expected, don't you think?"

McKean picked up his pen. "When was the last time you saw Mr. Sutton?"

"Hmm. Eons ago. Three weeks? He dropped by the drugstore to chat but not for long. He had a meeting – business, always business. Henry doesn't permit himself many breaks."

"To your knowledge, did Mr. Sutton get in touch with Lillian Fenniwick on that visit to Nelson?"

"I think they went out for dinner but that would have been business too. Lillian acted as banker for our little investment club. Henry didn't stay in town long. He never did. He had commitments back in the US, Idaho mainly."

"Do you know what date he left Nelson to return to the States?"

"I assume it was the day after he had dinner with Lillian. Towards the end of May, if memory serves."

"You assume. You don't know for certain the date he left?"

"As I said, it must have been late May. I haven't seen him this month."

"How was he travelling?"

"By car, presumably."

"Presumably. You don't know how he travelled in this particular instance?"

"He occasionally drove a small motor home. Listen, I know you're only trying to do your job. But all these questions about Henry Sutton are probably irrelevant. If foul play was a factor in Lillian's death, Henry would be the last person anyone should suspect."

"What makes you say that?"

Levitt looked away for a moment. "You're putting me on the spot..."

"Take your time, Ms. Levitt, lay it out for me. What do you think happened the night Ms. Fenniwick died?"

"I can only speculate, but I understand killers are often close to their victims. Henry was only an acquaintance of Lillian's – he hardly knew her." Levitt sighed an exaggerated sigh. "Who am I to say what happened to Lillian? Maybe if you look closely enough, the evidence will speak for itself." She laughed. "Sorry. I must have heard that on TV. I'm a big fan of those crime series."

McKean had no time for guessing games. He thanked her for coming in and made a note to find out what dates Henry Sutton had crossed the border into Canada and back into the United States.

* * *

Mid-afternoon Wednesday, Stella answered a call on her direct line. "You never printed my Letter to the Editor about the ignoramuses that don't clean up after their dogs," said a gruff voice. "I've seen you down at the soccer fields with your kids. How do you like stepping in dog poop?"

"Well, sir," Stella said, slightly creeped-out that the caller knew her family by sight, and that he'd called her line instead of Patrick's. "I'm not sure how that happened. But in the past month we've printed two letters about that issue."

"So what? I pay taxes. I got a right to see my letter in the paper. Whatever happened to freedom of the press?"

"Alive and well, I hope. We certainly –"

"I have half a mind to cancel my subscription but I guess I'd have to spend another half hour on your fucking phone directory."

Before she could reply, he hung up.

Seconds later, another call came in on the same line. Stella sighed and picked up. This time a voice she recognized said, "I'd like to know what you have against Henry, Stella. I hear you've been asking about him all over town."

Good old Vanessa, clearly irate but never profane. "That's definitely an overstatement, Vanessa."

"I just want to know what's going on. A little birdie told me you were at the Lakeview asking questions about Henry and Lillian."

Stella's eyes were on her computer screen; she had five minutes to tweak a press release. "Just doing my job as a reporter."

"Yikes, sweetie. Why are you so snappish? This is *me*, Vanessa. It just doesn't seem fair to malign Henry when he's not even around to defend himself."

"Sorry, Van. I'm on deadline and –"

"Listen, I know you're busy and I don't want to upset you, but another little birdie told me Nina spent a night in the city jail. Do you know what that was about? She's not answering her phone. I'm kind of worried about her."

"Jail? That doesn't make sense. I'll look into it, okay? Sorry – gotta go." Stella hung up.

Vanessa, Vanessa. She meant well, but she gossiped with anyone and everyone who stopped by the drugstore. Granted the remark about Stella making inquiries "all over town" wasn't too far off the mark. If she'd heard about the night Lillian and Henry spent at the Lakeshore Hotel that little factoid certainly would have distressed her. But more important, could her information about Nina be correct? Stella entered Nina's number and the call went to voicemail.

Before she left the office, Stella rang Joe to ask him to make dinner. "I think I should check in on Nina," she said. "I haven't been able to reach her since Lillian's funeral and now I've heard this crazy rumour –".

"For chrissake Stella, you run to that woman's side every time she passes gas. I'm sure she's fine."

"Well I'm not. Look, there's nowhere I'd rather be than home with you guys, but Nina could be in trouble. Joe, listen, I heard she spent a night in jail."

"The drama never ends, does it? You'll do what you want to, but I'm sick of the whole business." He hung up on her.

At the ferry slip, there was an overflow from the previous sailing. Stella had forgotten the regular vessel was in dry dock for repairs. The wait for the smaller, slower ferry was going to be fifty minutes. Stella pictured Joe grumpily thawing burgers, the boys nagging him for pre-dinner snacks, the evening wearing on. She would miss their bedtime again too. She paced and fretted, considered giving up and going home. But Nina still wasn't answering her phone. When the small ferry chugged up to the wharf, Stella got back into her car.

On board, she made an effort to see the situation from Joe's point of view. Fair to say she had been preoccupied with the murder investigation and not as attentive as usual. She resolved to make it up to him, and also to Matt and Nicky. She would pamper them all weekend. Cook great meals. Start a fun project with the boys. Buy new poster paints – they loved to paint – and special paper to make a picture book for Patrick's new baby. She would go to bed early with Joe. Leave the TV on so they could make a little noise without waking up their sons.

Stella was channelling goodwill toward the universe when she rumbled off the ferry and down the winding road to the yellow cottage. She planned to touch base with Nina, do what she could to cheer her up, then race back to Joe and the boys on the next sailing.

The Range Rover was in the driveway but not in its usual place. Stella pulled up beside it. Was Max still around? She sat in her car a moment then made a dash for the porch and knocked on the door.

No sound from inside. Maybe Nina had gone for a walk. Vanessa might have invited her over to pump her for details about the rumoured night in jail. If so, she hadn't taken the car.

Stella knocked again and this time the latch gave a little, which was odd. Since Lillian's death Nina had been obsessive about locking up.

"Nina?" she said. "Nina, are you there?"

A gentle push and the door swung open. Silence. The living room was in shadows.

"Nina?" she called again. Doors to both bedrooms stood open. Stella looked first into Nina's room then Lillian's. The beds were made; nothing seemed out of place. She approached the swing door to the kitchen and gave it a shove.

Nina was on her back on the floor, apparently unconscious.

Her insulin pump, a pager-sized black device, lay beside her, still attached by a length of narrow tubing. Her shirt had slipped up to expose the place above her low-rise pants where the tube connected to a disk the size of a one-dollar coin.

Stella dropped to her knees and shook Nina's shoulder, asked loudly if she was okay. No response. She grabbed her phone and keyed 9-1-1, hit speakerphone, and started chest compressions while she gave the dispatcher directions to the cottage. After thirty compressions, she performed a head-tilt/chin-lift manoeuvre to open Nina's airway. Gave two mouth-to-mouth rescue breaths and got no response. Thirty chest compressions and two rescue breaths later, there was still no response. God, she hoped she was doing it right. As a First Aid rep at her last job she had taken a course in CPR but only ever practiced on a dummy. Stella continued the cycle of chest compressions and rescue breaths, fighting off fatigue as time crawled by.

Close to an hour passed before the ambulance from Creston arrived. Drenched in perspiration, Stella moved out of the way to let a paramedic take over. A short time later he checked for a pulse. "She's gone," he said.

Stella went to the bathroom then returned to sit at the kitchen table and wait for the police. On a laptop open on the table, the screen saver flashed images of exotic landscapes.

25

AT THE HEADQUARTERS OF the Nelson Police Department, a framed copy of a mission statement hung in the reception area. Stella couldn't make sense of it. At that hour, there was no one behind the desk so she had come to the foyer to call home and speak to Joe in private. The wall clock struck midnight as she hit the number for their landline.

Ben McKean had brought an entourage to the scene of Nina's death. Outside an officer had unrolled yellow crime-scene tape. Inside the repeated flash of a camera had punctuated Stella's vigil in the kitchen. She had moved to allow a man and woman garbed in papery jumpsuits to check the position of Nina's body and take a series of measurements. The female officer tucked the insulin pump into Nina's pocket, closed and bagged the laptop on the table. Stella rode to the station in near silence in the front passenger seat of Ben's cruiser. On the way to town she had tried four times to reach Joe on the landline and his cell but he'd let all the calls go to voicemail.

Now, at last, he picked up on the third ring and the sound of his voice made her throat catch. When she told him about Nina he seemed subdued, almost apologetic. With the Pathfinder still parked at the yellow cottage, Joe offered to come to the station for her; he would call a neighbour to sit with the boys. Wiping her eyes with the back of her hand Stella told him not to bother. She was fine, and surely one of the cops would drive her home after hauling her all the way into town to question her.

Ben had interviewed her with a policewoman present. Stella described each step that had led to the discovery of Nina's body and her attempt at resuscitation. Constable Lewis, the female officer, appeared to hang on every word. She seemed almost too happy to lead Stella down the hall to fingerprint her.

After the call home, Stella caught up with Ben in his office. The laptop found near Nina Huber's body was open on his desk. Without looking up, he said, "Suicide note and murder confession rolled into one."

"I don't believe it. Show me the note."

"You shouldn't even be in here, Stella. You found the victim's body, which puts you in the frame for –"

"Ben. Show me the note."

With a gloved finger, he swung the computer around. "Don't touch anything."

The note, all in caps, read:

I KILLED LILLIAN. WE ARGUED ABOUT HER ROWING TO VANESSA'S HOUSE. I LOST MY TEMPER AND IN-JECTED HER WITH INSULIN. TO LILLIAN, I WAS ONLY A HOUSEKEEPER. HER FRIENDS DON'T REALIZE HOW SHE TREATED ME IN PRIVATE. YES, I KILLED LILLIAN. BUT I CANNOT STAND THE GUILT AND LONELINESS SO NOW I MUST TAKE MY OWN LIFE.

Stella dragged the worn oak armchair up to his desk and sat down. "What do you make of it?"

"The alleged argument doesn't seem like much of a motive for murder," Ben said. "Unless Huber had an awful lot of pent-up resentment. But more to the point, the way Fenniwick died suggests premeditation. The killer loaded a syringe with insulin and executed a complex series of steps. How does that fit with a spur-of-the-moment argument?"

"It doesn't. Maybe Nina didn't write the note – she was set up."

He looked sceptical. "Or she planned the murder then waited for an opportunity – or a trigger. The note's sketchy though, isn't it? Like it was written in a hurry. Why toss off a few disjointed lines when you have plenty of time to try to justify your actions?"

"Nina was a woman of few words but she was methodical. She didn't toss off anything. The computer belonged to Lillian, by the way. I've never seen Nina use it."

"If she didn't normally use a computer maybe that's why the note's all in caps. We'll check the laptop for prints and see what else is on there. Email, browser searches. How about the tone of the note? Does it sound as if Huber wrote it?"

"Yes and no. Something is off. For one thing, it sounds more like a disgruntled employee wrote it rather than a loving partner."

"For all we know the romantic slant was a figment of Huber's imagination. Did she strike you as unstable? She was flipping out when I took her into custody for dangerous driving."

"So it's true Nina spent a night in jail? I wish I'd known."

"Caught her swerving down the highway drunk. She was given permission to make a call," he said. Closed face.

"Oh, God," Stella said. "This was when – Sunday night? We let a call go to voicemail. The next morning when I saw NPD on the call display, I assumed it was from you. *God* – to think she might have tried to reach me, maybe at a time she was feeling low enough to kill herself…" Stella let that hang in the air. She didn't want to say out loud that a night in a cell could have pushed Nina over the edge. "I need to think about this." She pulled out her phone. "Let me take a picture of the note."

"Sorry. Can't allow that." He stood up. "I'll drive you home. I just need to step out for a moment."

* * *

Corporal Ray Eberly had been assigned to guard the crime scene near Give Out Creek. Punishment, as he saw it, for having bungled the apprehension of an ex-con named Max Huber. At least, in Ben McKean's humble opinion Ray had bungled the capture, simply by using his siren. McKean was an anal bastard. How do you relate to a guy like that?

Now Ray had to stay up all night to prevent anyone from entering the cottage where Nina Huber's body was found. Like that would happen. Why would anyone live out here? That was the question. It was near impossible to get to. Ray could see having a summer place on this side of Kootenay Lake. Get away from it all. Skinny-dip when the spirit moved you, smoke a doobie or two far from prying eyes. But live there year-round? Forget it.

Ray surveyed his surroundings. The place was unusually neat and orderly for a crime scene. Too neat and orderly. Why not snoop around to pass the time? He opened a desk drawer and found each pen, pencil, and postage stamp lined up in a designated slot. He opened another drawer – not a paperclip out of place. The bottom drawer was locked; he would get back to that later. Books were arranged on shelves alphabetically by author names. Sheets and towels in the linen closet were stacked according to size and colour. He opened the fridge. Spotless. Every nook and cranny in the kitchen was immaculate. The beds had been made with military precision. Jeez, talk about McKean being anal – you'd think the housekeeper might have slacked off once her boss had checked out.

Ray drifted back to the living room and sat down on the couch. Behind the front door was a serious-looking black leather handbag on its side, a few items spilling out. Not what you would expect to see in a compulsively neat home. He checked the contents: key ring, hairbrush, ballpoint pen, packet of tissues, one tampon, and a coupon for the car wash. No wallet or loose change. Now that was interesting. Ray liked a puzzle.

He put on gloves and went over the cottage again, rechecked every drawer, cupboard, and shelf, every purse and shopping bag in the closets. In a nightstand, he found a key to the locked desk drawer where an envelope held Lillian Fenniwick's passport, driver's licence, and assorted cards. Other than that: nothing. Not a bill or a coin. He took the key ring and went out to the car, a late model Range Rover. Not a bad ride for a couple of old ladies. He checked under the seats, in the glove box, in every compartment in the vehicle. Not a red cent.

Nina Huber had been robbed. Possibly by an intruder who had interrupted her while she took her insulin, which might have caused her to OD. Yessir, someone had paid Ms. Huber a visit, someone known to her because there was no sign of forced entry. Unless she'd left her front door unlocked, a common enough practice among folks who live out in the boonies.

Ray got a flashlight from the cruiser and took a gander around the yard. Thieves often ditched a wallet after taking what they needed. Ray checked out the periphery of the cottage, the garden, the shed, and the area around it. He picked up a stick and stirred the ashes in a big metal drum. And didn't he find what he was looking for at the bottom of the drum: an open wallet and a bunch of loose cards.

* * *

At the outskirts of Creston, Max hitched a ride in the direction of the Kootenay Lake Ferry. He'd hung out at an old motel and RV park for a spell, staying in a crap little unit in exchange for doing odd jobs. Wanda the owner was okay. She'd heat up some pork and beans, sit down and have a beer with him, jaw about the ex-husband who'd left her in that god-forsaken hole.

Then an obituary for the lawyer Nina lived with came out in the local papers. It gave him a jolt to see the details right there in black and white. But he took it as a sign the time was right to approach Nina again. Last time she was probably still stressed-out by all the rigmarole related to her boss's death. By now she should be ready to get on with her life.

He got dropped off short of the ferry slip, walked the gravel side road, then bushwhacked up to the prospector's shack – déjà vu all over again. He was hungry, but if he ever ate another can of Campbell's Pork and Beans it would be too soon. Anyhow, he expected to eat his next meal with Nina. He grabbed the towel and a bar of soap and headed to the stream. The water was colder than a witch's tit but Max didn't mind, not with the prize so close. He lathered up by the stream and shaved as best he could without a mirror. He was down to his last clean shirt and his backpack was stuffed with dirty laundry. Nina would offer to do his washing but he wouldn't let her, not that night. After she made them a bite to eat they'd hit the sack. He got hard just thinking about it.

Max walked down the mountain feeling like a million bucks. He didn't stop until he had a view of the cottage.

What the…? Cops again! Holy shit.

This time there was yellow tape around the building. But if this was a crime scene, what was the crime? The lawyer's death was old news. Had there been a break-in? If some dirt-bag had waved a gun in Nina's face he would find him and make him pay.

Max sat on his pack and tried to settle down as he waited and watched. After a couple hours, a uniform came out and nosed around, checked out the Range Rover, messed with a metal drum by the shed then went back inside. Still no sign of Nina. Max waited another hour then made his way back to the shack. What the fuck was going on? If Nina had taken off, how would he ever find her?

26

STELLA ACCEPTED BEN'S OFFER of a lift home from the police station. Neither of them had much to say during the twenty-minute drive. When he pulled up to the darkened cabin, she thanked him and got out before fishing in her bag for her keys. Inside Joe wandered out of the bedroom in his boxers, his chest bare, and pulled her into a hug. She held on until he loosened his grip. "Get you anything?" he said.

She shook her head. "Go back to bed. I'll join you in a minute." She was too wound up to sleep but didn't feel like talking. The hug had felt good though.

Teeth brushed, face washed (some habits die hard) she dropped her clothes on the bedroom floor and crawled under the covers, snuggled up against Joe's back. He groaned softly; she stroked his chest until he drifted off again.

When she rolled onto her back the horror crept back in.

Nina was dead. Sprawled on the floor of that spotless kitchen she had worked her heart out to maintain. A secluded death scene that couldn't have been more unlike Lillian's at the City Wharf. It would have been too easy, too glib to say each woman died as she had lived, Lillian in the spotlight, Nina in the shadows. No, for Stella the difference came down to an uncomfortable truth: she had let Nina down.

Back when Lillian's body was discovered, Stella hadn't even considered going along with the police to notify Nina. She simply hadn't thought of her as Lillian's next of kin. Then she'd drifted into the vacuum left by Lillian's death without really grasping that Nina had no one else to turn to. Add to that the suspicious syringe, which Stella had turned over to Dr. Antoniak without first taking Nina aside to discuss the implications. And maybe worst of all, Stella had allowed Nina to depend on her without making a genuine commitment to follow through. Even that evening when she'd gone over to check in on her, she had fully intended to hustle back to her own family as soon as she could get away.

When the self-flagellation got to be too much, Stella reached for a flashlight and her Louise Penny book and slipped out to the kitchen for a glass of milk. On the way, she stubbed her toe on the edge of the cast-iron, wood-burning stove and had to bite back a stream of four-letter words. Once she had settled into a wicker chair on the porch, the refrigerator came on with the force of a locomotive and Stella wondered whether that was normal – to hear the fridge from outside. Or was it on its last legs? Another expense they couldn't afford. She read the first page of the mystery novel, read it again, and closed the book. She went back inside for her phone and scrolled through her photos to find the alleged murder-suicide note.

I KILLED LILLIAN. WE ARGUED ABOUT HER ROWING TO VANESSA'S HOUSE. I LOST MY TEMPER AND IN-JECTED HER WITH INSULIN. TO LILLIAN, I WAS ONLY A HOUSEKEEPER. HER FRIENDS DON'T REALIZE HOW SHE TREATED ME IN PRIVATE. YES, I KILLED LILLIAN. BUT I CANNOT STAND THE GUILT AND LONELINESS SO NOW I MUST TAKE MY OWN LIFE.

Her friends don't realize how she treated me in private. It was true Lillian could be imperious at times; she had been used to taking charge. She might have lorded it over Nina when they were alone, treating her more like a servant than a companion. Other than dabbling in the garden, Lillian had rarely lifted a finger around the place. And when Nathalie or Amelie dropped by the cottage, the conversation most likely switched to French, leaving Nina out in the cold. Bottom line: regardless of how Lillian's relationship with Nina might have evolved, it had begun as that of employer and employee – and some routines may have stuck.

At 1:55 a.m. Stella forced herself back to bed, slipped under the covers, and lay as still as possible so as not to wake Joe. An hour later she got up for another glass of milk. In bed again, she took a series of deep, cleansing breaths to try to release the tension that had crept into her neck. No good – the muscles remained tight as a spring. Joe made a spluttering noise. Joe never had trouble sleeping. She tried not to hate him for it. She tossed and turned, dozed a little.

The clock read 3:16 a.m. when she sat up, grabbed her phone, and lurched outside.

After four rings, Ben picked up and muttered something indecipherable. Stella kept her voice low. "Nina didn't write that note," she said. "Ben? Did you hear me? There is no way she wrote that note." In her mind's eye, she saw him sit up and swing his long legs over the side of the bed, run his fingers through dark tousled hair.

"What?" he said, groggily. "How do you know?"

"I finally figured out what was wrong with that so-called confession. The fourth sentence reads, 'Her friends *don't* realize how she treated me in private.' At first, I got side tracked thinking about the meaning of that sentence, the implications for Nina. But it's the grammar that doesn't ring true, the word 'don't.' Nina would have written 'do not.' Nina never used contractions."

* * *

McKean checked his watch. In seven minutes' time he was slated to brief the Chief of Police, who would expect him to affirm that Nina Huber had confessed to the murder of Lillian Fenniwick then killed herself, thereby saving the department a great deal of time and trouble. Too bad he wouldn't be able to oblige. In her late-night call, Stella had insisted Huber didn't write the note left at the scene of her death. If that hunch proved correct, there would be no hope for a quick wrap-up to the investigations.

With a heavy heart, McKean cancelled his flight for the weekend trip to Fort St. John. He put off calling his wife; that would come later, at home, over a cold beer. Dutch courage. He thought about his son, gone now for more than two weeks, and all the things he must have missed with the little guy growing up so fast.

But he couldn't let himself get all soppy. He had to focus on the job. With another suspicious death there would be another autopsy. The coroner had recalled Dr. Antoniak, who was due to arrive Friday, the following day.

McKean checked his watch again. Time to face the boss.

Upstairs, a secretary waved him through. The Chief was backlit by his picture window as he shook hands with Ray Eberly. "McKean," he bellowed. "While you've been pushing paper around, your colleague here has been getting his hands dirty. He found an empty wallet in Huber's trash that could crack this case wide open."

27

TO LET HER FRIENDS at book club know about Nina's death, Stella asked the remaining members to meet her at Oso Negro Café. Vanessa, Carli, and Nathalie agreed to be there. Amelie had to decline; two of her three children were home with strep throat.

Stella had called ahead so their standard orders would be ready when everyone arrived. The server did her usual, "Who's the skinny decaf latté?" routine as the four women settled at a window table in the half-empty coffee shop. The sound system was off. A tap dripped in the background. The latest Art Walk paintings featured haunted human faces that crudely resembled *The Scream* by Edvard Munch.

"Creepy pictures," Carli observed. "Who buys that stuff?" She added a few grains of sugar to her espresso. "So, Stell, what's up? What's with the mysterious meeting?"

Vanessa called the server back to order a muffin, preferably bran, with a small pat of butter on the side. "Just a heads up," she said to the others. "I can't stay long. My Maybelline shipment is blocking the rear exit of the store."

Stella waited for the server to bring Vanessa's muffin before she brought up the reason for the gathering. "I'm afraid I have sad news," she began. "And there's no easy way to break it to you... Nina is dead. I found her body at her cottage yesterday."

Vanessa's knife clattered to the floor. She put a hand to her mouth.

Carli said, "Nina – dead? What happened?"

Stella described her visit to the cottage, the unlatched door, and Nina collapsed in the kitchen. Leaving out any mention of the insulin pump or the laptop, she went on to tell them about the arrival of the police and her trip to the station. In stunned silence, the women let her talk on and on until she finally grew quiet too.

"How did she die?" Carli said. "Does anyone know at this

point?"

"The police are investigating," Stella said.

"*Mon dieu, mon dieu*," Nathalie muttered. My god, my god.

"You don't think she killed herself?" Carli said quietly. "We know she was crushed over losing Lillian. I guess we all worried about her. But dead..."

Vanessa shook her head. "Nina didn't do living alone well, did she? But still, to take her own life..."

"Unless someone killed her," Carli said. "The police still don't really know what happened to Lillian, do they?"

"Probably best not to speculate at this point," Stella said.

"Well, yes," Vanessa said. "Hopefully there's some kind of cut-and-dried explanation."

"Christ, Vanessa," Carli said. "What kind of cut-and-dried explanation could there be? Two of our friends are dead. Any of us could be in danger. I'm surprised you're not freaking out. What if there's a serial killer going after women on the East Shore?"

Nathalie blanched.

"Carli, stop. That's awful." Vanessa fluttered her hands in front of her face. "Don't say things like that. You're upsetting Nathalie. No. I knew Nina well and she was not happy. Full stop." She grabbed for a napkin and brushed at her eyes. "But why did she have to die? First Lillian and now Nina – I've lost my best friends. Present company excluded, of course."

Stella reached across the table and squeezed Vanessa's arm. "All we can do is be there for each other," she said, inwardly cringing at the hackneyed expression. "I guess we have another funeral to plan. Not today though."

"No, not today," Carli said.

Vanessa sighed, palms flat on the table as she pushed herself to her feet. "Well, ladies, I'm sorry to do this given the circumstances, but I really have to get back."

"Your Maybelline shipment," Carli said drily.

Vanessa sighed again. "It isn't going to unpack itself, Carli."

* * *

Early Friday morning, the business offices at the *Times* were deserted and Stella was alone in the newsroom. She turned on the lights and opened a window then checked her voicemail. Jade was on some mysterious assignment in the Slocan Valley. A message from Patrick indicated he would be late; the baby looked jaundiced and needed a blood test. There was no word from Ben, not that Stella particularly expected to hear from him.

The office door banged open and a gravelly voice called, "Anybody home?" Stella peeked around the corner for a view of the front counter. The voice belonged to a stocky, thuggish-looking man, probably early fifties. She flashed on the irate caller whose Letter to the Editor they had failed to publish. What a fool she'd been to leave the main entrance unlocked – Patrick told her to lock that door when she was alone. "Good morning," she said, moving across the room and behind the counter, forcing a smile, her mind racing. "Can I help you?"

"Um, maybe." His neck was a trapezoid that began at his jawline and ended mid-shoulder. Bulging triceps and pectorals gave shape to a faded Gold's Gym T-shirt, which was tucked into his jeans. "I have this long-lost cousin who lives around here," he said. "A second cousin. I wanted to get in touch with her and I just wondered… I don't think she's missing or anything, but maybe I could put an ad in the paper? Do you have boxes a person can write to?"

"Sure," Stella said, breathing a silent sigh of relief. "But it'll be faster to reach your cousin if you put a contact number or email address in the ad."

"I'll use a box." The man shifted his eyes around, glanced out the window then back at Stella.

She rummaged in a drawer for a classified ads form. "The business office isn't open yet but I can take your information," she said. "Name?"

His left eye twitched. "Campbell. Bob Campbell."

"Okay, Mr. Campbell. Phone number?"

"I lost my cell. I'm just passing through so…"

"No problem. What's your cousin's name, by the way? I might know her."

"Second cousin," said the beefy stranger. "Nina Huber."

Fight or flight? The choice was obvious but, God help her, Stella couldn't move. Frozen in place, she made herself look Max Huber straight in the eye. "Would that, uh, would that be Huber with an H?" Her breathing was slightly laboured but she made herself keep talking. "Don't think I've met the lady. But I'll tell you what, Mr. Campbell. Jot down what you want to say, okay? I'll come back in a sec and let you know what the ad will cost. The price, uh – that'll depend on how many words you use and the number of days the ad runs. I'll be right back, okay? I'll be back in one second."

He accepted a pen and gazed down at the form.

Stella gradually regained movement in her legs and made her way back into the newsroom to grab her phone. Curbing an impulse to pelt down the back hall and scream for help, she slipped into the washroom and locked the door. Fingers trembling, she entered Ben McKean's personal number and prayed he would pick up.

28

TWO DAYS AFTER NINA Huber's body was found at the yellow cottage, McKean went back to his notes for the Fenniwick case. If Stella's theory proved correct – if the note left at Huber's death scene was a fake – all bets were off for both investigations.

On the original list of possible suspects there was a big question mark beside Henry Sutton's name. In McKean's interviews with book club members, Carli DeLuca had painted a picture of a sleazeball embezzler while Vanessa Levitt seemed to do everything in her power to deflect suspicion from him. All in all, Sutton seemed like a man worth talking to.

Through IBET, the Integrated Border Enforcement Team, McKean determined that Sutton had entered Canada from the United States four days prior to the murder of Lillian Fenniwick. His stated purpose for the visit was pleasure and he had cited "retired life coach" as his occupation. Sutton had crossed into British Columbia in a Ford Focus registered to his name at an address in Coeur d'Alene, Idaho. He had gone back to the States in the Focus at 10:17 a.m. on the day Lillian Fenniwick's body had been found. After that date, there was no evidence Sutton had returned to Canada, which made it unlikely he was in the country on the day Nina Huber died.

But something else popped up in the system that was noteworthy. Sutton had entered Canada at the border crossing close to Nelson on his last trip, but returned to the United States at the crossing farther east, near Creston. Did Sutton have contacts over there? McKean made a note to investigate; he would put Eberly on it. Regardless of hearsay, Sutton's relationship with Lillian Fenniwick and the timing of his movements at the border qualified him as a person of interest in her death.

McKean was vaguely aware of the protocol required for a Canadian police officer to question someone residing in the US. He would first have to convince the Chief to contact the RCMP in Ottawa who – if they saw fit – would then notify the FBI in the States. The Chief wouldn't like it. He'd ask why the FBI would want to be bothered with Sutton when there wasn't enough evidence to arrest him in Canada. Good question. Was it enough that Canadian authorities considered a US citizen a possible murder suspect? If federal agents in the States were willing to do a background check and set up an SIP, Special Interest Police, entry on their national computer system, they would be notified if Sutton was located or had any dealings with American law enforcement. But without grounds to arrest him, the Bureau could only request an interview with Sutton; he would have to be willing to cooperate. McKean made some quick notes for his pitch to the Chief and prepared himself to be thrown out of the big guy's office.

Before he went upstairs, McKean called the hospital to see if Dr. Antoniak had arrived back in town. An administrator confirmed he was there. The forensic pathologist was scheduled to perform the autopsy on Nina Huber's body that afternoon.

What would he find? The insulin pump on the floor near the body pointed to the possibility of another insulin-related death. But McKean was not about to jump to any conclusion. The pump could simply have fallen out of Huber's pocket when she collapsed. Alcohol had been implicated in the Fenniwick murder, but Nina Huber was found dead in her kitchen with no drinking glasses or open bottles or any other evidence of alcohol use in view. No sign of a struggle either, or of forced entry into the cottage. What had gone wrong?

McKean's cell rang. Stella Mosconi told him in a frantic whisper to get the hell over to the *Times*.

* * *

At the newspaper office Max read over his ad for the third time. He'd settled on: "Attention Nina Huber. A long-lost relation wants to see you. Send your phone number. You won't be sorry." Max crossed out the last sentence and put down the pen. The gal with the long hair was nowhere in sight. Must have gone to the can. Max wandered over to the window just as a panda car pulled up in front of the building and – *fuck* – two frigging uniforms jumped out and thundered up the stairwell.

"Max Huber?" said the tall, swarthy-looking one, as they barged in. "We'd like to talk to you."

The paper with the ad was forgotten as the plods hustled Max down to their car.

At the station, he recognized Sergeant McKean as the cop who'd visited Nina at the yellow cottage. The other guy, a Corporal Eberly, was the one he'd seen the other day when the cottage was covered in crime scene tape. Eberly was skinny as a rail. How did a guy like that pass the physical to be a cop?

McKean said, "We've been looking for you, Mr. Huber."

"Yeah, well, I been down at the Coast," Max said.

"Oh, that's right," Eberly piped up. "Her Majesty put you up in one of her fine establishments."

Max would have paid money to slam Eberly's bone-rack body against a wall, but he kept his head. "If you talked to my parole officer, you know I've done my time. I'm a free man, okay? All I wanna do is find my wife. Last time I checked that wasn't a crime."

"Your wife?" McKean said, glancing pointedly at his notebook. "At the *Times*, I believe you referred to Nina Huber as a second cousin."

Max thought fast. "Guess that was just my foolish pride, officer. A man doesn't like to say he has to put an ad in the paper to find his wife."

"When was the last time you saw your wife?" McKean said, his tone suddenly irritable.

Was the cop having woman trouble too? That made Max feel a bit better. "Not since I was locked up a little over a year ago," he said.

"You haven't approached her since you came to town?" McKean pressed.

"Haven't had the chance – I was planning to surprise her."

"Which was it?" Mr. Bag 'o' bones. "You haven't had the chance – or you wanted to surprise her?"

Max ignored him. McKean moved on. "You've been in the area how long now?"

"A day or two," Max said.

"Describe your whereabouts over the past forty-eight hours, Mr. Huber," McKean said. "Take your time. We'll need you to account for every hour."

"Well, let's see now." Max leaned back in the chair and scratched his chin. "Few days ago I went to Creston and then –"

"Why Creston?" Eberly again.

"I was hitching, see. Got to talking with the driver and before I knew it he was on the cut-off to Creston. And I thought, what the hell? I have an old friend in Creston, name of Betty Martin. She's having a hard time with her motel so I stayed and helped her around the place before I came here. She appreciated it but she knew I wanted to see my wife. Said to be sure and give Nina a big hug for her." *Nice touch,* Max told himself, *very nice touch.*

"We'll need contact information for Betty Martin so she can back up your story," McKean said. "But for now, go on. You were in Creston…"

"Yesterday I came over to Nelson. Hitched a ride with a kid in a pickup just passing through. I wasn't sure where to find Nina. Looked in the phone book for a number. No listing under Huber."

"You didn't know where she lived?" McKean said. "Or who she lived with?"

"She was helping a nice lawyer-lady out on the lake, wasn't she? But damned if I could remember exactly where they lived. These addresses out in the sticks…" Max shrugged.

"Where did you spend the night?"

"Let's see now." He scratched his chin again. "Guess I kind of slept rough in the woods outside of town. Don't think I broke any laws. No 'Private Property' signs that I could see."

"There's a shack up behind the lawyer's cottage – maybe you know it." Eberly's grin was so wide Max could have reached in and yanked out his frigging tonsils. "Don't suppose we'll find your prints on anything in that shack, huh?"

Max started to get up. "I don't know anything about no shack. Are we done here?"

McKean took back control of the interview. "Sit down please, Mr. Huber. We're just getting started."

* * *

It was Friday afternoon and true to form the Chief was still dragging his feet about sending a request to the RCMP in Ottawa. "They'll want more evidence implicating your Mr. Sutton before they go to the FBI," he told McKean. "From where I sit, if Nina Huber didn't kill Fenniwick – and that's a big if – her husband likely did. Max Huber is a more plausible suspect than Sutton. Makes no sense to bring in National Division if the killer is sitting right under our noses."

Max Huber was still on the radar all right, but finding no grounds to arrest him, it had been necessary for McKean to let him go. But not before Eberly leaked the fact the poor bugger's wife was dead. Huber fell apart at the news – or appeared to.

You never knew what would come out of Eberly's mouth next, and if you couldn't trust his judgment, anything he did was open to question. For starters, how thoroughly had he searched the yellow cottage on the night of Huber's death? Once he'd found her wallet in the metal drum he was probably so pleased with himself he didn't look any further. You'd think he'd found the Holy Grail the way he scampered back to tell the Chief, yet they were no closer to solving the case.

McKean decided to check out the place himself.

He caught the next ferry to the East Shore and bent down under the police tape to let himself into the cottage. The black handbag still lay on its side behind the front door. It was hard to connect a robbery with a body found some distance away in another room – and nothing disturbed in the space between.

McKean began a search of the bedrooms. In Nina Huber's room it was soon obvious that Eberly the Great hadn't pulled out the dresser drawers. Taped to the bottom of an underwear drawer was an envelope, inside it *The Last Will and Testament of Nina Katrin Huber*, dated three years back. McKean sat down to peruse the short document. In it, Huber named Lillian Fenniwick executrix of her estate. The sole beneficiary was none other than Huber's now estranged husband, Max.

McKean made a dash for the ferry and made it back to Nelson before five o'clock, hoping to catch Fenniwick's lawyer before the end of his workday. But Arthur Nugent had left his Baker Street office. A note on the door read, "Gone fishing. Back Monday unless enlightenment achieved."

Enlightenment. Odds were Nugent would be back on the job after the weekend. Still, McKean thought, must be nice to have nothing better to do than contemplate your navel.

* * *

After the run-in with Max Huber, Stella spent the rest of Friday looking over her shoulder. She had been hiding out in the restroom when Ben and his corporal burst in to nab him. Now she wondered if they'd made an arrest. Otherwise, as the one who called the cops, she was vulnerable.

That afternoon as she cycled along the lakeshore highway, a dark grey pickup swerved onto the shoulder and almost ran her off the road. The driver, a guy of indeterminate age wearing a ball cap, didn't stop. She'd been too flustered to catch his plate number. Maybe it was a case of distracted driving. Or maybe Max Huber had gotten his hands on a truck and come after her.

At home Stella was disappointed not to find Joe waiting. On her way up the porch steps, her phone dinged with a text indicating he'd be late; she shouldn't delay dinner. After the babysitter left, Matt and Nicky played a noisy, aggressive game of cops and robbers until Stella, her nerves shot, put a stop to it and sent them outside.

The house phone rang and the call display read "Unavailable." Stella picked up. No one spoke but she could hear what sounded like heavy breathing. She wanted to sit down and cry.

It happened again after Joe got home, a call from Unavailable. "Telemarketer," he said. "Leave it."

Stella waited for the ringing to stop then checked for a message. "The caller let the recording run but didn't speak," she said. "Maybe it's not a telemarketer."

Joe frowned. "Could be a prankster. If you turn off the caller ID on a disposable phone, it shows up as Unavailable."

"I don't like this," Stella said. "I'm going to keep track of the calls."

29

SATURDAY MORNING MCKEAN WALKED to the station and from the evidence room, signed out the laptop on which Nina Huber's alleged murder/suicide note had appeared. As Stella had predicted, the computer found near Huber's body had been registered to Lillian Fenniwick.

According to the department's IT guy, McKean was in for several hours of tedious reading. Minutes from hospital board meetings, personal email dating back three years, a host of Google searches – the most recent on investment clubs in Idaho.

McKean watched for references to Henry Sutton, particularly any that touched on his relationships with the deceased women. But even after spending the better part of a day and evening bent over the laptop, he had little to show for his efforts. Sutton had been cagey in the handful of email notes he had sent to Lillian Fenniwick. Nothing but social niceties and vague allusions to when he might visit; no messages related to finances. For a person with limited eyesight, Fenniwick seemed to have a lot of favourites on Google. Maybe Nina Huber read aloud to her, which might explain Henry Sutton's reticence to say much in his emails.

Shortly after midnight McKean fell into bed, his brain fried. When the phone on the bedside table rang, he let the call go to voicemail. The phone rang again. He picked up.

"It's me," Miranda said. "Aiden and me kind of miss you."

McKean propped himself up on one elbow. "Come home then," he said.

"Two days of driving? Don't think I can hack it. Aiden cried all the way here."

"I could fly up and drive you back. But I don't know when I can get away."

"Can you make it next weekend? Ma is driving me nuts."

* * *

On Saturday Zoe took the ten o'clock bus that went out of town along the lakeshore road to the ferry terminal. Kieran met her on the other side. She could have died happy when he took her hand to lead her to his uncle's place. He was out on tour with his band in Kelowna that weekend.

The cedar house was about half a kilometre from the ferry dock. Tall trees everywhere – you could hardly see the front door. At the back, a hot tub bubbled on a deck that had a peek-a-boo view of the lake. Right away Kieran pulled out a baggie of weed and rolled a joint. He lit it, took a drag, and held it out to her. She felt nervous, but what was the big deal? Her own mother snuck a cigarette almost every a day, which she thought no one knew about. Zoe took a small puff and immediately started coughing from the smoke. Kieran laughed, but not in a mean way. He showed her how to hold in the smoke and let it out slowly. She took a few more pulls.

"Want a tour?" Kieran said.

"What's 'ahture'?" she said. They laughed hysterically.

Kieran led her around saying, "This is the living room, that's the dining room. Bathroom's in there." Despite being slightly buzzed, Zoe was wary of the tour ending up in his bedroom. But Kieran suggested they go back outside and sit in the hot tub. He grabbed a couple of glasses and a bottle of red wine from a wooden rack in the kitchen. Out on the deck he twisted the cap on the bottle and filled both glasses to the brim. Then he pulled his shirt over his head and undid the top button of his jeans.

Zoe said, "Oops – I didn't bring my bathing suit."

"Who cares, suits are optional," Kieran said.

Oh. My. God. Zoe had just smoked weed and was prepared to drink a little wine – her parents drank wine every night – but there was no way she could take off her clothes in front of a boy.

Kieran pulled off the band that held back his amazing hair and kind of shook his head. When he unzipped his fly, Zoe stared at her fingernail polish. He folded back a blue vinyl cover, stepped out of his pants, and eased himself into the hot tub. "I'll close my eyes while you get in," he said.

"That's okay," Zoe said, thankful she was wearing shorts instead of skinny jeans. She kicked off her shoes. "I'll just dangle my feet in the water. I get kind of overheated in hot tubs."

"Yeah?" Kieran splashed her and she splashed him back. "So how long can you stay? There's a party tonight." He reached for his jeans and pulled out the baggie of weed.

"That would be so cool except I have to catch the 3:30 bus back. My mom thinks I'm tutoring a friend today. If I'm late for dinner she'll have a coronary."

"No shit… I could call you a cab so you could stay longer."

"A taxi? Are you serious? That would cost like fifty or sixty dollars."

"I'm good for it."

"Your uncle must be generous."

"My uncle? You gotta be kidding." He inhaled and passed her the joint. Zoe shook her head. "Money's not hard to come by if you keep your eyes open," he said. He grabbed her leg and pretended to pull her in.

She braced herself and splashed him with her other foot. "What do you mean? Sounds like you just find it or something."

"Zoe," he said slowly. "Somebody leaves cash lying around they might lose it. Law of the jungle."

She didn't ask him what he meant by *lying around*. "Are you hungry?" she said. "We could get a burger or something at the ferry slip."

"There's leftover pizza."

Zoe studied a thermometer on the side of the house while Kieran got out of the hot tub and wrapped a towel around his waist. "You want to listen to some music?" he said, picking up his pants and the wine bottle. "C'mon. I'll show you my room."

* * *

Carli had been a wreck ever since she had heard about Nina. A second death coming days after Lillian's accident (if that's what it had been) seemed downright sinister. Carli would wake up in the morning and remember, then feel all helpless and weepy, which was not like her at all. She decided to move up her appointment at the hair salon, her happy place. What she needed was to feel a little pampered, gossip with her stylist, lose herself in some trashy magazines.

And now it was Saturday. While Zoe helped a friend with math and Tim played squash, Carli sat paging through the latest edition of *Us*. Her stylist was in the back, mixing her tawny blond tint. Carli wasn't paying much attention to the hum of salon chatter until one particular conversation made her prick up her ears. A woman sitting a few chairs down said, "I told Cassandra. Forget it, I said. That Kieran Corcoran is trouble with a capital T. You are forbidden to date him. Don't even think about it." Kieran was the name of the boy who had been at Stella's place the day of the canoe incident. He'd turned up more than once, apparently, and Stella seemed to think Zoe was the draw. Carli and Tim had followed up with a little talk to their daughter about the responsibilities of a babysitter.

"Trouble as in sex, drugs, and rock 'n' roll?" said the woman's stylist.

The patron laughed. "That about covers it. Cassandra sulked for a week but she knew I was right. He must have messed up bad for his mother to send him all the way out west from Toronto. And that uncle of his is not up to much, a second-rate guitar player who works summers at the nursery. He lets the kid do whatever he wants."

Carli peeked sideways down the row of chairs. She couldn't place the mother although like most people in Nelson she looked familiar. Carli's stylist returned and applied her colour and put her under a hairdryer. Taking up her magazine again, Carli turned to a page with photos of three starlets in identical gowns and tried to decide which one wore the dress best. But it was impossible to enjoy herself now that she had even more reason to be concerned about this Kieran character.

Carli was grateful for one thing: Zoe was an outstanding student, completely self-directed with aspirations to become a palaeontologist or a doctor or something of that calibre. Not many teenagers would give up a Saturday to tutor a friend in geometry. Zoe said it would take the entire day, maybe Sunday too. Shelby was seriously in danger of failing eighth-grade math.

Someone passed Carli a cup of herbal tea that smelled of peaches and cinnamon, Lillian's signature brew, and now she felt sad again. She hoped to hell Sergeant McKean was on to Henry Sutton as a suspect. The old phoney had gotten away with bilking his clients out of an obscene amount of money but could he get away with murder? Tim thought it unlikely Sutton had bumped anyone off. "Financial cheats don't kill their clients," he said. "Ruin their retirement, yes. Turn their lives into a living hell, by all means. But murder? I don't think so. Too much exposure." Tim was an idealist; that was one of the things Carli loved about him.

Later, outside the hair salon, a mob of teenagers was blocking the sidewalk. A voice from the crowd said, "Hi, Ms. DeLuca."

Carli looked up. "Shelby? What are you doing downtown? I thought Zoe was helping you with geometry."

"Um, we finished early?" Shelby's ears turned bright red. One of the other girls snickered behind her hand.

"Awesome," Carli said, pleasantly. "I expect you know where Zoe went after you finished your homework. Spill."

The girl couldn't have told a lie to save her life. She said Zoe had taken the bus to visit Kieran Corcoran over on the East Shore. Carli believed Shelby when she claimed not to know the exact location of the house or the uncle's name. Undaunted, she got into her Lexus and drove up the lake. She only had to approach five cars in the ferry line-up before she found an acquaintance of the musician who had taken in a teenaged nephew. The driver told her to follow him after they disembarked; he would flash his hazards when he came to the uncle's house.

Carli waved at her guide, parked the Lexus, and walked up a path to a flat-roofed cedar home. The doorknocker was a crudely carved woodpecker. She rapped on the front door. No answer. Knocked again, this time with a closed fist, again to no avail. At the back of the house, steam rose from an uncovered hot tub and a sliding door stood open to a kitchen. Carli leaned inside and called her daughter's name. No response. The kitchen featured an old butcher-block island gouged with knife marks and strewn with empty pizza boxes. But the place didn't smell of pizza – somebody had been smoking pot. Christ Almighty. A thumping sound came from the interior of the house. "Zoe!" Carli called again, more urgently now. "Zoe, are you here?"

She followed the thumping to a closed door, tapped, waited a second or two then turned the knob and eased the door open a crack. "What the fuck!" Kieran Corcoran was in her face, shirtless, the top button of his jeans undone. Zoe had her hands behind her back. With a start Carli realized her thirteen-year-old was doing up the clasp on her bra.

30

SUNDAY JOE WENT TO the high school to finish his report cards while Stella stayed home with Matt and Nicky. Unrelenting rain made her almost stir-crazy in the cramped quarters of their cabin. What their two-storey home in Vancouver had lacked in charm, it had made up for in space, for each son, a bedroom; for Stella, a study all her own. Today with extra time on her hands, all the worries she had pushed to the back of her mind came flooding to the forefront. The mysterious man with the brown dog, the silent caller, the irate letter writer, the driver of a pick-up that had run her off the road. She didn't even want to think about Max Huber.

The boys played Monopoly on the covered porch, whining that the wicker furniture stunk like an old basement. Back inside they continued to hold their noses claiming the smelly trash bins in the mudroom made them want to puke. Stella suggested a trip to the dump but the little princes declined and begged to watch Netflix. The pounding of rain on the tin roof put the kibosh on that. "I wish we still lived in Vancouver," Matt whinged. "Or at least right in Nelson where there's something to do."

"Yeah." Nicky mimicked his brother's tone. "All our friends live in town."

"The three of us can have fun together," Stella said, forcing a bright smile. To her credit, she'd checked the weather forecast in advance and prepared for a rainy day at home. Now she brought out construction paper, brushes, and new paints and suggested the boys make a picture book for her boss Patrick's new baby. She reminded them of the story she'd told the day they hiked up the hill behind Nina's cottage. The one about the mother bear and cubs, the little girl lost in the forest. "We should brainstorm the storyline first and all the names," she said. "Do you think the little girl should be named after the baby?"

"I'll paint but I don't want to brainstorm," Matt said.

"Same here," said Nicky.

"Be my guests," Stella said. "But remember how the small bear scattered flowers so the girl could find her way back to the beach? How about I make tissue-paper flowers and glue them on for a 3D effect."

Everyone set to work but when the rain finally let up at around two o'clock, all three of them were more than ready to escape the cabin. The boys argued about what to do next. Nicky wanted to go to a playground, Matt didn't feel like it. The only thing they both seemed to want was a store-bought treat. Stella craved a hit of adult company. In the end they drove to town, stopped at the grocery store for a small carrot cake, then continued on to Mountain Lake Centre for a pop in visit with Will Irwin.

Will took a while to answer Stella's tap on the door. His hair was mussed and the bedclothes rumpled. "Will – I'm so sorry to disturb you," Stella said.

"We have cake," said Matt.

"It's for you," Nicky added. "But Mom says you'll probably share."

Will smiled. "Come in, come in. You boys will find dishes and cutlery in my efficiency kitchen over there."

While Matt and Nicky looked for plates and forks Will had a quiet word with Stella. "I read about the latest death, the woman from over on the East Shore. Former housekeeper of Lillian Fenniwick."

Stella said, "You guys go wash your hands in the bathroom. And don't forget to use soap." She dropped her voice to a whisper. "Nina Huber. I found her body, Will. I'll tell you the whole sad story one day when you-know-who aren't with me."

At home that evening Joe admired the boys' storybook. "Whose idea was it for the bears to leave a trail of flowers?" he asked.

"Mom's," said Matt. "The whole thing was Mom's idea."

Later, when the boys were in bed, Joe said, "Scattered flowers. Really? Even the stories you tell the boys have echoes of Lillian's death. You can't let it go, can you?"

Stella turned up the radio and dropped her voice. "Give me a break. The boys liked the story and enjoyed making the book. And, okay, I *am* curious about the flowers in Lillian's rowboat. For one thing, they were strewn all over the place. Lillian usually tied her bouquets with string. I forgot to mention that to Ben."

"Oh, it's 'Ben' is it? You're obsessed – you know that? God help us now that you have a second death to fixate on."

"So you're a shrink now?"

"It doesn't take a shrink to recognize a faraway look, like you're not completely here. You're not even physically present as much as you should be. That paper doesn't pay you enough for the hours you put in. Other people seem to be able to work at the *Times* without letting it take over their lives."

"Oh, like your friend Jade?"

"Oh, for chrissake. You're not listening, Stella, you're not hearing me. But since you bring up Jade, well, yeah, she seems to be able to balance work and play. Doesn't take herself too seriously."

"And you're well enough acquainted with Jade Visser to know all that?"

A beat. "It's a small town."

Stella switched off the radio, picked up her handbag, and walked out the door.

* * *

After a long, hot shower, Zoe DeLuca wiped the steam from the bathroom mirror with the side of her hand then hunched her shoulders together to see how her cleavage was coming along. She hoped she was growing. On Saturday Kieran had touched her. The memory of him grabbing and squeezing made her feel funny, but in a good way. If only her mother hadn't walked in on them at his uncle's place. She had absolutely forbidden Zoe to see him again.

But what could her parents do anyways – lock her up in her room? Worst case scenario she'd have to sit through another little talk.

Alone in her room Zoe took Kieran's gift from the secret compartment in her school bag and slipped it around her neck. He'd found a tiny piece of driftwood with a hole in the centre and threaded a length of purple raffia through the hole to make her a necklace. Purple was his favourite colour, he said. Zoe loved purple too. Still naked except for the homespun choker, she leaned her desk chair against the bedroom door and lay down on her bed to call Kieran. He sounded stoned when he answered the phone. "You must spend a fortune on weed," she said, then immediately regretted being dorky. Not so much dorky, as preachy – like her mom.

"For a little rich girl, you talk about money a lot," he said. "Maybe that's normal for little rich girls."

"I'm not rich," she said. "You're the one with all the money. You told me you find it lying around." She normally wouldn't have been so rude but she hated him calling her a little rich girl.

"How about you? Ever steal anything?" His voice was lazy and teasing.

"I stole some gum once when I was a kid," she said. "My dad wouldn't buy it for me so I took it." She left out the part where her mother marched her back to the store to apologize to the owner.

"No shit," Kieran said. "Good girl. I'll have to take you along on a heist."

"Oh sure."

"I'm not fucking with you – I mean it."

Zoe didn't like where the conversation was going but her curiosity got the better of her. "So, what's the biggest thing you ever stole?"

"I found a hundred bucks in a wallet last week."

"Whose wallet?" Zoe asked in a small voice.

"This is lame. Do you want to meet me downtown somewhere?"

"You know I'm grounded."

"Later then." He hung up.

* * *

Sunday evening McKean ended up on traffic patrol. He'd traded shifts with another member so he could take off the upcoming Friday and fly to Fort St. John to bring back his family.

On a straight stretch on the lakeshore road he set up a speed trap, then slid the front seat of the cruiser back a few notches and settled in to compare and contrast the facts of the two murders.

A car zipped by going twenty clicks over the posted speed.

McKean activated his lights and took off after the vehicle, cursing when he realized he was in pursuit of a familiar white Pathfinder. The Pathfinder pulled over. McKean got out and approached the driver side.

"Hi. Sorry." Stella handed over her driver's license and car registration. "I hate it when people speed along here."

McKean leaned in the open window. Her hair smelled of a meadow. "Aren't you going in the wrong direction?" he said.

"I had a fight with Joe."

"Follow me to the pull out under the power lines," he said. "You can help nab your fellow speeders."

Stella followed him, parked her car, and slid into the passenger side of the patrol car. "Is this legal?" she said.

He gave her a look. "Why the fight with your husband?"

"He thinks I'm *obsessed* with Lillian and Nina's deaths. I am obsessed. I'd rather sit here and talk about the investigations than pretty much anything else. That's the sick truth."

He had no response to that.

"How did it go with Max Huber?" she said.

"He's been cautioned not to leave town."

"Do you think he killed Nina?"

"His prints were all over the shack near her cottage, yet he denied knowing where his wife lived. He also couldn't tell us how long she'd been diabetic, or when she started using the insulin pump. Claimed he stopped in Creston to help out a friend – then gave us a false name for the so-called friend. So, we caught him in a bunch of lies but found no evidence he'd killed anyone. One of our members found Nina Huber's wallet in a trash burner out behind her place. No cash. Max denied any knowledge of that too."

"Could he have taken the money to make the murder look like a robbery gone bad?" Stella said.

"His prints weren't on the wallet or anywhere in the cottage, although he might have worn gloves. That laptop found at the scene had been wiped clean."

"You mentioned a friend in Creston…"

"Apparently he stayed a few nights at her motel in return for handyman duties. My colleague Ray Eberly tracked down the motel and its owner. She recalled the time and date Max left her place to return to Nelson, which coincided with the day you found his wife's body. Time-wise, he could have done the murder."

"If Nina told him about her relationship with Lillian, he wouldn't have been happy," Stella said. "Let's say that festered a while, he returned and killed her. Or Nina told him about her feelings for Lillian some weeks ago and he killed Lillian first. I wonder if she was still alive when he approached Nina after his release from prison."

"I still don't rule out the husband and wife colluding to kill Fenniwick. Neither of them had an alibi for the night she died."

"But Nina's dead too. And if Max killed her, why place the ad in the paper? To cover his tracks?"

"Possibly." McKean rubbed the back of his neck. "Although if he knew she was dead, he's a good actor. He went to pieces when Eberly let it slip during the interview. That guy never knows when to keep his mouth shut."

"Any news about Henry Sutton?"

"Still in the States. He was in Canada when Fenniwick was killed, but returned to the US the next day at the crossing near Creston. No record of his being in the country when Huber died."

"Could he have hired a hit man?" Stella said.

Ben looked at her. "I suppose," he said.

Stella clammed up for a while, frowned into the distance, alone with her thoughts. "What if the killer is someone we haven't even thought of – an outsider, say? Lillian practiced family law. Think of the thorny divorce and custody battles she would have stickhandled."

"She retired a long time ago though. What's it been now – ten years?"

"For a person bitter about a result, ten years could seem like yesterday. I might do some digging."

"In your spare time."

"Probably the least I can do. If Nina was innocent I'd hate to think I stood by while the authorities took that murder-suicide note at face value."

"Thanks for the vote of confidence," McKean said.

"Sorry, that didn't come out right. But I let Nina down when she was alive and now... well, I just wouldn't want her memory to be unfairly tarnished." She looked at him. "You're rubbing your neck again. When can you go home to your family?"

"No time soon. Wife took the baby to Fort St. John, her hometown. Left a note."

"That sounds... complicated."

"Yup." He kept his eyes front. "I'm going to fly up Friday and drive them back over the long weekend."

"I almost forgot Monday is the first of July. Well, that's good. It'll be good to have them back."

"Think your husband's getting worried?"

Stella shrugged. "Guess I should be on my way. But haven't you forgotten something, officer?"

"I'm letting you off with a verbal warning. Go home. And drive safe."

* * *

Alone on a Saturday night, Vanessa Levitt liked to crank up the volume on her sound system, eat and drink whatever struck her fancy, and get a little high. It amused her to think her naughty little secret would have blown the minds of even her closest friends.

But Sundays were different. Sunday evenings were set aside to plan her wardrobe for the week ahead, check for loose buttons, iron garments in need of pressing, polish shoes, make handbag changes. As her mother had drilled into her, a woman who carries the reputation of three generations of Levitts has a responsibility to look presentable in the public eye. On Sundays Vanessa gave herself a mani-pedi and a facial and consumed nothing stronger than Twinings Earl Grey tea. The routine was sacrosanct.

So, when the hospital pharmacist sent her a cutesy invitation to a bridal shower to be held that Sunday evening at seven, Vanessa was less than thrilled. But how could she decline? The guest of honour was one of Vanessa's favourite employees, a bright, efficient pharmacist who was fun to have around the store. She had lived with her boyfriend for five years though, and Vanessa had to wonder what the happy couple could possibly need after half a decade of co-habitation. She combed the kitchen shop, settled on a pair of tea towels with matching pot scrubber, and reconciled herself to a break in routine.

At the shower, Vanessa had to endure silly games and even sillier refreshments, including a vulgar cake decorated with male genitalia made out of marzipan. Most of the guests were thirtyish and the generation gap yawned like the Grand Canyon. Well, she had done her bit for staff harmony. At nine o'clock she took her leave and headed toward the ferry, slowing down when she spied a speed trap on the lakeshore road.

And there, parked a discreet distance from the police car, stood Stella Mosconi's white Pathfinder. Inside the cruiser, two heads instead of one. It was all Vanessa could do not to pull over and haul Stella away by the scruff of her neck.

31

HOME AFTER TRAFFIC DUTY, McKean beat himself up for inviting Stella Mosconi into his vehicle. His excuse had been her usefulness to the investigations. But he'd crossed a line when he made her privy to confidential information. Then crossed another when he allowed the conversation to drift into personal matters.

Too wired to sleep, he logged onto Netflix and watched multiple episodes of *Longmire* until he passed out on the couch. Just before everything went black, he realized the character Henry Standing Bear never uses contractions.

The following morning, McKean woke with a stiff neck. After a long hot shower and a full pot of black coffee, he drove directly to the morgue to speak with Ralph Antoniak, the forensic pathologist.

"Hate to tell you, but we have another death by insulin overdose," Dr. Antoniak said. "Only this time the victim had diabetes. Sadly, it's not unheard of for a diabetic to commit suicide by upping the dose of insulin, sometimes in combination with alcohol and pills. Depression is common among these folks. Imagine having to constantly monitor your blood sugars. Give yourself several injections a day and watch every bite you take. The victim had an insulin pump, which would have made life easier. But a pump doesn't entirely relieve the daily burden. Not by a long shot." He grimaced. "Pun not intended."

"Could you tell where the excess insulin came from?" McKean said.

"Easily. You could see the pump had been programmed to deliver a large bolus at once, enough to kill her. Seems consistent with the note found on the laptop."

"Trouble is, the validity of the note is open to question," McKean said. "Stella Mosconi, the local reporter you met last time you were here, maintains that Huber didn't write it. The note contains a contraction and Huber apparently never used contractions. Which puts us in the woolly realm of literary forensics, in this case QDE, Questioned Document Examination. Not sure how it would hold up in court. But if Stella's correct – that Huber didn't kill herself – that would also put us back to square one with the Fenniwick case."

"QDE is a legitimate arm of forensics," Antoniak said. "But unless Ms. Mosconi is an expert in it, I wouldn't jump to any conclusions."

"She's no expert in forensics but she is a reporter with a good eye for detail."

"Point taken. But I'd say the odds still favour suicide in the Huber case."

"Maybe, but there are a couple of other irregularities worth noting," McKean said. "On the night Mosconi discovered Huber's body, the front door of the cottage was unlocked, not even properly latched. Seemed this was unusual. After Fenniwick's death Huber never left the door unlocked. And another thing: on the night she died, her wallet was found outside with the cash missing."

"Any theories?"

"Her estranged husband has been spotted in the area. He's an ex-con with a history of injection drug use – steroids, apparently. Huber might have opened the door to him. But would he have known how to manipulate the insulin pump? I had him in for questioning and he claimed he didn't even know she had a pump, which was likely a lie."

"On the chance this was a copycat murder, I checked the body for injection sites," the doctor said. "Couldn't find any. No, the insulin was delivered via the pump. As for time of death, seems the body was discovered not long after the victim expired. Paramedic who took the call didn't notice any signs of rigor. Blood alcohol showed the victim probably had a drink or two before she died."

"A drink or two," McKean said. "She was falling down drunk when I picked her up last week for dangerous driving. But on the night she died, there were no tell-tale glasses or open bottles of booze at the cottage. She could have taken a drink elsewhere. Or the killer – if there was a killer – might have brought the booze to the victim then cleaned up any trace of it."

"That raises another question then," Antoniak said. "A second party, if there was one, might have spiked the drinks. Has to be easier to kill a person with her own pump if she's confused or sleepy. Seems convoluted though, doesn't it? Why use two drugs to kill her when one would do? We'll see. I've sent samples to the lab. While we wait for the results there's no reason I can't release the body to the funeral home."

* * *

Late Monday morning Stella received a text from Ben: *Nina Huber's body delivered to funeral home. Cremation today.*

Stella once again rallied the book club to plan a funeral. That afternoon the five remaining members met for an early supper at Jigsaw's Bistro in downtown Nelson. A birthday celebration was in full swing inside, so they took a table on the patio to hear themselves think. Amelie and Nathalie slipped indoors for a moment to extend their good wishes to the guest of honour, a transplanted Québécoise like themselves.

The first order of business was to settle on a date, and Stella wondered out loud if there was sufficient lead-time to hold the event late afternoon that Wednesday. "If we can pull this off in two days, the moon will be full again," she said. "The last full moon was on the night Lillian died. I think Nina would have liked that connection."

"Nina and her superstitions." Vanessa shook her head. "But I see no reason why we can't do this on short notice. The event is bound to be low-key." She rolled her eyes as the singers inside the bistro belted out an energetic rendition of *Bonne Fête*.

Carli offered to look after refreshments and stepped out of range of the singing to call her caterer. When Nathalie and Amelie came back outside they agreed to the proposed date for the funeral. Nathalie said, "We will arrange the flowers, eh, Amelie? Flowers from *le beau jardin de Lillian*." Lillian's beautiful garden. It occurred to Stella no one ever thought of the garden as Nina's, although even when Lillian was alive, she had done most of the work in it.

Stella took out her phone and booked the small chapel at the United Church, along with the assistant minister. Vanessa volunteered to line up an organist and to put up a notice on the front door of the drugstore.

"We're getting too good at this," Stella said, as they gathered up their belongings to leave.

"*Ah, oui,*" Amelie said. "*C'est triste.*" How sad.

The women broke off to go home but unlike Amelie and Nathalie, Vanessa seemed in no hurry to catch the ferry back to the East Shore. "I suppose you need to get home too, Stella," she said, wistfully. "But we never did get together for that drink we talked about."

Stella felt a twinge of guilt—here was another friend she never seemed to find time for. "I think the guys can get along without me for another hour," she said. "Let's do it. Where should be go?"

Vanessa beamed. "They make great Caesars at the Lakeside. Is your car parked behind the *Times?* Leave it there and we'll take mine. I'll just slip into the little girls' room first."

From an outdoor table at the Lakeside Hotel, Stella and Vanessa watched the sun set and sipped their drinks. Across the patio, a middle-aged couple leaned toward each other, hands clasped across the table.

Vanessa absently stirred her Caesar with a celery stick. "It's been a long time since a man looked at me like that," she said.

"Oh, Van," Stella said. "I guess I've never met any of the men in your life. In high school, I knew you as the pretty girl at the drugstore who gave me tips on make-up. But you must have broken a few hearts during those years I was away at the Coast."

"I don't know about that." Vanessa chuckled, but her smile was sad. "There've been a few men over the years, but no one really 'took.' A teacher still living with his mother at age forty. He moved to Ontario to get away from her. What a wimp." She made a funny face. "Then there was the ferry captain who ran off to work on a cruise ship… Not long ago I met a drug rep with a whole raft of kids – your typical travelling salesman, after only one thing." She took a big gulp of her drink. "Don't laugh. But would you believe I'm still a virgin, Stella? I am. A pre-menopausal virgin."

Stella struggled to hide her amazement. "I'm not laughing, Van. I'm just surprised. You have so much going for you." She shook her head. "That sounded terrible – sorry. Is it a religious thing? I mean, not that I would question your principles…."

"I once loved someone very deeply," Vanessa said. "And lost him to another woman. After that… Well, better to have loved and lost, and all that."

A waitress came by and asked if they wanted another round. "We're good," they said in unison, which made them laugh.

"What about Henry Sutton?" Stella asked, carefully. "Do you see any future with him?"

"Oh, sweetie. I'd like to think so. He's such a gentleman. And just old enough to be interesting – and to make me seem young to him. Younger." She laughed. "This is just between you and me, okay? Carli wouldn't understand."

"Absolutely. Just between you and me."

"I've never told anyone about the virginity thing. You must think I'm a real loser."

"Oh, Vanessa, we all have our little secrets. I never tell friends about my water phobia. I hinted about it the day we talked at the pool. Kind of downgraded it to a breathing issue. But put me in the deep, dark lake and I fall apart."

"Oh, that's awful. I'd love to help you with that," Vanessa said. "Seriously. We'll meet at the pool, or at the beach when the lake warms up. I really appreciate you trusting me with your secret. Doesn't it feel good to talk about something other than *death*." Stella lifted her glass and they clinked. Vanessa spoke again, "But since it is the elephant in the room at the moment, I have to ask, Stella. Have the police been able to establish the cause of Nina's death?"

"Who knows, Vanessa?" Stella said. "I don't have any insider information if that's what you're after."

"No?"

Stella met her eyes but remained silent.

"You and the good sergeant seem – how shall I put it? Close." Vanessa's tone was light-hearted but she stirred the remains of her drink nervously. "Tight, as the youngsters say."

Where is this coming from? Stella wondered. "I think the term is collegial," she said, pushing aside her glass. "Hey, we should probably get going. For one thing, you have a ferry to catch." She looked at her watch. "You need to hustle, my friend."

"Oh, sweetie. I just hope..." Vanessa seemed at a loss for words, which, in Stella's experience, was rare. Obviously flustered, she fumbled for her wallet.

"This one's mine," Stella said, plunking a bill on the table as she stood up. "Are you okay?"

"It's you I'm worried about," Vanessa said, incongruously. The

Caesar talking, maybe.

"No need to worry about me," Stella said. "Hey, let's do this again. Soon."

They got into Vanessa's Honda to drive to the newspaper building and retrieve Stella's car. But when they turned into the parking lot, Vanessa clamped her hand over her mouth. "What the hell?" Stella said. All four tires on the Pathfinder were flat.

32

STELLA'S TIRES HAD NOT been slashed: that was the good news. But someone *had* intentionally let the air out. Vanessa drove her home, clucking all the way about what the town was coming to, particularly with all the hippies passing through during the summer.

The next morning, Stella cycled to work.

Fortunately, Patrick owned a compressor and he straight away went home for it and returned to inflate the tires on the stranded Pathfinder. Stella was grateful; she tried to focus on Patrick's kindness rather than speculate on who had pranked her. But it was getting harder and harder to overlook all the petty, unsettling incidents.

That afternoon, Ben sent a text asking her to drop by the station. He looked serious when he stood up to greet her in the interview room. "Thanks for coming," he said.

Stella smiled at his formal manner. "You're welcome. Why am I here?"

"The manager at the mall delivered a package some kids found in a dumpster. Have a look." Ben held up a clear plastic evidence bag.

"Syringes," Stella said. "Here we go again."

"Identical to the one found on Huber's beach."

"Fairly common type and size, I would think."

"We found a clear thumbprint on the packet," he said, all business. "A match with Nina Huber's prints."

* * *

Thirty or so friends and acquaintances attended Nina Huber's funeral, along with a few curious onlookers. A Vancouver tabloid had referred to Nina's death as the probable suicide of the former live-in companion of Lillian Fenniwick, retired lawyer and popular community activist. How Lillian would have laughed at that take on her life and volunteer work, Stella thought. But who had leaked the suicide theory? It could have been mere conjecture, of course, the sleaze factor put into play to sell newspapers.

Stella was surprised when Colette Fenniwick made an entrance. It hadn't occurred to her Lillian's niece would still be in town. This time Colette had skipped the fascinator she'd worn to Lillian's wake and swapped the sheath and heels for clingy black separates and matching ballerina slippers. Heads still turned as she dabbed at her eyes with a black lace hanky and steered her son into the side chapel of the United Church. Stella shared the narrow front pew with Vanessa and Carli while Amelie and Nathalie sat behind them. Ben McKean took a seat at the back with Corporal Ray Eberly. Joe had stayed away, insisting it would be better for the boys to kick around a soccer ball than to attend another downer funeral.

A slight murmur erupted when Max Huber barged up the aisle and squeezed in beside Stella. She tried not to recoil as his rock-hard shoulder connected with hers, and avoided looking at him when she got up to deliver the eulogy. When she spoke of the sad death of a gentle, quiet woman, his shoulders shook.

The assistant minister spoke next. "Let us pray for our sister Nina," she intoned, and Max Huber rose to his feet.

"You're a bunch of hypocrites," he said, his voice catching. "Where were you when Nina was dying out there in that frigging cottage? Shame on you." He was shouting now. "Shame on every goddamn one of you."

Ben came forward and took his arm. "Come on, Mr. Huber," he said. "Time to go." Max brushed off his hand and fled from the church.

* * *

Colette Fenniwick felt like a fly on the wall at Nina Huber's funeral. She had hardly known the woman but felt she needed to be there; Colette had a sixth sense about these things. She and C were the only Fenniwicks left in the family, the only ones with a right to her uncle's cottage on Kootenay Lake. As far as Colette was concerned, his second wife had only held it in trust for his natural heirs. Strange the housekeeper had expected to remain in the cottage after Lillian died. Well, too bad, so sad, the housekeeper was gone now too.

Colette hoped to claim her inheritance without much delay. Apart from a townhouse in Calgary and the BMW, a purchase she didn't regret for one second despite the exorbitant upkeep, she was cash poor. A few more nights at the Lakeshore Hotel, even without room service, could push her Visa over the limit. She didn't need another scene like the one in Lethbridge where a waiter cut up her Master Card in front of a restaurant full of people. The jerk.

She had just elbowed C to put away his phone when a stocky guy in the front pew – mucho rough around the edges – stood up and started to rant. He'd barely gotten started when a stud in a suit got up and ushered him out. The Suit called the guy Mr. Huber. He must have been a brother because Colette couldn't see Nina as anybody's wife. She pegged the Suit as the strong, silent type. Tall, dark, lean, and loose limbed – definitely a man worth sussing out.

Not long after Mr. Huber's dramatic exit, people stood up and hugged and filed downstairs for coffee. Colette touched her hanky to her cheeks, discreetly, as if she didn't want anyone to notice, then leaned on C and manoeuvred him into the crowd, such as it was. Well, Colette could schmooze with the best of them. She extended her hand to a half-dozen people saying things like, "Poor Nina. Aunt Lillian would have been devastated to lose her," or "Completely selfless, wasn't she? Born to serve." At times Colette simply shook her head and swallowed hard as if words failed her.

Outside on a smoke break, she spotted C on the church steps with a cute blond girl of twelve or thirteen and an older boy who was quite the hottie. Colette considered having a little fun with him to see if he'd sneak a look at her chest, but she decided to leave them alone. Her son didn't make friends easily and it warmed her heart to see him mixing with kids his age. She stubbed her cigarette out on the sidewalk and left them to it.

Back inside, Colette went to the restroom to powder her nose. The stalls were both occupied. From behind one closed door, a voice said, "I wonder what'll happen to the yellow cottage now."

From the other stall, a younger voice said, "My money is on the husband. I heard he's been in jail at the Coast. But as far as I know he and Nina never legally separated."

The husband. Colette snapped her compact shut and went back to blend with the mourners.

* * *

Zoe had risked the wrath of her mother with the brilliant idea to invite Kieran to Nina Huber's funeral. "It's a free country," she'd told him. "My mom can't keep either of us from paying our respects." Zoe was wearing the homemade necklace Kieran had given her, tucked under a buttoned-up shirt. The string scratched a little, but Zoe didn't care. Throughout the service, her mother kept an eagle eye on her but it was easy to get away during the reception and meet Kieran outside. The only other young person was a boy called C who sort of followed them out. Zoe asked him what the C stood for.

"Whatever you want it to," he said. "My mother takes a lot of liberties with my name."

"How come?" Zoe asked.

"She's a liar," he said, and began to fiddle with his phone.

Kieran visibly perked up. "Your mom sounds like quite the lady," he said.

The boy called C shrugged. Zoe asked if he lived around there. It turned out he was from Calgary. "My mom wants to move here though," he said.

"How do you feel about going to school in Nelson?" Zoe said.

"School would probably suck as much here as it does anywhere else," he said.

Zoe involuntarily fell into dork mode. "I think Nelson's schools are pretty good compared with others in the province," she said. "Even Vancouver."

"Even Vancouver," Kieran said. "Woo." Kieran could never resist showing off about Toronto, the only cool city in Canada as far as he was concerned. But then he put his arm around her and gave her a squeeze, which almost made up for the mean remark. He dropped his arm when C's mother came outside for a smoke. Zoe hoped and prayed *her* mother wouldn't come out.

Just then Stella Mosconi emerged from the church, holding her car keys. She absently greeted the group, crossed the street, and walked once around her car, peering down her tires. She must have clicked the key fob several times because the lights on the Pathfinder kept flashing. On her way back inside, Stella stopped to ask if they had "partaken" of the refreshments. That was the word she used, partaken. As the door closed behind her, Kieran kind of smirked. Zoe tried to keep a straight face.

33

THE DAY AFTER NINA'S FUNERAL, Max wandered up and down Baker Street in a haze until some sort of impulse for self-preservation kicked in. He found a passable one-man tent at a thrift shop and made his way to the City Campground. Max set up his paltry camp among a bunch of big RVs and trailers. Most of the other tent dwellers were hippies, strumming guitars and playing with their mongrel dogs. He was tempted to tell them to cut their hair and get a job as he would have done at their age, but he just didn't have it in him.

With Nina gone, Max was at a dead end. For one thing, without her money, his hopes and dreams to buy the gym in Fruitvale were crushed all to hell. It hurt to think he'd never have a bunch of body-builders looking up to him. Or a line of of T-shirts and coffee mugs with his name on them. He slumped in front of his tent like a straw man. Hell, even in the slammer he'd been able to motivate himself to do a set of push-ups. Now it was an effort to put one foot ahead of the other.

In this sorry frame of mind, Max idly watched a bodacious blonde and teenage boy get out of an old BMW not twenty feet away. Must be lost. Or looking for somebody, a friend of the kid's probably.

You could have knocked him down with a feather when the boy pulled a tent bag out of the trunk. The blonde stomped around, puffing on a fag and waving her arms, finally settling on a site. She wore a scoop-necked shirt that gave Max an eyeful as she leaned over to spread out a ground sheet. The kid emptied a sack of poles and stakes. When his mother knelt to position the tent, her pants exposed the top of a scarlet thong. Damn, but she was a fine-looking woman.

"You gonna just sit there gawking or do you want to make yourself useful?"

Max took a moment to realize she had him in her sights. "You talkin' to me?" he said.

She laughed. "This isn't the movies, wise guy."

Lord above. He scrambled to his feet. "Max Huber. Pleased to make your acquaintance, Miss…"

The woman looked stricken. "Huber? Oh, God. Now I know where I've seen you. The funeral. Listen, I'm sorry about your wife. And for giving you a hard time just now. I'm Colette Fenniwick and this is my son, C."

"No need to apologize, Colette. Classy lady like yourself must get tired of men looking at her. Me I'm kinda out of it these days." Max extended his hand to C. "Hello there, young fella. Good your mother has you to keep away the riffraff."

The boy allowed his hand to be shook then sat down at a picnic table and pulled out a fancy-looking phone. Colette said, "I thought C needed a taste of the outdoors. We've been staying at the Lakeshore but a kid feels cooped up in a luxury hotel. Once a Boy Scout, always a Boy Scout, right C? I think he was still in diapers when his dad bought him this tent."

The kid looked up from his phone. "I was six, mother. I didn't wear diapers when I was six."

Colette ignored the remark.

They settled in for the afternoon. Colette was a talker and Max was happy just to chip in every now and again. After a while the boy wanted to go look for somebody down at the mall or on the beach. His mom reminded him he had a curfew, 11:00 p.m. She slipped him a twenty and told him to text her hourly. Hell, Max would have given the kid a couple sawbucks himself if he'd known C's social plans would free up Colette to join him for a beer and sandwich at a joint down the street.

Strolling down High Street with a good-looking woman made Max feel like a human being again. And the hours zoomed by in the old Civic pub, yakking with Colette. Max had forgotten how good it felt to hang out in a crowded bar, shouting over the music, ordering a few rounds. At eleven o'clock, the kid sent a text to say he was back at the campground and Colette picked up her handbag. By then she was starting to slur her words. "So, Max," she said, "we've been beating around the bush all day, but I guess we're after the same thing."

Was she coming on to him? Well, no. Not with the kid back at the campground. Max half-nodded, half-shrugged, not sure what to hope for.

"You don't know what I'm talking about, do you?" Colette said. "The cottage out at Give Out Creek. My uncle's family built it. My son and I are his heirs. No disrespect to your late wife, but there is absolutely no way she had a legal claim to the property."

Max blinked. "Say what?"

"After my aunt passed, Nina wouldn't have been entitled to keep the cottage. She must have been deluded if she thought she could. I'm sure Lillian was fond of her, but come on. Again, no disrespect, but Nina was only the housekeeper."

Holy Mother of God. Had the lawyer left her property to Nina? "Well, Colette." Max struggled to find the right words in spite of his own beer buzz. "Whatever Nina wanted – that's all that matters to me."

"You're a nice man, Max," Colette said, and now she appeared to have sobered up too. "I'd hate to see you left with diddlysquat. But I guess we'll find out where we stand with respect to the law, eh?"

* * *

Late afternoon Thursday, Stella heard loud knocking coming from the street-level entrance to the newspaper offices. She looked down through an open window to see two girls step back into the parking area and wave up at her. She went downstairs and let them in. The girls wore short, patchy clothing that revealed full body tans and tattoos in sensitive places. They had come to the *Times* to place a display ad for a summer music festival but the business office was closed for the day. "We hitched all the way here," groaned the taller of the two.

"If you could help us that would be amazing," said her companion.

Stella told them to follow her up to the office. While she calculated the cost of a full-page ad, the pair spoke together as if she wasn't there; their banter made her feel about a hundred years old. The steep price of the ad didn't seem to faze them. "So," said the girl whose left shoulder and neck were inked with mythical creatures, "You're a reporter, right? Do you think you could cover the event?"

"Why wait 'til the event?" interjected the girl with a unicorn on her chest. "It would be awesome publicity if you could come ahead of time. Check out the set-up for the stages. Kind of visualize the whole scene? It's really beautiful up on the land. You could swim in the creek, bring your boyfriend or whatever."

"I'm guessing that would annoy my husband," Stella said, and the pair tittered politely. "I'll see what I can do though. I understand this will be the first of its kind in Nelson. Shangri-Lectric – catchy name. I like it. I notice you've chosen July third, partway between Canada Day and the Fourth of July. Guess you hope to attract people from the States too. How big a crowd do you expect to draw?"

"Three-four thousand, right Starshine?"

"Three-four thousand easy," replied Starshine.

"And what about drugs?" Stella said. "Do you have a plan for keeping them out or will it be pretty laissez-faire?"

Two pairs of eyes grew large. "Oh, drugs will be totally verboten," said Starshine. "We'll check everyone at the gate. *No problemo.*"

"No offence, but festival organizers always say that. Yet people seem to find a way to get high. Aren't you worried about fentanyl? It's a huge problem– people all over the province are dying from taking laced drugs."

The second girl said, "Not gonna happen, not on our watch. This'll be a drug- and alcohol-free event. Where you get high on the music and nature and all."

"Okay." Stella drew out the word. Best not to say she also believed in the tooth fairy. "Just out of interest though, what's the flavour of the month these days? Ecstasy, GHB, LSD?"

"Oh, gee. I wouldn't have a clue – not my thing," Starshine said. Her friend shook her head vigorously. "I guess you could look on the Internet."

Stella thanked the girls for their business and showed them out. Street drugs were changing so fast, it was a perfect topic for a news feature, a series maybe. The parents among her readers would be riveted, but first she'd better find out which drugs were making the rounds in Nelson that season. A few years back something bad had happened at a nearby rave, a death maybe. Ben might know.

It was just past five and Stella hadn't stepped out of the office all day. Recorder in hand, she jogged up to the police station and asked to speak to Sergeant McKean. The woman at the desk asked the nature of her enquiry. "I'd like the department's take on drug use at music festivals and raves," Stella said. "Several thousand people are about to descend on Nelson's first-ever Shangri-Lectric."

"I'll page Corporal Eberly," the woman said. "He covered the raves on the other side of the lake until they banned them after that kid ODed."

Corporal Ray Eberly, Ben's nemesis. Stella stifled her disappointment and sat down to wait. A few minutes later Eberly sauntered into the foyer like he owned the place and ran his eyes over her body. She asked for a quick primer on the drugs most likely to circulate at the upcoming music festival. "How much time you got?" he said. Cocky bastard.

"Whatever it takes," Stella said, curtly. "I have kids of my own. I want to know what's going on right under our noses. I think a lot of our readers would like to find out too."

"Yes, ma'am." He led her to an interview room.

With fifteen minutes of Q and A on tape, Stella went back to the *Times* to dig deeper online. From what she read, weed and booze were still the go-to drugs at music festivals – some things never changed. But ravers posted on social media about Lucy and Molly and poppers and a bunch of other substances Stella couldn't identify off the top of her head. Ecstasy still came up and, more rarely, cocaine and ketamine. Fentanyl use seemed to be almost accidental – people were clueless about what their street drugs were cut with.

Patrick came in to get something from his desk. "You still here?" he said.

Stella told him about the rave. "I'm overdosing on drug warnings, never mind the drugs," she said.

"Don't get bogged down. Your job isn't to educate the public on the minutiae of street-drug use. Focus on the upcoming event and find out what the cops plan to do in the way of harm reduction."

"Guess I'll have to talk to know-it-all Eberly again, damn it."

"That's the spirit." Patrick turned to leave, then stopped. "Suspicious deaths up the lake on the back burner?"

"Out of sight but not out of mind. No one's going to get any closure until we find out what happened, starting with Lillian Fenniwick. The more I think about it, the more I wonder if the perp could be an outsider, someone from Lillian's past."

"The perp. You still hanging around McKean?"

"Oh please," Stella said. "Don't you start. But hear me out. Lillian practiced family law down in Vancouver. Divorce settlements and custody battles can bring out the worst in people."

"You cast a line all the way to Vancouver and you'll push yourself over the edge. Tip McKean, but don't take on this line of questioning yourself. I mean it, Stella. Go home. Good night."

"See you." She put aside the drug notes, refreshed her browser and keyed in CanLII. No harm doing a quickie search on the database of the Canadian Legal Information Institute.

The phone rang, Unavailable again. This time on her work phone. She let the call go to voicemail and replayed the message. Again, there was nothing but breathing. She deleted the non-message and called it a day.

34

THE NEXT MORNING STELLA found a moment to call the offices of Honeywell & Smart LLB – formerly Fenniwick, Honeywell & Smart – and introduced herself to the receptionist. She asked to speak to someone who would remember Lillian Fenniwick.

"Ms. Fenniwick hasn't worked at this firm for a long time." The woman's tone was cool. "We were sorry to hear of her death. But I'm afraid all the partners are either in court or –"

"Please," Stella said. "This is important. I don't need to speak to a partner. What about an associate, or someone Lillian might have mentored?"

The receptionist put her on hold. Stella switched to speakerphone and turned back to her computer. A good ten minutes later, a voice said, "Jeff Quinn." Stella reached for the receiver.

Quinn had articled under Lillian and later become an associate at the firm. He and Lillian had been friends, he said, in as much as a senior partner and junior associate could be.

"Lillian and I were close too," Stella said. "I'm looking for background that might shed some light on her untimely death."

"She died too young for sure," he said. "But I don't know what I can tell you. We lost touch in recent years. I missed her when she first left the city. Her decamping to a small town, especially one so far from Vancouver, seemed odd at the time."

"Well, she fit right in. Lillian was well-liked in the community."

"Good. Great. I'm pleased to hear that."

Quinn had spoken with such feeling Stella's reporter instincts clicked in.

"You sound surprised," she said.

"No, not really. Her emails about Nelson were positive. But then Lillian had a way of putting a good face on a situation. You have to remember she was my boss in the beginning, so that would have coloured my perception."

"I don't mean to pry, but was Lillian popular at the firm?"

A pause. "She wasn't unpopular. Lillian more than pulled her weight. She was well respected."

"But…" Stella waited.

"I assume you know her husband brought her into the firm. Let's just say the transition wasn't altogether smooth."

Stella made a stab in the dark. "Clark was in another relationship at the time."

"I guess it was no secret," Quinn said. "But it didn't sit well with some people upstairs. Look, I think we've strayed off topic. Anything else I can do for you?"

She wanted to keep him talking. "Lillian left Vancouver quite soon after Clark's death. Almost abruptly."

"She did. But what does that matter now?"

"I'm sure you're busy so I'll get to the point," Stella said. "The police have evidence Lillian was murdered." The silence at the other end of the line was deafening. "Sorry to drop that on you, Jeff. Do you need a minute?"

"Carry on."

"So far the investigation has focused on suspects connected to Nelson. But it seems reasonable to broaden the search. I wonder if Lillian ever had any particularly disgruntled client, or spouse of a client. Someone unhappy enough to nurse a grudge for ten years or more. I know I'm reaching here."

"Family law can be adversarial, as I'm sure you know. Any number of clients or their ex-spouses might have been unhappy with a judgment Lillian got for them. But not many people commit murder. If Lillian ever received a threat, she kept it to herself."

"I've scrolled through the websites for CanLII and the Courts of British Columbia but I can't seem to get to first base. Even in public records, parties are often identified by initials only."

"That's right, and what you find on CanLII isn't necessarily representative of a lawyer's career," Quinn said. "Most of our cases settle, and even the ones that go to trial aren't necessarily noted. In this province, judges decide whether a trial is important enough to be posted."

"Can you help me, Jeff? Can you think of any particularly challenging case Lillian might have handled toward the end of her tenure? Let's say a husband got hit with a mega divorce settlement and also lost custody of his kids. A person in that situation might be bitter enough to seek revenge against his ex-wife's lawyer."

"Look – Stella, is it? I'd like to help. I owe that much to Lillian. But client information is privileged. That will be one obstacle. Anyway, leave this with me. Give me your number and I'll see what I can do."

Stella felt optimistic as she left the office at the end of the day. Jeff Quinn hadn't turned her down outright. She would give him time to check his files then follow up. After stopping for groceries, she arrived home in a good mood. After all, it was the last day of school before summer vacation. Joe and the boys were bound to be on top of the world.

* * *

Colette Fenniwick drove to the nearest gas station and locked herself in the restroom while C combed the shelves for granola bars and energy drinks. The facilities at the campground were passable, but Colette was a lady who liked her privacy. She first cleaned the sink and counter with disposable wipes and then unpacked a zipper case of beauty essentials. Next, she spread paper towels on the floor, stripped down, and embarked on a leisurely sponge bath. Twice someone pounded on the door. Twice Colette sang out, "Almost done!" Not that she hurried to finish her toilette. You could buy the finest creams and lotions, but if you let yourself get stressed your looks suffered; that was a scientific fact. Tomorrow she would find a gym or community centre and wash her hair at her leisure but for now she pulled it into a French twist.

From her Samsonite roller suitcase, Colette selected an off-the-shoulder sundress in tomato red and a pair of sparkly gold flip-flops. Next on her agenda was a trip to the Nelson Public Library to brief herself on estate litigation. She was smart enough to know she needed Max Huber's cooperation to cash in on the property at Give Out Creek. On her own, she probably didn't have a leg to stand on.

* * *

When Stella pulled up outside the cabin, Matt and Nicky were on the roof of an old tool shed wearing loaded backpacks. She flew out of the car as Matt began to swing his arms. "Hey, you guys," she called across the yard. "What are you doing? Don't jump off that thing, especially with backpacks. You could break an ankle or worse."

Air bound, Matt said, "We're being careful." He stumbled onto his knees as he hit the ground.

"Matt! What did I say?"

"Guess what, Mom," Nicky called from the top of the shed. "Dad is taking us camping."

"Yeah? Well for now pass me your pack and I'll help you down."

Inside, Joe was cramming a sleeping bag into a stuff sac. "Guess the cat's out of the bag," he said cheerily as Stella carried in the bags of groceries.

"You told them you'd take them camping?"

"Little wilderness adventure will be good for them. Male-bonding thing."

"No girls allowed?"

"You seem to have a lot going on. And now that school's out, the boys and I could take off anytime."

"Wow. Okay. I could join you for a weekend though. What campground did you have in mind?"

Joe pulled a face. "Might as well stay home as go to a campground. I want to backpack with the boys, carry all our food and gear. Maybe do a traverse on Buttercup Ridge. The guys are into it. They've been wearing those packs since we got home."

"Buttercup Ridge? Isn't that in the back of beyond?" Stella said. "No cell phone signal for one thing." Matt and Nicky had never slept away from her. An outdoor adventure with their dad would be fun, but a multi-day trek?

"No cell phone signal," Joe said with mock horror. "C'mon. It'll do them good to have a break from electronics. I figure a week, ten days tops, before everyone needs a shower and a real bed."

"I could probably get time off in August. If you wait, I could come too. I mean, how much do you think Nicky can carry?"

"Nicky can carry his own clothes. Why wait until August? All I need is some maps and supplies. We can leave after the long weekend and still be back for me to teach summer school."

"You seem to have it all figured out," Stella said. No comment from Joe. "I guess I'll whip up some mac and cheese for supper."

She put the bags down next to an object she'd never seen before, a cube-shaped wooden apparatus with rows of shallow trays. "What is this – a food dryer? Looks expensive."

"Borrowed it from Caleb – Jade's boyfriend," Joe said. "No artificial commercial stuff for those two. Caleb probably doesn't care what he eats, but Jade –"

Stella clicked on the radio. "Let's catch the weather report for the long weekend," she said, putting an end to any more chatter about Jade Visser and her balanced, childless, and no doubt mortgage-free life.

On CBC, listeners were calling in music requests to celebrate the first long weekend of summer. The announcer said, "Here's an oldie that should bring back memories. Going out to a special girl in Nelson – *Step by Step* by New Kids on the Block."

"Hey!" Stella laughed and turned up the volume, Jade Visser forgotten. "I loved this when I was a kid." She pranced and twirled, marking time with two wooden spoons. The boys dropped their packs on the front porch and bounded in kicking and leaping and grabbing at each other, not quite in time to the music. Even Joe got into the act, tapping out the rhythm on Caleb's wooden food dryer.

"Are you the special girl in Nelson, Mom?" Matt asked.

"You bet she is," said Joe. It was the nicest thing he'd said in a long time.

Stella blew him a kiss. She'd been missing sweet nothings like that. Maybe with school out now, she and Joe would find the time to make things better. Step by step.

35

MCKEAN'S LITTLE SON AIDEN, home after the long visit at his grandma's house in Fort St. John, burbled in his highchair. Miranda tucked the phone under her chin and poured infant cereal into a bowl. "The drive back was a living hell, Ma," she said into the mouthpiece. "The baby cried the whole time." She added a generous dollop of formula and stirred vigorously. After a beat, spoke again. "Well of course he did all the driving – so what? I was a wreck. I miss you already, Ma. Nothing here has changed. Today is the first of July – freaking Canada Day – and he's going to the station, as per usual."

McKean looked at his watch: 7:15 a.m. Having taken Friday off to fly to Fort St. John and driven two days straight to bring his family home, he would have to play catch-up at work. He took the plastic bowl from Miranda and spooned cereal into Aiden's mouth. The little guy hummed as he lapped up his breakfast. Miranda interrupted her conversation to tell him to wipe the baby's chin. He picked up Aiden and carried him outside to watch the black-capped chickadees at the bird feeder next door. Aiden giggled and filled his pants. McKean took him upstairs to change his diaper.

Back in the kitchen he told Miranda he had to leave and handed over the baby. With an exaggerated sigh, she ended her call. "Will we see you again this calendar day?"

"Cut the melodrama," McKean said. "I'll be home about 6:00 – 6:30 at the latest."

"Sure, like eleven hours from now. Great. Pick up a pizza on your way home."

McKean drove away in a state of – what? Despair didn't seem too strong a term. To say he loved his son – well, love wasn't a big enough word for how he felt about Aiden. For Miranda, indifference more or less summed up his feelings.

Miranda. His wife, the mother of his child, the woman whose

body once drew him into a deep well of pleasure. Now the well was dry. No warmth, no tenderness, not even a little playfulness. Even with the baby she often seemed aloof. Could post-natal depression kick in at this stage? Because a few months back Miranda had seemed reasonably satisfied, content to breastfeed and play with Aiden, to make love to her husband every now and again. Before the move south, life had seemed, if not blissful, fine. About as good as he hoped for, at any rate. Maybe she should talk to a counsellor, maybe they both should. But McKean couldn't see himself getting all touchy-feely with a therapist, not in a town where everyone knew his name. Besides, he wasn't sure there was anything worth reviving with Miranda.

When he pulled up at the station he had no idea how he'd gotten there – bad form for anyone, but for a cop, inexcusable. In the parking lot, Eberly shot him a mock salute. What was that clown's excuse for working on a public holiday when he didn't have to? Likely another bid to brown-nose the boss.

* * *

On the Tuesday morning after the long weekend, Stella crept around the cabin to avoid disturbing her sleeping family. Her plan was to get away early. The bike ride into the office that brilliant summer morning – boats whizzing by on Kootenay Lake, other cyclists shouting greetings – felt like a guilty pleasure.

Over the three-day weekend, she'd helped Joe dry food for the upcoming trip to Buttercup Ridge, which had meant no escape from cooking smells, day or night. Much like living in a 24-hour diner, and a basic one at that. Small bags of kibble-like spaghetti sauce, curried chicken, coleslaw, and other tasty treats accumulated by the day. Matt griped about the menu. Twice Nicky got her up at night to discuss the possibility of meeting a bear on the trail. Joe kept adding items to his list of supplies, his good mood unwavering.

At work that morning, Stella got back to Jeff Quinn, an associate at Lillian's former law firm. "Good timing," he said, not wasting time with preliminaries. "Might have something for you. I've narrowed the field to one high-profile case."

Having checked out Quinn's photo and profile on the Honeywell & Smart website, Stella pictured a good-looking guy in his early thirties, expensive haircut, well-tailored suit. "You have my attention," she said.

Quinn continued. "A divorce, heard in January of the year Lillian left the firm. I juniored for her on the file. In the division of assets, the wife received a generous settlement and full custody of the three minor children. There'd been allegations of abuse with respect to the daughter but the charges didn't stand up in court."

"Hold on," Stella said, scrambling to capture the details. "Three children..."

"Two boys, ages seven and twelve, and a girl of fourteen. The husband tried without success to get shared custody. When the judgment came down he was not a happy camper. He made a complaint against Lillian to the Law Society. Also attempted to bring a suit against her. She hadn't broken any rules so nothing came of it. Challenges like those come with the territory, but Lillian didn't take criticism well and his claims upset her. The guy was a hot-shot doctor and the media was all over it." Quinn paused. "I don't know about you, Stella, but here reporters jump on a case like this as soon as it's filed."

Stella smiled at the friendly dig, but something else had quickened her pulse. "Wait – a doctor. Lillian's killer injected her with insulin. A doctor would know how to do that. I want to find this guy."

"Hold on now. Doctors aren't the only people familiar with insulin. Have you considered the killer might be diabetic?"

"You're quick, Jeff. Lillian's housekeeper had diabetes and when the insulin connection came to light she drew police attention. But about three weeks after Lillian's death, someone killed her too. Nina Huber was her name. The killer left a fake murder-suicide note."

"How did the police determine the note was fake?"

Stella paused. "I made that call. I knew Nina well enough to realize she hadn't written it. What it came down to was her manner of speaking. She never used contractions and the note contained one. I reported my reasoning to the police."

"And they bought it?" He sounded incredulous.

"They didn't discount it. Tell me more about this doctor."

Jeff paused a moment. "Look, he may fit your profile, but why would he have waited ten years to kill Lillian and then another three weeks to kill her housekeeper?"

"I have no idea but I still want to pursue this lead. Can you help me identify him?"

"So that you can write your story?"

"So that I can help the police find Lillian's killer. I don't identify sources, Jeff. Anything you tell me will be kept confidential."

"Look, Stella, it's been nice talking to you. Your calls have reminded me of Lillian. We spent a lot of time together, Lillian and I, tonnes of overtime. I miss those midnight chats. She gave me advice at a time when I was struggling with a personal issue. But to name this doctor would break the rules I'm bound by. Still, as I said, the doctor drew media attention. The archives of the *Vancouver Sun* should give you plenty to go on, a full name, possibly a place of employment."

She groaned. "The *Vancouver Sun* archives. I'll have to plough through a mountain of material."

"I bet you're good at that," he said, and brought the call to a close.

* * *

Stella's message light was flashing when she hung up from Jeff Quinn. Carli had called to ask if she had packed a lunch. "Meet you on the bench outside your building at noon. I have news."

When Stella went downstairs at lunchtime, Carli was already tucking into the contents of her Tupperware container. "You're not going to believe this," Carlie said, with her mouth half full of food.

"Try me," Stella said.

"I have returned from a little sleuthing south of the border," she said, with a broad grin. "In Coeur D'Alene, Idaho. I found an address for the notorious Henry Sutton and you won't believe who pulled up in front of his house virtually ten seconds behind me." She paused to heighten the suspense. "One Vanessa Levitt. And don't expect to hear any of this from her because she was mortified to see me. Are you ready? We clump up to the front door and an older woman opens it. Dark wispy hair streaked with grey, multi-colour reading glasses on a chain around her neck. Vanessa nearly passes out – she must have thought this was Henry's wife.

But no, she's the mother of a guy who bought the house *about a month ago*." Carli paused for a reaction. "Quite something, isn't it? This lady knew the previous owner was Henry Sutton but that's all she could tell us."

Stella was rapt. "So, what happened to Henry?"

"Well, back at the curb Vanessa could barely hold it together. 'I'm sure there's a perfectly reasonable explanation,' she says. I suggested we grab a bite together but Vanessa was full of excuses. I thought, hell, I didn't drive all the way to Coeur D'Alene to shop at Costco. I rang a neighbour's doorbell and when no one answered I went to the next house. On the third try, a young cutie in just his boxers and a Dallas Cowboys T-shirt opened his door. 'Oh, the old guy,' he says. 'The wife talked to him once or twice. Thought he was sweet.'"

"I'd kill Joe if he called me 'the wife,'" said Stella. "Did you talk to her, the guy's wife?"

Carli raised another heaping fork of rice pilaf to her mouth and chewed for a moment. "She was at the gym. Personal time, he called it. I went downtown for coffee and while I waited I tried to think where a bankrupt Henry Sutton might have moved to – a rental apartment, a trailer park? Remember how he sometimes drove that little motor home? I did a search on my phone of campgrounds near Coeur d'Alene and the closest was an upscale RV park. The host said rental records were confidential so I made out I was planning a family holiday so I could snoop around. But when he asked what kind of RV we owned I drew a blank. The creep wouldn't let me past the gate."

"So then you went back to see *Mrs.* Dallas Cowboys."

Carli laughed. "You know I did. Turns out our Henry had been a fly-by-night neighbour. Lived there maybe three months before he flipped the house."

Stella took out her phone and added Henry to her list of unsanctioned research assignments at the paper. Whether or not Ben had managed to track him down, the slippery Henry Sutton was definitely worthy of closer attention.

* * *

Ray Eberly wore a T-shirt with the slogan "Nelson Rocks" splashed across a photo of a rock face popular with local climbers. To make the shirt look well used, he'd cut off the sleeves and backed over it a few times with his truck. He spared his hundred-dollar distressed jeans a similar assault. Ray applied extra hair gel then appraised the total effect in a full-length mirror. The image that grinned back looked like a guy who'd just won the lottery. Ray was on orders from the Chief to attend Shangri-Lectric *undercover*. Plain clothes was the term the Chief used, but why split hairs? In Ray's wildest dreams he hadn't expected an undercover assignment this early in his career. And here it was on a goddamn silver platter. Corporal Raymond Eberly, undercover cop.

Ray lingered in front of his mirror, turned this way and that. He'd worked out nine consecutive nights on a contraption he bought from an infomercial, but his arms looked as scrawny as ever. Now he regretted the hatchet job on his T-shirt. He rooted in his closet for a denim jacket and, for good measure, choked back another glass of skim milk laced with whey powder.

Shangri-Lectric was to be held south of town on a piece of property once slated for development. When the zoning didn't work out, the owner built a big fence, erected a couple of stages, rented a row of port-a-potties and – Bob's your uncle –had a venue for a music festival. The organizers swore up and down there'd be no drugs or booze at the event but the Chief wanted one of his own on the inside. "Leave your weapon at home," he'd told Ray. "But take a phone."

Ray stuffed his ID down the front of his underpants in case he got checked for drugs then drove to the festival grounds and lined up at the gate with all the other music lovers. When the girl at the turnstile asked if he had any drugs or alcohol, he held up his hands and said, "Want to frisk me?" She rolled her eyes and waved him through. Amateur hour. Ray would have employed a couple of brawny bouncers.

No stranger to raves, he inserted a pair of silicone earplugs and set out to case the grounds. The freaks were already gyrating to the electronic music booming from speaker towers on stage. He recognized one of the *Times'* reporters, Jade Visser, dancing all by herself, curly hair flying. Now there was a babe he'd like to help with her research – unlike that other one, Ms. Stuck-up Mosconi.

Ray found himself getting into the groove. He turned a blind eye to the joints being passed around. No need to kill the vibe over a little weed. He felt… Ray searched for the word. Accepted. Like he belonged. It had to be the clothes. No one could tell he was a cop. When he spied Max Huber with a sexy-looking blonde he turned his face so as not to blow his cover. Jeez, how did a loser like Huber make it with the ladies?

Ray edged closer. He jumped when a hand came down hard on his shoulder. A voice said, "You the cop?" The speaker, of uncertain gender, wore a pink fright wig and tie-dyed clothes. "You're needed at the First Aid tent," he or she said. "Some girl is flipping out."

36

CARLI DELUCA NEVER THOUGHT a daughter of hers would be admitted to an emergency room for a drug overdose. Under the guise of attending a sleepover at Shelby's, Zoe had hitched (hitched!) to the music festival with Kieran Corcoran. He hadn't even stayed with her. In the line-up for a port-a-potty, Zoe accepted a drink that apparently looked like a shot and ended up in the First Aid tent with a boy called C.

If Zoe could be believed, C was a friend who didn't do drugs. He'd been at the rave with his mother when he noticed Zoe on her own, acting kind of out of it.

The emergency doctor didn't look old enough to shave. "Her drink was probably laced with MDMA which makes you dehydrated," he said, in a blasé tone. "She seems fine now. The officer who brought her in might be able to tell you more."

Carli left Zoe to rest and went out to the waiting room. A thin man in plainclothes jumped to his feet and held up his ID. A Corporal Raymond Eberly. "My daughter is thirteen," Carli said. "Any point trying to press charges against a boy of sixteen?"

"Did he coerce her in any way?" Eberly said.

"I suspect he crooked his little finger and she followed him like a puppy. But I don't think he gave her the drugs."

"That's what she told you?"

"I take your point, officer. We'll deal with this at home."

Carli thanked him for his help and in near silence drove Zoe home and put her to bed.

* * *

Jade Visser had talked Patrick into letting her cover Shangri-Lectric for the paper. "I'm going anyway," she told him. "I'm in the target group. It's perfect."

Her story, which was to run under the headline, *Drugs flood Shangri-Lectric – Organizers to face the music,* included a reference to an anonymous thirteen-year-old admitted to the ER with a bad reaction to drugs. Jade had already spoken to the girl's mother. Now on the morning after, she was interviewing Corporal Ray Eberly, who had attended the rave in an official capacity. The pair seemed to have a mutual admiration society going on. For some inexplicable reason Jade put Eberly on speakerphone and Stella had to listen to the entire gag-worthy exchange. Patrick found an excuse to leave the office.

Still, Stella kept her impatience to herself. She had anticipated problems at Shangri-Lectric the moment she'd met the organizers, but now she was too busy chasing leads on other stories to care much. For the past two days, she'd spent every spare moment at both work and home searching the archives of the *Vancouver Sun.*

Jeff, the lawyer at Lillian's old law firm, had alluded to a high-profile doctor who had lodged a complaint about Lillian with the Law Society and also attempted to sue her. Jeff was bound by rules of client confidentiality and couldn't name the doctor, but he had let slip the fact the trial had taken place in January of the year Lillian left the firm. That helped, although Stella still found herself at one dead end after another.

Finally on day three she stumbled onto a name that fit the facts of the case: Doctor Graham Perry. Her browser had several entries for Dr. Perry, an Internal Medicine specialist with an office in a prestigious tower in downtown Vancouver. Stella considered notifying Ben but decided to start the ball rolling on her own. Dr. Perry wasn't in when she called at nine; his receptionist couldn't say when he'd be back. "Would you like to speak to his locum?" she said. "She's with a patient now but I can take a message."

"I need to speak to Dr. Perry directly," Stella said. "Is there another number I could try?"

"All I can do is take your information," the receptionist said.

Stella was in and out all day but carried her cell. No calls from the doctor's office. At four o'clock, having left a second message for Dr. Perry's locum, she called Ben. She was tempted to ask about his trip to pick up his family in Fort St. John, but decided to keep it professional and simply report on her calls to Jeff Quinn and the pursuit of the doctor. Ben had little to say. He just asked her to keep him advised of developments. She wondered why he seemed so distant. Maybe someone else was in the room or – and this thought smarted a little – he regretted that cozy conversation in his car.

At the end of the day, Stella tried Dr. Perry's office again and this time his locum answered the phone herself. "You still working?" she said. "Sorry I haven't had a chance to return your calls." She sounded tired. Stella pictured a stressed-out working mother with a backlog of patient notes to enter into the files.

"And you're still at work too," Stella said. "Look I hate to bug you, but I have an urgent issue to discuss with Dr. Perry. It's personal. Do you know when he'll be back?"

"He expected to be back after the long weekend," she said. "But his wife put her foot down. Can't say I blame her. Five weeks isn't a lot of recovery time for a hip replacement."

"Gosh," Stella said, reaching for her calendar. "Has it been five weeks already?"

"Give or take. His surgery was on the twenty-sixth of May. Poor guy has an acute case of cabin fever. Should I ask him to call you when he's in the office again?"

"Um, no, that's okay. I'll give him time to settle in. Take care." Stella put aside the calendar. The doctor had undergone hip surgery two days before Lillian's murder. She reached for her notebook and drew a large cross through his name.

She texted Ben: *Doc lead is a dead end.*

He texted back: *Thanks. Assignment in Vancouver. Back Monday.*

* * *

Max wrestled with a drycleaner bag that encased the only non-denim pants he owned along with a shirt in a solid colour. Blue, to match his eyes, as Colette said. He'd planned to take his rumpled clothes to the laundromat but she wouldn't hear of it. "Standards, Max," said the bossiest broad he'd ever met. Colette had taken it upon herself to contact some lawyer named Arthur Nugent who represented Nina's old boss. Max hated lawyers – all they'd ever done for him was get him locked up. But Colette said this Nugent guy could help them if they played their cards right. She'd spent a whole afternoon in the public library preparing for Max's appointment with him. Max wasn't sure how he felt about Colette putting herself in the picture.

Now they sat side-by-side in the lawyer's office, Colette cool as a cucumber in a sleeveless white dress while Max sweated bullets in the blue shirt. Nugent was short and paunchy, grey at the temples, sixty if he was a day. White shirt, striped tie, suit pants held up by suspenders. The suit jacket drooped from a bent wire hanger on the back of his office door. That wire hanger did it for Max; he relaxed enough to shoot the breeze. "Pleased to make your acquaintance, Mr. Nugent," he said. "I hope you'll excuse me if I get a bit choked up. I'm kinda lost without my wife."

Nugent didn't beat around the bush. "I understand you and your wife were estranged."

Estranged, that frigging word again. Max sat up straighter. "I made a mistake that tore us apart. But that's behind me. I expected Nina and me to have a long happy life together until …" Max shook his head. He waited for the lawyer to jump in.

Nugent allowed the silence to stretch before he spoke again. "For a period of some sixteen months, Nina Huber was the live-in companion of Lillian Fenniwick." He glared at Max over heavy horn-rimmed glasses. "In her will, Lillian Fenniwick named Ms. Huber as her primary heir. But the timing of Ms. Huber's demise complicates things. Ms. Fenniwick's will had a fifteen-day survivorship clause. These clauses are put in place to simplify matters if a beneficiary dies within a few days of the person who made the bequest. If Ms. Huber had passed away within the fifteen-day period, she wouldn't have inherited." Nugent paused. "You follow?"

"Yes sir," Max said, hoping Colette knew what the hell he was talking about.

Nugent went on. "Now Ms. Huber survived the fifteen-day period. But she died only seven days later. Twenty-one days from the date Ms. Fenniwick died. Had the survivorship clause been a little longer, Ms. Huber would not have inherited. And it's worth noting, survivorship clauses are commonly one month or longer. Still with me?"

Max hesitated. "Yeah, I think so," he said.

Colette had been scribbling in a small black notebook. This was the longest Max had known her to stay quiet but she wasn't asleep at the switch. "Did Nina have a will?" she asked.

"I was coming to that," Nugent said. "Ms. Huber had a will,

signed and witnessed about three years ago. In it she named you, Mr. Huber, as her sole beneficiary."

Max's left leg began to jiggle. He placed a hand on his thigh to keep it still.

The lawyer continued. "But as executor of Lillian Fenniwick's estate, I have a responsibility to proceed with caution. First there's the issue of Mr. and Mrs. Huber's separation. To further confound the situation, Nina Huber appointed Ms. Fenniwick as her executrix and failed to name an alternate in the case of Ms. Fenniwick predeceasing her." The creases in Nugent's forehead deepened. It occurred to Max the lawyer might be closer to seventy than sixty. Guys like that never retired; they liked the power. Nugent went on. "Therefore, we're left with a number of legal questions. I can tell you off the top that a separation in excess of one year presents a problem."

Max momentarily lost his head. "But I had no choice, don't you see? They threw me in prison. I tried to get in touch with Nina as soon as I got out."

Nugent looked at Max for a long moment then nodded. "You have a point, Mr. Huber. Involuntary separation. Yes, that could make a difference."

Max was still reeling when Nugent brought the meeting to a close. "I'll need to look into some details before I can provide you with more information," he said.

Colette jumped up and led Max out of the lawyer's office. Chipper as ever, she suggested a coffee at Oso's – her treat. "I have a good feeling about this," she said.

"Good for me – or for you?" Max retorted, seizing the upper hand for a change.

Colette smiled kindly. "Let's not think that way, Max," she said. "This could be win-win for both of us." She talked about lawyers that specialize in the validity of wills. Estate litigators, she called them, your go-to people if you wanted to challenge a will. "Let's say I were to challenge Lillian's will," she continued. "We'd both end up spending a shitload of money on legal fees." That must have been a slip, the foul language, because Colette flushed slightly before she forged on. "Like with divorces. The lawyers on both sides typically power through the assets until there's nothing left."

Max's spirits sagged even further. "A regular Joe like me doesn't stand a chance with those bastards," he said.

"But don't you see, Max? Lawyers don't intimidate me. I went after my ex for a sweet settlement and didn't blow a lot of cash in the process. I can help you negotiate with Nugent. On the other hand, a legal challenge could hold up your inheritance for years. And even if a judge eventually ruled in your favour, there might be nothing left. But if we work together, we can get our hands on the property and sell it. Split the proceeds fifty-fifty."

Max thought before he spoke. "Sell it – the whole thing? What about all that business you gave me about your family and Uncle Clark? What would he think about that?"

Colette lifted her chin. "Well, he'd realize times change and understand I had no choice. And there would be comfort in knowing at least some of what he'd worked for would go to his blood relations."

But Max Huber was nobody's fool. "Fifty-fifty, huh?" He shook his head. "No can do, Colette. If I were to take you on as a business partner – that's an 'if,' okay? – I'd have to think about the split."

Colette said, "By all means, Max, but you do need my help. And don't forget that parcel is worth big bucks. There's plenty for both of us."

"Could be," he said, but he was thinking, *Nina would have hated her guts.*

* * *

Stella answered a call on her bedroom extension. "Has the entire town gone loco?" said a familiar voice. "Did somebody spike the water?"

Stella smiled, shoved aside a heap of clothes still warm from the dryer and made herself comfortable on the bed. "How's it going, Carl," she said. Three backpacks, one each for Joe, Matt, and Nicky, stood propped against the wall. The countdown was on: one more day before the three of them were to leave on their wilderness adventure.

Carli continued. "First the ER rings to ask me to come pick up my thirteen-year-old after she took drugs at that music festival. Then this Jade person calls here looking for a scoop. I thought that was your job but I guess you have your hands full these days with

Ben McKean."

"Carli –"

"Christ, Stella. Parking with him in his patrol car. At night, with the Pathfinder in plain view."

Vanessa's strange comments over drinks the other night started to make sense. "Did this come from Vanessa?" Stella said. "It might explain why she asked me about my quote/unquote 'insider status' with the police. I guess she passed the speed trap Ben set up on the lakeshore road Sunday evening. I'd stopped to talk to him for about two minutes. It was nothing, a non-incident. Forget about it." Stella knew that was asking too much even as the lies tumbled out of her mouth. "But what about Zoe? Tell me what happened."

"Not so fast, pal. Zoe is fine. It's you I'm concerned about."

"Like I said, forget it – there's nothing personal between Ben and me. Comparing notes on the two cases is part of our jobs." Stella looked in the mirror across from her and tried to sound casual. "Good old Vanessa. I should have asked what she was on about and straightened this out at the source."

"I don't buy it. Tim saw you with him too. Down at the park, sitting together on a bench."

"You're joking, right? Crimes are newsworthy. I might point out the park is a public place – he suggested we meet there."

"No doubt."

"Carli, this is ridiculous. C'mon. You know me better than that."

"So why did you bow out of a camping trip with Joe and the boys if not to stay home and play detective with the good sergeant?"

Stella stood up so fast she knocked over the backpacks. "I wasn't even invited on the camping trip. Joe wants to do a male-bonding thing. And you know what? I'm fine with staying home to do my job, even though I'd rather be with my family."

"Don't try to use the guilt card with me, Stella. I'm Catholic. I grew up on my knees. What the hell are you playing at?" Carli's voice had moved up another octave. "Joe is a wonderful husband and father. Think of your sons."

"I never stop thinking of my sons. And I would never cheat on my husband. Got that? I wouldn't do anything to hurt..." Stella's voice failed her. She swallowed. "I would never hurt my boys."

"Stell – you're crying. And you know why? Because I struck a nerve. No, listen. I'm going to hang up and this is what I want you to do. Wash your face and drink a tall glass of water. Then tell your husband you love him. And insist on going on that damn camping trip."

"You're not listening, Carli. He doesn't want me to go. Besides, I can't take a week off work without giving Patrick notice."

"Stella, just do it. Or you'll be sorry for the rest of your life." She hung up.

37

FRIDAY, WHILE JOE WAS home making final preparations for the trip, Stella bluffed her way through her assignments at work, trying not to dwell on Carli's call. She could see how Vanessa might have jumped to the wrong conclusion about her and Ben. Vanessa was a good person and a loyal friend, but having spent her entire career in a drugstore on the busiest corner in town, gossip and intrigue were food and drink to her. Carli was her own woman, and a friend since childhood. It hurt to think Carli believed the worst about her. Yet Stella was not about to give up on the murder investigations and the connection with Ben McKean that entailed. Not for Carli, not for anybody.

Ironically, at a time when her friends thought she was carrying on with Ben, he seemed to be distancing himself from her. Case in point: the mysterious trip to Vancouver he briefly referred to in his last text. She wondered if he had gotten anywhere with Henry Sutton. Carli's visit to Coeur D'Alene seemed to have reinforced her suspicions about Henry. Meanwhile, dear naïve Vanessa was likely as enamored as ever. Especially with her chequered history with men, the last thing Vanessa needed was to get involved with a criminal.

Stella picked up her desk phone and called a few church offices in Coeur D'Alene to enquire about Sutton. She struck gold with the junior pastor of a large Baptist congregation. The pastor recalled a brief acquaintanceship with a man called Henry Sutton. He wasn't prepared to discuss details, although he implied Sutton had ingratiated himself to a number of parishioners who had subsequently lost money investing with him. The congregation hadn't exactly run the man out of town, but Stella got the impression the pastor had been happy to see the back of him.

Stella skipped lunch to do more digging on the Internet. Having gotten nowhere with past searches, she tinkered with his name. *Lo and behold* (one of Sutton's catch phrases) she found a brief news report in a small-town Montana paper that referred to an Arnold H. Sutton. Maybe the "H" stood for Henry. This Mr. Sutton had been detained by the Sheriff's Office following an altercation with an irate husband whose wife had business dealings with him. No criminal charges were laid, but the husband came out of the exchange with a black eye and filed a civil suit against his attacker. Was Arnold H. Sutton the man known in Nelson as Henry Sutton? Stella emailed the news clip to Ben and received an automated out-of-office reply.

On the way to get her bike at the end of the workday, Stella noticed Max Huber at the coffee wagon across the street from the paper. He stared back belligerently. She fumbled with the combination lock on her bike and escaped up Baker Street.

At home the Pathfinder stood in the middle of the drive, doors left open, half-packed for the adventure to begin the following day. Inside the walls almost vibrated with the boys' anticipation. For dinner Stella cooked a family favourite: teriyaki chicken with oven-roasted potatoes and steamed broccoli, the only green vegetable no one complained about. And despite misgivings about one adult taking two small children on a multi-day hike in an isolated area, she did her utmost to stay positive.

But after she put the kids to bed, Joe picked a fight when Stella alluded to being left out of the plans. "From day one you've done your best to sabotage the trip," he said, "but this martyr act is worse."

Too tired to see straight, Stella waded right in. "Okay, so I harped a little – *mea culpa* – but you have no idea how often I bit back my concerns."

"You're right. I have no idea what goes on in your head, period. From where I stand, you're totally wrapped up in your own world."

"Really? I'm surprised you'd notice. Considering you're usually off at a meeting or hanging out with your mountaineering friends." *Good going, Stella: pathetic and needy.* But before she could change tack, he stormed out. The door slammed. Then a scraping sound as he dragged the canoe across the gravelly beach, the splash as he launched it into the lake.

* * *

Stella was a basket case the following morning. For the boys' sake, she feigned a sunny mood and in their excitement, they seemed to buy it. Every toy they owned was brought out then cast aside while Joe left trails of dry goods all over the kitchen. By departure time, the place looked as if it had been vandalized.

Matt gave his mom a quick hug then rushed to claim the front seat in the Pathfinder. Nicky clung to her but didn't cry. From his place in the back, he swung around to blow her a kiss and continued to blow kisses until she lost sight of the car. Matt never once looked back.

After Joe's late-night caper, he'd left the canoe upright on the beach and now, unable to face the mess in the cabin, Stella climbed into the stern and gazed out across Kootenay Lake. She thought about her aborted attempt to paddle across the lake after Lillian died. Wondered if she would ever again try to make it to the other side solo. Likely not. Not in this lifetime.

The lake level had peaked and begun to drop. An orange Frisbee that had been underwater now lay exposed on the beach. About a paddle's length from shore, a smattering of driftwood marked the high-water line. So now there was enough space for one of Joe's famous beach fires. Had he noticed last night? Or had his anger at her blinded him to anything good?

Around the bend on the opposite side of the lake, the yellow cottage would be empty now – no one left to hear the rush of Give Out Creek. On one side of the stream two women had lost their lives. On the other, Vanessa Levitt carried on, seemingly as usual.

Give Out Creek. The mining boom of a century ago had left a legacy of mining-related place names like that. Give Out had been associated with silver mining and likely the hopes and dreams of countless prospectors, each after some sort of "give out" of his own.

And Stella? What kind of give out did she hope for? All she'd ever wanted was a family of her own – a happy family – although she hadn't foreseen how tall an order that might be. The kids were all right, more than all right. But the marriage needed work. She felt a sort of ache to speak to Joe, to hear his voice. But he was driving, and to pull over on that winding road would be risky. Soon the car would be out of cell range and there she sat in a grounded canoe.

"I have to get out of here," she said aloud. "Stop moping and do something useful." She looked back at the old cabin and thought of Will Irwin, wondered what he would be up to on that beautiful Saturday morning. Well, she knew where to find him.

Once again Will took some time to answer the knock at his door. He was dressed in his usual slacks and check sports shirt but looked dishevelled, as if he'd been lying down. "Just the person to cheer me up," he said, running a hand over his bristly white hair. "What brings you out so early?"

"I need cheering up too," Stella said. "Joe took the boys up to Buttercup Ridge."

"And you miss them already. But wilderness is good for kids, isn't it? They'll have a ball."

"I worry about them though, Nicky especially."

"Now why is that?"

"You could say I'm a little overprotective. More than a little, I guess. But why do you need cheering up this morning?"

"Doc's making noises about taking away my licence. I'd planned to go to Kelowna today for my daughter's birthday but she doesn't want me to drive. Whole business is damned frustrating – I know that road like the back of my hand."

"Well I'm not doing anything," Stella said. "I could take you to Kelowna."

"My goodness, Stella, that's kind of you. But it's more than four hours' drive."

"No biggie. I'd enjoy it. Joe left me his sporty Subaru. It'll be fun. Could your daughter bring you back home when you're ready?"

"Don't see why not, or I could take the bus. And if you wanted to stay overnight Verna would find a bed for you." The smile on Will's face made him look years younger. "You sure about this?"

"Absolutely. I expect I'll just turn around and drive back this afternoon. But we'll cross that bridge when we come to it. Pack your bags, mister."

Outside by the car, Stella lifted her face to the sun. What could be better than putting a smile on Will Irwin's face, not to mention grabbing a brief respite from Unavailable and the rest of the problems in her life.

38

ON THE DRIVE TO Kelowna, Stella remarked on how good it felt to get out of town, even for a day. Will asked if she missed the Coast. "I miss the privacy for sure, the anonymity of a larger city. And I miss friends at my former job, the old neighbourhood. Wah, wah, wah."

Will said, "Now that's not trivial, Stella. A person mourns old times, old contacts. And in the short while you've been back, you've lost two new friends to tragedy."

"I've alienated one too, and I'm not sure where I stand with Vanessa. It's hard to be annoyed with her though. She's probably lonely over there on the East Shore."

"Vanessa should get herself a dog. Her parents had dogs. Cocker spaniels. Her mother was devoted to them."

"My kids want a dog."

"Every kid wants a dog."

After a pit stop at Rock Creek, Will nodded off. Stella thought about how easy it was to talk to him. It touched her how much he seemed to care. *The father I don't have,* she thought and gave her head a shake. *A shrink would have a field day.*

When the Subaru began to descend the rolling hills above Kelowna, she gave Will a gentle nudge. At his daughter's home, Stella accepted a cup of tea but declined a bed for the night. She drove back towards the highway and stopped at an intersection where a left turn would take her in the direction of Nelson. A road sign arrow pointed right towards Vancouver. The car's left turn indicator blinked as Stella stared at the sign. The road home led back to her messy, empty cabin. The car behind the Subaru blared its horn and Stella instinctively turned in the direction of Vancouver. In less time than it would take to drive back to Nelson, she could treat herself to a hit of the city. Why not? She hadn't been back since they had moved.

Okay, Ben was in Vancouver for the weekend but she told herself that was of no special relevance. No, this wasn't about Ben. This was about being spontaneous, bending the rules a little.

She pulled over and rang Patrick at home. "I'm in Kelowna," she said, "and I just had an idea that would require one day of leave."

"I'm listening." Patrick spoke over the wails of his infant daughter.

"In four hours, I could be in Vancouver and have a face-to-face with a contact for a story. Thing is, my source won't be available until Monday morning then I'd have to drive back. This is outrageously short notice, but a couple of stories were leftover on Friday, and the coordinator for the Homelessness Conference promised to submit a piece Monday, photos too. Could you manage without me for a day?"

Silence. Stella said, "Patrick? Are you there?"

"Just mulling," he said. "I don't think I can justify travel expenses."

"My dime, okay? I love road trips and Joe hates any long drive that doesn't end at a trailhead. I need this right now, Patrick. Say yes."

The baby started to hiccough. "All right. Bring back something good, yeah?"

"You got it."

She sent a text to Jeff Quinn before pulling back on to the highway. Although the doctor hadn't panned out as a suspect, Quinn might be a good background source. He had liked Lillian and seemed open to talking about her. A short one-on-one might shed some light on her sexual orientation, for one thing. It seemed important to know if Nina was telling the truth about their relationship. Jeff's profile on the Honeywell & Smart website included contact info, and if Stella had read the young lawyer correctly, he would check his phone often during the weekend.

* * *

The final hours of the drive to Vancouver took Stella through the Fraser Valley where Max Huber had served his time at Matsqui, the medium-security prison not far from the freeway she now travelled. Reflecting on her run-ins with Max, she tried to deconstruct the threat he posed. Clearly, he'd made some bad choices, but was he capable of murder? Putting aside the steroid use , did he have the daring or knowledge to inject Lillian with a syringe of insulin or manipulate Nina's fragile insulin pump? Hard to say, although there was no denying he scared Nina, and Stella too. It was going to be pleasant not to have to look over her shoulder for a couple of days.

Closer to Vancouver now, and despite the heightened volume of traffic, Stella half-enjoyed deking back and forth between lanes – she hadn't lost her touch. In no time, she had crossed the Port Mann Bridge and entered Vancouver's city limits. She took the First Avenue exit and shortly after checked into the YWCA Hotel on Beatty Street.

The desk clerk looked past Stella's shoulder and asked if she needed a luggage cart.

Stella patted her handbag. "Travelling light," she said.

After a total of eight hours in the car, she was ready to recharge. By foot, she zigzagged to Davie Street and covered another twelve blocks to English Bay, filling her lungs with the tangy salt air, grooving on the palm trees and larger-than-life bronze statues of laughing men. She dodged in-line skaters on the seawall and fell in step with the dog walkers and couples cruising the restaurants after a day at the beach. Along Denman to Robson then, she passed a Korean restaurant where a boisterous party of four grilled a platter of sizzling beef on a patio table. Hunger had snuck up on her.

Stella went inside and ordered a meal. Checked her phone. No reply from Jeff Quinn, nothing from Joe, although scattered reception in the mountains was to be expected. What would Matt and Nicky be doing at that moment? Probably tucking into platefuls of reconstituted spaghetti.

A burst of laughter from a nearby table – four women apparently out on a spree, two open bottles of wine on the table. Animated chatter. They could have been Stella's friends from book club: the all-too-happily married Carli-clone with nothing to chip in about an errant husband, a Vanessa look-alike holding forth about a member of the group who'd begged off that evening. For Stella, the book club had been one of the brightest sparks in her routine. But how could it ever be the same with Lillian and Nina gone – and now Carli and Vanessa disappointed in her?

At the table of women, the Vanessa double said, "Josie's so darned wrapped up in being a cop she lets everything else slide.

That's just not healthy."

Gossip. Everyone scorned it, but who could resist jumping right in? Stella vaguely recalled a blog that extolled the benefits of gossip in building social cohesion. Might be a story in it. She made a note on her phone.

Whoops. One of the women must have noticed her eavesdropping and now raised a glass in Stella's direction. She pretended she'd been trying to catch the eye of a waitress then followed through by ordering a pricey glass of Chardonnay.

More excitement. A tall brunette dashed in and skirted around a server, nearly toppling her tray of drinks. Must be the missing friend from the chatty group because the noise level at their table went up. A waiter was summoned to find another chair. Vanessa's doppelgänger remained unrepentant. "You decided to join us after all, Josie," she remarked in a faux-friendly tone. "Will the mean streets of Vancouver be safe without you tonight?"

That was bitchy, Stella thought, although perhaps she was being unfair. Maybe, like the real Vanessa, the woman had the best interests of her friends at heart. Stella settled back and enjoyed her meal. She wondered where in the city Ben was eating that evening, wondered if he was alone.

* * *

Waking up Sunday morning in the quiet, darkened room at the YWCA Hotel in Vancouver, Stella forgot for a moment where she was. No birdsong at an open window – no open window, for that matter. No kids spilling cereal in the next room. But there was no sense getting homesick; this was supposed to be a fun getaway, a retreat from her routine. Stella yanked back the heavy blackout draperies and shielded her eyes against dazzling sunshine. The sky behind the surrounding glass towers was the bright blue you'd find in a child's paint box. After a long, leisurely shower, Stella dressed and hit the lobby. Grabbed a rosy red apple from a bowl at reception and struck out again on foot.

Back on Robson Street she stopped at the Blue Horizon Hotel for brunch. When she checked her phone, she was rewarded with a text from Jeff Quinn: *Monday tight. Court at 10. Prep before*

Stella texted: *Law Courts on Robson? Could I walk with you?*

While she waited for the bill, Jeff replied: *Foyer my building, 9?*

She texted back: *Perfect*

The waitress slid her Visa into the card reader. "You look happy," she said.

"I am happy," Stella replied. She left a good tip.

A glorious open-ended day stretched out before her. Seize the moment, she told herself. No brooding about Joe, no worrying about the kids, no dwelling on gossipy friends – and absolutely no obsessing about murder. Seriously.

Still, with Ben McKean somewhere in Vancouver, it seemed almost dishonest not to reveal her whereabouts. She scrolled through her contacts and hit the little message bubble under his name.

Okay, what to say? Every phrase that popped into her head was either trite or inane. Forget it.

She continued down Robson to the entrance to Stanley Park at Lost Lagoon and proceeded past the Vancouver Rowing Club to the sea wall with a plan to circle the park. At Lumberman's Arch, she sat on a bench and took out her phone. In the iMessage box still open at Ben's number, she keyed in: *Hey, still in Van? Me too.* Feeling like a teenager, she sent it.

She checked for a reply every ten minutes and was back at the Lagoon staring at the ducks when her phone rang.

She closed her eyes. *Let it be Joe.* A call from Joe would make life so much easier.

But it was Ben McKean. She took the call. "Ben. Hi. Where are you?"

"At a meeting in Richmond. I had to escort a prisoner to YVR yesterday after a drug bust in Ymir. A guy we arrested is wanted in Winnipeg so I brought him this far. A Mountie met me to take him on the next leg. Why are you down here?"

"Well, I'm having a bit of R and R at the moment. But Monday I'm going to talk to that lawyer about Lillian."

"Sounds good," Ben said.

"When's your meeting over?"

"I could get away anytime."

What the hell. "I could be at Waterfront Station in fifteen minutes," said Stella. "Why don't you hop on the Canada Line and meet me there?"

"Roger that."

She loved it when he talked geeky.

39

WATERFRONT STATION, A GRAND red brick building once a terminus for the Canadian Pacific Railway, serves as a transit hub for downtown Vancouver. Stella got there first and slipped into a restroom to quickly fix her hair.

In the crowd spilling from the train, Ben McKean stood out. No uniform, yet no mistaking him for anyone but a cop: grey slacks; white open-collared shirt and navy blazer; black briefcase stamped with a subtle NPD logo. Probably armed.

She could tell when he saw her because he smiled then looked away. When he got close she thrust out her right hand. He squeezed it.

"Where to?" she said.

"Hungry? Kind of early for dinner, but we could find a nice place on the water to sit a while."

"Lead the way."

The patio at Cardero's in Coal Harbour overlooks a marina filled with yachts. They started with iced teas, chitchatted like a pair of college kids on vacation. Ben suggested a look at the menu and after a quick glance settled on the wok squid.

Stella laughed. "I wouldn't have figured you as a wok squid man. I'll be boring and have a salad, the Mediterranean looks good."

After giving the waiter their orders, they watched the activity in the harbour in companionable silence. Ben said, "So the doctor didn't pan out as a suspect."

"Nope. Two days before Lillian was murdered Dr. Graham Perry was under the knife for a hip replacement."

"Good alibi."

"Solid." Stella smiled at the waiter as he filled her water glass. "Disappointing though."

After the server left, Ben said, "You wanted a solve that would exonerate Nina Huber."

"I did." She clasped her hands together on the table. "I'm almost certain Nina didn't kill Lillian. And I can't help thinking…" She paused. "If I hadn't let Nina down maybe she'd still be alive. I just wasn't there for her." She sipped some water to compose herself. "Not sure about Max though, no warm fuzzy thoughts about him."

"Did you hear he made a bid for the Fenniwick property as his wife's beneficiary?"

"What?" She put down the glass. "Does he have a legitimate claim?"

"Arthur Nugent seems to think he might. That is unless Max Huber is convicted of murder, in which case the taxpayers will have to pay for his room and board. Seems he's joined forces with Colette Fenniwick to go after Nina's inheritance. They make quite the pair."

"Wonder what Colette was doing the night Lillian died."

"We checked. Witnesses put her at her son's school in Calgary. Parents' Night. Sorry, Stella. All roads seem to lead to Nina Huber. I'm not convinced a single contraction in the murder/suicide note is enough to rule her out as a suspect. Especially in light of her dumping those syringes at the mall."

"Can you picture her doing the crime though? I can't get my head around it."

Ben took a moment. "Both women were slim. But Nina was wiry and considerably younger. Say she gets Fenniwick tipsy. Then as the older woman climbs into the rowboat, Nina jabs her with the syringe. A small shove and she's in the boat, another shove and the boat's in the lake."

Stella twiddled with a fork. "Okay, that's not utterly implausible. But getting back to the packet of syringes, Nina had a valid use for needles before she got the insulin pump. And what about the wallet in the trash burner? Someone besides me visited Nina the day she died. Didn't you tell me Max denied being there?"

"He did. But if you put Max in the scenario I just presented, he and Nina could have dispensed with Lillian without breaking a sweat."

Their meals came. The waiter hung around offering extra bread, fresh-ground pepper, and drink refills before he finally left them to it. Stella looked at her plate. "I seem to have lost my appetite."

"You have to eat," Ben said.

"Let's talk about something more pleasant," Stella said.

"Like a drug bust?"

She smiled. "Can you give me anything on that for the paper?"

"I emailed you some details from the train into the city."

"Oh, thanks. I should write up something and file it later to-night. Earn my day off tomorrow. By the way, have you caught up with Henry Sutton?"

"Not even close. Still waiting for my boss to put in a request to the RCMP in Ottawa."

"Did you see my note about the altercation in Montana?"

"Yeah, I did. Safe to say there are a lot of Suttons in the US, but I added your info to the slim file on the Mr. Sutton in question."

Stella picked up a small vase and held the single yellow rosebud to her nose. The fragrance was faint. "I haven't explained why I really came to Vancouver. The chance to talk to the lawyer at Lillian's old firm was more of an excuse than a reason."

He smiled. "So why *did* you to come to Vancouver?"

"Joe and the kids went camping and I felt left out."

He must have picked up on the strain in her voice. "Murders wearing you down?"

"Murders plus collateral damage." Stella twirled the bud vase. "I'm beginning to think someone is after me – tell me that's normal." She tried to smile. "And Carli is upset with me, in part due to a silly rumour. I think Vanessa Levitt saw us parked in your patrol car that night."

Ben shook his head. "That was my fault. I'm sorry. Bad optics all round."

"No need to apologize. I was more than willing."

He gazed out at the harbour again. "That night in the car… you said you were obsessed with the investigations. The sick truth, you called it."

She grinned. "You have to admit it's twisted – to think about murder all the time."

He hesitated. "I never stop thinking about you."

Her hand shot across the table and he nearly toppled the vase to reach out to her. The hand that now engulfed hers wore a plain silver wedding band. "We can't do this, can we?" she said. "I mean, both of us…" To look directly at him would have been like staring at the sun. "What now?" she asked the rosebud.

"Let's get out of here." He signalled the waiter who looked alarmed at their almost-full plates and asked if anything was wrong. "Everything's fine," Ben said, tossing his card onto the table.

On the waterfront, they didn't touch. A dog yapped on a float at the marina while its owner fastened the tarp on a boat. A small floatplane made a noisy landing. Ben seemed about to say something but stopped himself. She felt shaky, disoriented. She almost collided with a toddler whizzing along the walkway on a coaster bike, the parents full of apologies.

In that moment, there was nowhere else she wanted to be; no one she wanted to be with more. But what was she willing to risk? Not the boys, not their happiness. After some time, she broke the silence. "Maybe we need to go back to where we started. Make this about work."

"Is that what you want? Because I don't know where to go with this. It's all a foreign country to me."

"Me too. I can't believe we're even having this conversation."

He touched the small of her back to steer her around a threesome on the sidewalk.

"So, do you want to talk about the investigations?" she said. "When you're alone do you go over and over the same facts, waiting for the final piece of the puzzle to click into place?" She took a breath. "Say something if only to shut me up."

"Sure, I go over the facts in my head. But I'm not much of a talker. That's one of Miranda's beefs. How about Joe? Does he talk to you?"

"Joe is Italian – what can I say?" She managed a wobbly smile. "Only we don't have enough privacy these days to hash things out, that's the problem. Not the only problem, obviously."

The constellation of huge white sails at Canada Place came into view. Ben said, "I'd suggest a drink, but…"

"But." To keep her hands busy, Stella pulled her hair into a ponytail and fastened it with a rubber band from her pocket. "Where are you staying – out by the airport?"

"Yup. Booked the first flight back tomorrow." They kept walking toward Waterfront Station.

"Well, it's early yet." She nudged him gently with her elbow. "We could have that drink before you get on the train."

She didn't have to ask twice. He shifted his briefcase from one hand to the other and guided her back toward Canada Place and the Pan Pacific Hotel. Their table in the lounge overlooked Stanley Park, the seawall she had walked along only that morning, a lifetime ago.

He ordered a beer; she asked for a glass of white wine. She felt conspicuous, as if they were performers in a play. Or still in Nelson, where a public conversation could set tongues wagging. Their glasses were still half full when he put a bill on the table and said, "Let's walk."

They covered block after block as if they had a purpose, rarely speaking. At intersections, he took her arm. She considered how they must look together: a man with a briefcase, a woman carelessly dressed, neither a West Ender nor a tourist. At the approach to the Burrard Street Bridge, she suggested taking a side street to catch the outlook to Granville Island.

Despite the sparkle of sunshine on False Creek, a cool breeze rippled its surface. "Warm enough?" he said. Without waiting for a reply, he draped his jacket over her shoulders. She pulled the jacket close, arms tucked inside. He leaned down to kiss her.

Panic. "I can't do this," she said. "I want to. It scares me how much I want to, but ..."

He stepped back a little but kept one arm around her as they watched the small blue ferries sail back and forth to Granville Island. "Those little boats look like bathtub toys," he said.

"My boys love riding the ferries to the market," she said. "It won't be long before your little guy will want to run around the kids' market – ever been there? Great toy stores."

"We carried him around the whole island once when he was tiny. Grabbed a coffee on the wharf. Bought him a souvenir T-shirt. Aiden slept through the whole thing."

"If I were my own best friend, I'd ask myself what the hell I was doing here," Stella said.

He squeezed her shoulders.

She let out a deep breath and handed him his jacket. "I should go back."

"I'll get you a cab," he said.

"No, it's okay. I'll walk. My hotel isn't far."

"I'll walk with you."

She struck off blindly in the general direction of the YWCA Hotel. He took her hand and slowed the pace. After two false turns, they came to the brightly lit entrance. "I was hoping it would take longer to find this place," he said.

She hugged him. When she started to let go, he held on. They stood like that for a short eternity. When he loosened his grip, it took every shred of moral fibre for her to let go and watch him walk away.

She made herself smile at the man behind the front desk, as if he would care about her state of mind. Back in her room, the image in the bathroom mirror looked like the "before" picture in a fashion makeover. Cock-eyed ponytail. No trace of makeup. The white summer-weight pullover worn for two consecutive days had a tear-shaped salad-dressing stain just above her left breast. Yet she felt beautiful, sexy. "You're a crazy person," she told the stranger in the mirror.

40

HALFWAY THROUGH A RESTLESS night, Stella checked her phone and found Ben's email. The subject line: Ymir. The content was a short, factual report on the drug bust. Nothing personal – not even a salutation. But then he had sent the note hours earlier, before meeting her downtown. Now it was 3:14 a.m. and she was wired. She got up, washed her face, turned the note into a five-hundred-word piece, and sent it to Patrick. After that she finally slept. She got up at seven, grateful to have a work-related commitment, an anchor in her otherwise conflicted state. After checking out of the hotel, she walked resolutely to the business district to meet lawyer Jeff Quinn. When he stepped out of an elevator in his building, hefting two oversize brief cases, she recognized him from the Honeywell and Smart website.

On the way to the Law Courts, she got Jeff talking about Lillian as a co-worker and friend, finally seguing into hotter issues, such as her relationships with Nina and Henry. Stella tried to be tactful when she broached the question of Lillian's sexual orientation.

Quinn didn't buy the premise Lillian had been gay. "She liked men," he said. "When I knew Lillian, she was in her late forties, early fifties, and in love with Clark. Would it sound too sappy to say it showed on her face whenever he entered a room?"

"She only had eyes for her husband," Stella said, thinking, *as I once did.*

Quinn laughed. "How would I know? My husband is going to crack up when I tell him you've come to me about this."

Okay, so Jeff was gay, which possibly make him a bit more of an expert on the subject than her, but probably not.

"Look," he continued. "I think Lillian loved her husband. But she clearly enjoyed the attention of other men. We had our share of heart-to-hearts, particularly when I was considering coming out to my family. I think I would have known if she was gay. Absolutely

231

I would have known. As for the investment dealer you mentioned, he doesn't sound smart enough for Lillian. When they checked into that hotel after dinner, are you sure they shared the same room?"

Stella groaned. "No, I'm not sure. I just assumed. That was stupid."

"Honest mistake. Should be easy to check though." They had reached the Law Courts. Jeff Quinn wished her luck. Then he lugged his bulky cases up the concrete stairs and slipped into the glass atrium.

* * *

Stella left Vancouver and after eight hours on the picturesque, twisting highways of southern British Columbia arrived home. Thanks to her adventuring husband, the kitchen counter with its dusting of flour, rolled oats, and two kinds of sugar was alive with ants. She slammed around killing ants, disinfecting counters, returning jars to their rightful places. When she spied a pair of Power Ranger action figures on the floor she picked them up and held them to her cheeks.

After she had put away assorted toys and about a thousand minuscule pieces of Lego, she boiled two eggs, toasted a slice of bread, and poured a glass of lukewarm Chardonnay. At ten o'clock she fell into bed exhausted but not sleepy, her head and heart still wrapped around Ben McKean, damn him.

Prior to that weekend, she'd barely registered the attraction. Well, that wasn't entirely true. She had felt a little steamy about Ben ever since he handed her those binoculars on the lakeside road. And if she had to be brutally honest, she had picked up signals from him. But God, now she was on fire. For the first time in her life she knew first-hand why a happily married woman might be tempted to stray. And for the first time questioned whether the phrase "happily married" applied to her and Joe.

Again, she asked herself what she was willing to risk and again the answer was: not the boys' happiness. She wanted the impossible: to be with Ben in a place and time exclusive to them, to have a relationship that in no way impacted her family or his. This was why people had clandestine affairs, she thought, they didn't want to choose. Brilliant insight, that. Her naivety was stunning, her lack of desire for Joe disturbing. The honourable choice seemed to be the painful, empty choice. It was a long night.

Dawn came before she drifted off. The last thing she heard was the early morning train rattling along the tracks on the opposite side of Kootenay Lake. When the alarm clock rang two hours later, she woke with a splitting headache, almost too tired to cycle to town, yet determined to take the bike as a penance for lusting in her mind.

Outside she did a double take. The canoe had been moved. On Saturday morning, it had been upright and closer to shore. She had sat in the stern and let herself get quite maudlin before leaving to visit Will Irwin. Now the canoe had been turned over and positioned closer to the house. Had someone "borrowed" it? Kieran Corcoran came to mind.

She preferred to think a Good Samaritan had noticed it from the water and reckoned it was too close to shore. Or was it a threat? A signal that said, *I'm watching you.*

41

STELLA ARRIVED AT THE *Times* still bothered by the repositioned canoe, and nervous about her re-entry to the newsroom. She had only missed one workday, yet the weekend in Vancouver seemed more like a year in Kazakhstan in terms of the change in her.

Surprisingly, change had been afoot at the *Times* too. Patrick had shaved off his goatee, which left him looking like a slightly wizened teenager. Even the furniture had been rearranged, Jade's desk moved under a window where a hot shaft of sunlight picked up the cobalt blue highlights – also new – in her auburn hair.

Jade's exposé about drugs at Shangri-Lectric had prompted so many hits on the website and likes on Facebook, Patrick assigned Stella to help with the follow. Aglow with self-importance, Jade asked her to do a sidebar on new street drugs popping up in the local area, adding bossily, "Be sure to include ketamine. It's called Special-K on the street. Someone broke into the vet's office on the East Shore over the weekend and cleaned them out of it."

"Have you spoken to the vet?" Stella said. "I know her book-keeper."

"Good," Patrick put in. "Follow up on that."

"What about the Ymir drug bust?"

"Posted. I combined what you sent me with the NPD press release. You get something good in Vancouver?"

"What? Oh, yeah. I need to track down a few more details, but yeah, good meeting. Tell you more later but now I'd better call that vet."

Patrick rubbed his hands together. "Okay people, let's get to work."

A phone message at the East Shore veterinary office indicated the clinic was closed; in case of emergency, callers were directed to the animal hospital in Nelson. Stella rang her friend who kept the books for the clinic. "Hey, Amelie," she said. "What can you tell me about the break-in on the weekend? Can you put me in touch with the vet herself?"

"Lou-Ann isn't taking calls right now," Amelie said. "I got an update when I stopped by the clinic. *Crisse*, what a mess! Those douche bags really trashed the place. Less than fifty bucks in petty cash but they were looking for the meds. Addicts are after ket – that's vet-speak for ketamine."

"Have the cops been around?"

"A Corporal Everly or Eberly? Off the record, Lou-Ann found him annoying."

Stella put in a call to Ray Eberly. The receptionist said he would get back to her. He didn't. Stella called again and agreed to be put on hold. Four minutes later Eberly came on the line to say the Chief would make a statement once the investigation was complete.

"Any connection with a possible robbery at the gas station on the ferry slip a while back?" Stella said.

"Like I said, still investigating."

Stella got to work on a sidebar about drugs, including ketamine, which seemed to have a million street names – K, Special K, Kit Kat, the list went on and on. The stuff could be injected, snorted, smoked, or dissolved in drinks, as in the case of date rape. The experience of taking it was known as the K-hole. Stella shuddered to think whose hands the clinic's supply might have fallen into.

Despite Amelie's attempt to shield the vet, Stella wanted to talk to her. She found her personal telephone number and managed to get a living, breathing person on the other end of the line. Dr. Lou-Ann's daughter called her mother to the phone. "Amelie told me you'd called," Lou-Ann said, wearily. "What would you like to know?"

* * *

On her way home, Stella almost cycled past Zoe DeLuca on Baker Street. She jingled the bell on her handlebar and pulled the bike up onto the sidewalk. "I haven't seen you since school let out for summer," she said "How are you doing?"

The girl looked embarrassed. "Okay, I guess."

"Your mom mentioned you had a bad experience at the music

festival. She didn't go into details."

"It was no big deal. She's still mad at me though."

"If it's any comfort, she's mad at me too."

"Yeah, I kind of heard."

Stella gestured to a bench in front of the kitchen shop. "Can you tell me about that?"

Zoe sat down beside her. "I probably shouldn't say anything, but I overheard my parents whispering about you and Joe."

How to explain to a thirteen-year-old what Stella failed to understand herself? "Marriage is complicated, Zoe. You're a smart girl so you may have picked up on that. But I don't want you to worry about Joe and me. We're fine." *Liar*.

Zoe nodded. After a moment she said, "You remember Kieran?"

Stella smiled. "How could I forget Kieran?"

"We broke up." A beat. "I'm not sure he noticed." She grinned bravely.

"Are you all right with that?"

"Yeah. I liked him but… I don't know. My mom hates him. She thinks he's a bad influence. That's her code for sex and drugs. But that wasn't even a big thing with Kieran. You know what we fought about? Money. We were like some old married couple."

"No kidding. What's the deal with Kieran and money?"

"He can't get enough of it. He told me he once ripped off Lillian. She gave him two bills stuck together and he didn't speak up – he figured she could afford it. I think he tried to make up for it by working for Nina but I know he steals. He says if people leave cash lying around they can expect to lose it. He kind of bragged about finding a wallet with a hundred dollars in it."

So, Kieran had "found" Nina's wallet. Had he rummaged through her purse while she lay dying on the kitchen floor? Maybe his handyman act at Nina's had been an excuse to case the place for valuables. Kieran was a screw-up, although he didn't seem twisted enough to kill someone for a bit of cash. He might have crossed paths with the killer though, possibly without knowing he had. To Zoe, Stella said, "Sounds like you're better off without him. Breaking up is hard though."

"Yeah."

Stella could have said so many things. She might have sympathized. Told Zoe there was something about dark, edgy men that can be hard to resist. Maybe someday she would. But for now she said, "You know, I'm glad we had this chance to talk. I've been wanting to clear the air after that incident with the boys in the canoe."

"I still feel bad about that."

"Please don't, Zoe. I overreacted. I apologized to your mom but I should have spoken to you too. Let's forget about it, okay?"

She shrugged slightly. "I'm good with that."

"Would you like to look after Matt and Nicky when Joe's teaching summer school? I know the guys would be pleased."

"Sure. That'd be great. It was nice talking to you but I better go."

On the bike ride home Stella watched a ski boat make loops on the lake. The skier – a girl about Zoe's age – took a tumble and the boat circled back to pick her up. Sweet Zoe. Stella hoped there would always be someone around to catch her when she stumbled.

* * *

Stella parked her bike outside the cabin and glanced at the overturned canoe. Maybe Kieran *had* come by and taken it for a spin. She wouldn't put it past him. If he helped himself to cash that didn't belong to him, why not "borrow" a canoe?

Blame it on her immersion in street drugs that day, but as Stella cooked dinner she grew more and more convinced the missing piece in the murders might be a second substance. A drug which, mixed with alcohol, could have rendered Lillian and Nina helpless enough for their killer to administer an overdose of insulin. Ketamine would have done the trick. The murders had occurred before the robbery at the vet's office, but there were other ways to get hold of the drug. Stella's conversation with Dr. Lou-Ann had been instructive. Doctors, dentists, and veterinarians have access to legitimate sources such as pharmacies, where there are strict controls to prevent abuse. As for illegitimate means, anyone with enough street smarts or Internet savvy could likely find a back door.

The pathologist Dr. Antoniak would have sent blood and tissue samples from the murder victims to the RCMP lab to be tested. But, as in the case of the syringe on the beach, the process could be speeded up if there was evidence that pointed to a specific substance to look for.

Stella drained her single portion of pasta and topped it with stir-fried veggies. When she sat down to eat, she glanced at her phone. No message from Ben, disappointing but just as well. Nothing from Joe either, but then what did she expect? He probably hadn't even taken his phone on the hike. With little likelihood of cell reception on the ridge and nowhere to charge it, he'd probably locked the phone in the glove box of the Pathfinder before he and the boys set out.

Matt and Nicky were never far from her thoughts but she had to stop obsessing about them. Will Irwin's subtle advice had been spot on. Wilderness is good for kids; she knew that full well. Realistically she couldn't protect them from every hazard known to man, and she couldn't put Joe in a bubble either. Why was she such a control freak – because her mom had been anything but? She had always considered herself the polar opposite of her unpredictable, disorganized mother and related more to her dad. The parent who left.

After dinner Stella took her tea out to the porch. She pictured the boys racing across a meadow on Buttercup Ridge, scrambling over rock screes, playing and laughing and tussling until they wriggled into their sleeping bags and fell into that deep oblivion only a kid can experience. Joe would be relaxing by a campfire, perfectly content.

She sipped at her tea.

Across the lake, an enormous grey thunderhead began to build over the mountains. More clouds scudded into view. The sky grew darker than it should have at – she checked her watch – nine o'clock. A fork of lightning flashed over the mountains, followed two seconds later by a rumble of thunder. Over the next hour Stella was treated to a full-fledged light show. But she couldn't just sit there and enjoy the spectacle – not when her family was on a ridge high in the mountains, possibly the worst place to be during a thunderstorm.

The next crash was deafening. The smoke alarm chirped a warning and the dim porch light went out. Power failure. A deluge of rain spilled over the edges of the tin roof.

Stella went inside to do an Internet search on lightning storms. Thankfully her phone had a data package that didn't require a power source, provided the cell tower hadn't been hit, and the odds of that were slim. But even as she groped on the kitchen table she remembered her phone needed charging. The cabin was black as a pit. She felt her way into the bedroom, found the flashlight, and scanned the bookshelf for Joe's favourite mountaineering book. In the section about lightning, she shone the beam on the first page.

Dangers to hikers, she read, include direct strikes, ground currents, and something called "induced currents" in the vicinity of strikes. She read on.

"Avoid moist areas," the author advised. But how is that possible for a hiker caught in a rainstorm?

"Stay out of small depressions and caves and away from overhangs. Sit, crouch, or stand on an insulating (meaning dry) object." Like that was going to happen.

Stella felt ill. Fearing she might throw up, she took the book and flashlight to the bathroom and continued to read perched on the edge of the tub. Nothing in the book reassured her.

At midnight the lights flickered once, twice, and stayed on. The wind continued to whistle outside the small, wood-frame cabin. Stella didn't consider herself a true believer, but that night she prayed for the safety of her family. On Joe's side of the bed, she arranged several pillows end-to-end and snuggled up to them as she waited for sleep to come.

A few hours later a gunshot-like sound catapulted her from the bed. The windows had rattled, the bed skittered along the floor, her reading lamp fell off the night table. She peeked behind the curtains. Nothing. Stella grabbed the flashlight and stepped tentatively onto the porch. The leafy top of a birch tree enveloped the wicker chairs.

A tree had toppled over and crashed to the ground. The trunk had missed the cabin by mere inches. Taking care on the porch stairs, she climbed through the branches then walked the length of the tree, placing one foot ahead of the other to gauge its height. Standing, the birch would have been about thirty-three feet tall.

42

THE NEXT MORNING STELLA called a tree service and was told she would have to wait a week to have the fallen birch limbed and bucked. Last night's storm had brought down trees and snags throughout the area, from Nelson to the ferry terminal and beyond. Stella cycled to work on a slick highway littered with branches as thick as human arms and legs, conditions hazardous to anyone on two wheels. Twice she pulled over to snap photos of the damage. Yet overall, the shiny cleansed landscape gave her a lift.

In the bright light of day, she stopped worrying about her family. Joe would have known how to keep Matt and Nicky safe during the thunderstorm – he would have made an adventure of it. Why had she let herself get all worked up over what-ifs?

A police car passed but she couldn't make out the driver. If it were Ben, would he have stopped? Where Ben was concerned, she didn't know what to wish for anymore.

At the *Times*, the storm was the number one topic of conversation. Stella's first assignment was to investigate cases of serious damage in the area. The highways maintenance contractor recognized her name when she identified herself over the phone. A member of the church Lillian had attended, he asked if Stella knew of any progress in finding her killer.

"If there was a killer," Stella said.

"C'mon."

"Well the police haven't released a cause of death."

"You ask me," the contractor said, "that embezzler is their man. Sutton. The guy had no scruples. He used Lillian to establish his bogus reputation all over town. But if he'd thought for one moment she had something on him, he would have killed her as soon as look at her."

Patrick caught Stella's attention and mimed the act of drinking. She shook her head; he and Jade left for the coffee wagon across the street. Stella got the contractor back on topic.

After the call, she had all the information she needed on the cause of the power failure and other results of the storm, including a temporary road closure. But she kept mulling over the contractor's take on Henry Sutton. She hadn't realized other people in Nelson shared Carli's conviction about Sutton. It seemed obvious the guy was a crook. Now the question was how far he might have gone to protect his interests.

Alone in the office, Stella took a moment to follow up on Jeff Quinn's question about hotel room arrangements the night Lillian and Sutton dined at the Lakeshore. Harold the catering manager hedged and promised to get back to her. Five minutes later he reported the pair had taken separate but adjoining rooms. Harold couldn't say whether they'd asked to be next to each other, but they paid separately for their rooms.

In other words, whether or not Lillian had been intimate with Henry, she had been discreet. Unlike Stella, who had climbed into Ben McKean's patrol car on a quiet stretch of highway then traipsed all over the West End of Vancouver with him. Anyone might have witnessed the public kiss on the waterfront near Granville Island, all that handholding and hugging.

Patrick and Jade came up the stairs laughing. He was carrying a latté for Stella. Jade was going on and on about the upcoming mid-summer triathlon. Even the mayor was rumoured to be training for the event. Stella put Henry Sutton on the back burner.

Over lunch, another call came in from Unavailable. Stella's mind ran away with her as she slammed down the receiver on the heavy breather. What the hell was going on? The crank calls, the flat tires, the repositioned canoe – even the fallen birch tree might have been an act of sabotage.

She stood up and paced the newsroom, glanced out the window. Jade was sitting on a bench across the street, bare legs stretched out, her face tilted to catch the sun. And there – not twenty feet away –a dark grey pickup was parked, the driver in a ball cap talking on his phone.

Stella flew downstairs, crossed the street, and pounded with a closed fist on the passenger window of the pickup. The driver, a male of about thirty, got out and walked around to the sidewalk. "You got a problem?" he said.

"You bet I have a problem," Stella said. "You nearly ran my bike off the road a couple of weeks back on the lakeshore highway."

"You on something? Get lost."

Jade came over and snapped a photo of him. "Hey, knock it off," he told her. Jade took more shots of the truck, including the front and rear licence plates.

Stella said, "You swerved onto the margin and didn't even stop to see if I was okay. I'd like to see your driver's licence and registration."

"Fuck you." He started to return to the other side of the truck.

"Oh now, that's not nice," Jade said. "She's a reporter for the *Times*. Better do what she says or you might find yourself on the front page."

"Shit," the driver said. He reached in the truck for his registration, fished his licence out of his wallet. Jade snapped a photo of each document.

"I'm still waiting for an apology," Stella said. She was beginning to enjoy herself.

"Look, I'm sorry," he said. "OK? You happy?"

"We're fucking over the moon," Jade said.

* * *

That afternoon Stella cycled to City Hall to interview the mayor about her triathlon training, still basking in the afterglow of the sting she and Jade had pulled off. The look on Patrick's face when they high-fived in the newsroom had been priceless. And if the driver of the grey pickup hassled her again, it would be easy to nail him with all the documentation she had now.

The plaza outside the city offices was deserted except for a young woman pushing a baby in a stroller. With a start Stella recognized Ben's wife, Mrs. McKean, the woman she had once passed in the lobby of the police station. Miranda, Ben had called her. He clearly adored the little boy but seemed somewhat ambivalent about his wife. Unless Stella had imagined that. Today Miranda's dark hair billowed around her small, sharp face, her Snow-White complexion setting off full ruby lips. In the band of flesh between her snug tank top and micro skirt, a belly button ring glinted in the sunlight. This was a woman any man would look at twice. Resisting a temptation to cut across the plaza to avoid her, Stella slowed down and caught Miranda's eye. "Cute baby," she said.

"Oh, thanks." Quick smile. Nice teeth. "He's a little cutie, all right."

"Well, enjoy your outing." Stella guiltily coasted on, heart hammering in her chest. No sign of recognition, but when she glanced over her shoulder she caught young Mrs. McKean looking back at her.

43

STELLA STARTED THINKING ABOUT Henry Sutton again as she cycled back to the office after her interview with the mayor. If he was the Sutton who had beaten up a man in Montana, he was dangerous, and almost as worrisome was Vanessa's interest in him. Imagine if at age fifty – and still a virgin – you had pinned all your hopes on one man and he turned out to be a killer.

Sutton's name had come up over dinner in Vancouver, but then Ben had dropped the bomb about his feelings for her and put an end to any rational discussion. This much Stella knew from their conversation in his patrol car: Sutton had been in Canada for a while before Lillian was murdered and returned to the US the morning after her death.

On his return to the US, he had used the crossing near Creston, which seemed curious. But then the Creston crossing would have made sense if Henry had spent his last night on the East Shore because the drive was shorter. Had he gone there to see Lillian again – to continue whatever they'd started at the Lakeshore Hotel? Had they argued? Nina claimed not to have seen Lillian leave in her rowboat. Maybe Henry had waylaid her without anyone noticing. Stella pulled her bike over and sat under the shade of a tree to think.

* * *

That afternoon she wrapped up work early, hoping to catch Vanessa at the end of her day at the drugstore. Stella would suggest they grab dinner at Jigsaw's, a good place for a heart-to-heart. She wasn't sure how to broach the topic of Henry Sutton, but as evidence mounted against him, it seemed unconscionable not to say anything. Sutton could either find a way to use Vanessa or – rather than return to the scene of his crimes – disappear south of the border and leave her to a lifetime of unrequited love.

But when Stella arrived at Levitt Drugs she found Vanessa had left for the day. One of the pharmacists said she'd come in at seven that morning to re-organize the break room then taken off early.

Stella needed a Plan B.

* * *

When she cycled home along the lakeshore highway, the water was as smooth as silk. An older couple in matching blue kayaks glided past a becalmed sailboat, its jib flapping. A small aluminum boat putted up the lake, ignored by a flotilla of Canada geese.

At the cabin, Stella stopped to put away her bike. And there on the passenger side of Joe's cherished Subaru was a scar the length of the vehicle. Someone had keyed the car – and in broad daylight. If it had happened the night before, she would have noticed the damage that morning before she left for work. Although the fallen birch had been a major distraction. With no way of knowing exactly when the vandal had struck, the insurance claim was sure to be a headache. Joe was going to be apoplectic.

She wondered if it was too crazy to imagine someone was sending her a message: drop the murder investigations or else. It seemed there had been too many threatening incidents to chalk up to coincidence. For a second, Stella just wanted to go to bed and pull the covers over her head. But, no. She wasn't going to let them win, whoever the hell "them" were. No. She didn't want to spend the rest of her life looking over her shoulder.

And that was when she decided to paddle across the lake to Vanessa's and warn her about Sutton. If she didn't make it to the other side, well, it wouldn't be the first time. And if she *did* make it, she would at least prove to herself she could do it.

Before she had time to talk herself out of it, Stella marched inside to pack a sandwich. She checked the charge on her phone and rounded up two flashlights, a beach towel, a bottle of water, and her lifejacket.

Back on the beach, she scanned the sky. No sign of a storm brewing, only a few wispy clouds overhead. The lake level was still dropping, the beach about a metre wider than it had been on Saturday. The water was still calm. Amazingly, she felt calm too.

She flipped over the boat.

And there on the ground under the canoe was a manila envelope with Stella's name scrawled on the front in black letters. She carefully opened the flap – and pulled out a flyer from a paving company. She laughed out loud. Had some jerk put her through all that torment because he wanted to pave the damn driveway?

But the back of the flyer had a message, written in a hand she recognized. She sat down on the beach and began to read. *Dear Stella, I guess you never expected to hear from your old dad. Believe it or not, this is my second trip to Nelson in a month. Finally screwed up the courage to talk, and you don't seem to be around. See, I often read the local rag online. That's how I found out you were back in town a few months ago. I live in Fernie now, still working in the food service industry, off and on. Don't know what I'd do with myself if I ever retired, ha-ha. I want to see you but only if you want to see me, comprende? Call or text anytime, night or day. Love ya, Stellarina*

At the bottom of the page he had jotted a phone number.

Twenty-five years, and he comes to her house and leaves a note on a scrap piece of paper. She re-read the letter. Twice. She thought back to the older man with the brown dog seen at the school. Had that been him? Hanging back in the shadows, spying on her family, unable to face her in person. Not the most assertive person in the world, her dad.

Fernie. That was consistent with the BC area code in the phone number. Did he have a family in Fernie? The thought made her feel sick to her stomach.

What now? Was she supposed to drop everything and call? *All is forgiven, daddy dearest, let's start anew.* Like a quick note can make up for leaving your family and disappearing for more than two decades.

Stella rolled her shoulders back and forth a couple of times and skidded the boat to the water's edge. Wiping her eyes with the back of her hand, she stowed her gear and nosed the canoe into the water. She put on her lifejacket and cinched the straps.

You don't have to do this, said an inner voice. *Yeah,* she muttered to herself, *actually I do.*

The canoe almost tipped when she lumbered into the stern but it remained upright. She spent a moment visualizing the crossing then picked up the paddle and pushed off. The lake mirrored the feathery clouds overhead. A fish jumped, and then the surface was still again.

Partway across the lake, she put aside her paddle and bit into the sandwich. The damned note had taken away her appetite but she made herself eat. She had to stay strong for the evening ahead.

With no wind to fill its sails, a sailboat glided by under power. Stella waved. The people onboard waved back and slowed down. But she felt a stab of terror at the memory of the boat she'd crossed paths with last time. She dropped the sandwich and tentatively steered at right angles to the wake of the sailboat. This time she had the sense to drop onto her knees to lower her centre of gravity, which helped so much she almost wept with gratitude. The far shore seemed to rise up to meet her. She was going to make it this time.

Around the first bend, the yellow cottage came into view. It looked dark and neglected, the lawn and gardens already overgrown, the door to the shed wide open. Stella felt obliged to stop and close it to keep out animals. No harm taking a break to give her arms a rest, anyway. She pulled the canoe up onto the beach.

Inside the shed, a shadowy male figure startled then came at her.

She swung wide and connected with the figure. A stack of copper pots clattered to the floor. "Kieran Corcoran," she panted. "What the hell are you doing here?"

"Fuck," said Kieran.

"You're stealing *flower pots*?"

"What do you care? Or are you helping out your boyfriend cop?"

The message was clear: you caught me red-handed but I have something on you too.

"Outside," she said. It was all she could do not to add, "you little prick."

Kieran dropped onto the narrow wooden bench next to the shed and pulled out a baggie of weed. She plucked it from his fingers. "You can have it back," she said, as he grasped for the packet, "when you tell me what's going on."

"Nothing, nada. I just forgot something when I was, like, over here helping out."

"Forgot what?"

He shrugged. "A jacket? Yeah, I lost a jacket. Can I have my weed back now? Please?"

"Or were you hoping to find – I don't know – another wallet

maybe?"

His face was a sullen mask. "I don't know what you're talking about."

"No, of course not." She tossed him the baggie. "Get out of here, and don't come back."

He loped off. Stella secured the shed and returned to the beach. In the canoe again, she continued toward Vanessa's place but her heart wasn't in it. She had no idea of how to even begin the conversation, let alone warn her friend that her love interest was probably a criminal.

She had crossed the lake solo though. That was something – her personal Everest. Joe was going to be proud of her, a thought that loosened the hold Ben had on her heart. Her dad would likely be proud too, damn him. How did he get off deserting her then wandering back into her life is if nothing had happened?

Beyond the creek Vanessa's makeshift wharf came into view. At the end of it, a small table with two folding chairs. Stella rested the paddle across her lap and let the canoe drift. With the lake level so low, the water close to shore was shallow and clear. She used the tip of her paddle to steer around several large rocks that might have damaged the boat's hull.

About two metres from shore, a black object on the lake bottom caught her eye. She manoeuvered the canoe closer to get a better look.

Sunglasses. Lillian's unmistakeable, wrap-around shades, her signature accessory.

Stella stared into the shallows of Kootenay Lake, dumbfounded. The temples of Lillian's sunglasses were open, as if she had pulled them off and hurled them into the water in a panic.

The level of Kootenay Lake would have been much higher the night Lillian left home in her rowboat. She couldn't have known the glasses would be found some weeks later when the water level dropped. The gesture would have been the desperate act of a woman fighting for her life. Vanessa had been adamant that Lillian hadn't reached her destination. But now here was indisputable proof that on the night she died, Lillian Fenniwick had been on the lake, directly in front of Vanessa's cottage.

Stella glanced at the house. Strange that Vanessa hadn't noticed the sunglasses. But then the wharf had a swim ladder. Vanessa wouldn't risk wading into the lake and spoiling her pedicure on sharp rocks. She would stride confidently to the end of the last float, dive into the lake, then use the ladder to climb back out after her swim.

Stella's pulse throbbed in her ears. What the hell had happened?

Why wait to find out? She scrambled out of the canoe, manually turned it around, then clambered back on board and raised her paddle.

"Woohoo!" Vanessa was walking toward her with a tray of drinks, two full glasses and a pitcher.

44

AS VANESSA ADVANCED DOWN the beach, a small inner voice shrieked in Stella's head: *Go. Leave. Paddle like a maniac.* Yet she responded as the polite woman she had been brought up to be. "Oh, hi," she called out. "I thought you weren't home."

"I saw you coming," Vanessa shouted back, stepping onto the first float. "Fixed us a pitcher of Caesars. I'm already one ahead of you."

In a daze, Stella stepped into the shallow water and pulled the canoe carefully onto the beach. She removed her lifejacket and, treading warily, followed Vanessa to the canvas fold-up chairs at the end of the wharf.

"Lake's dropping fast." Vanessa said. She sat down and stirred both drinks with stalks of celery.

"I hadn't really noticed," Stella said. "Been away a few days." Her heart pounded against her ribs, the hair on her arms stood up. *Lillian had been right there.* But who killed her? And where did Vanessa fit in? Maybe she'd been a witness – or worse, an accomplice. Or maybe she'd been in the house, oblivious to what was going on right outside her door. That seemed the most reasonable explanation.

"I was going to have Kieran rake up the debris that accumulated at the high-water line," Vanessa said. "But when I saw you I sent him home." Right on cue Kieran appeared up by the house, cupped his hands around his mouth and yelled something Stella couldn't make out.

Vanessa waved. "He's left something inside – he'd forget his head if it wasn't screwed on. He'll get whatever it is and leave by the back door."

Kieran must have moved smartly to have crossed the footbridge over Give Out Creek and got there only minutes after Stella arrived in her canoe. "Kieran Corcoran," she said, happy to latch onto a

251

safe topic. "That kid is everywhere. Sometimes I wonder if he has a home to go to." She shifted in her chair, crossed and re-crossed her legs.

"You were looking into the water, sweetie," Vanessa said, gently. "I noticed those silly old glasses too but I was dressed for work and didn't want to get my feet wet. I should toss them before anyone gets the wrong idea."

Stella hesitated. "I *was* a bit curious about them."

"Well of course you were," Vanessa said. "I was there when you asked Nina about them. She told you Lillian wore the glasses the night she died." Vanessa stretched her arms upward, turned her head from side to side as if to loosen her neck. "It took me a while to catch on, but I'm afraid our friend Nina was unstable. For all we know, she dropped those glasses into the lake to implicate me in Lillian's death. Isn't that awful? I hate to even think it. But it's quite obvious Nina killed Lillian then killed herself. The whole thing just breaks my heart, Stella. But I think we have to accept it – there's no other explanation."

Stella lifted her cocktail then put it down again. "Why though?" she said, slowly. "Why would she do that? Lillian was good to Nina."

Vanessa shook her head sadly. "This is going to sound terrible, sweetie. I know you were fond of Lillian, but I don't think you had any idea how much she used people. She used Henry then betrayed him to Carli and the rest of you." She gulped down half her drink.

Stella stared helplessly at Vanessa, took a sip of her drink, then stopped and put it down. Maybe it was spiked. A crazy thought, but given recent events it wasn't out of the realm of possibility. "Speaking of Henry," Stella said, carefully. "Did he come by to see you the night Lillian died?

"The night Lillian died..." Vanessa looked out across the lake for a moment. "I don't think so. He came by so rarely I would have remembered. It isn't fair he has to work so hard. Lillian didn't ap-preciate that. But then Lillian never had to worry about money."

"You and Henry..." Stella let the words trail off. She felt slightly dizzy. She looked at her glass. Vanessa had polished off her drink and was pouring a refill from the pitcher.

"My turn has come, Stella," she said, rubbing a hand sloppily across her mouth. "I've waited so long for a shred of happiness..."

Her eyes glistened.

"Oh gosh, Vanessa," Stella said. "I don't want to see you hurt again."

"Lillian never got hurt. Lillian always got her man."

Grasping for her meaning, Stella didn't know what to say.

Vanessa continued. "She was ruthless, you know. Long before Lillian made a play for Henry, she seduced Clark. Clark was in love with me before she came along."

Clark? *Clark Fenniwick?*

"God, Vanessa," Stella said, finally putting it all together. "That... that must have hurt."

Vanessa snorted. "The perky, fast-talking lawyer knew how to get her way. Well, I didn't have the benefit of a university education. When I should have been attending pharmacy classes at the University of British Columbia, I was in Saskatoon having a quasi-legal abortion."

What?

Vanessa barely skipped a beat. "Yes, Stella, I got pregnant. Clark was the father. I was so ashamed – I'm still ashamed. Despite the feminist crap we get shoved down our throats these days, I still feel shame. And sweetie, you gotta believe me, I am a virgin in my heart. There hasn't been anybody but Clark. I longed for him for years and years. Until I met Henry I never found a man worth giving myself to like that."

"You went to Saskatoon for the abortion," Stella said, the reporter pinning down details.

"My parents sent me on a little trip to 'help out' a great aunt who put me up. There had to be a respectable reason for dropping out of university. We couldn't take a chance on sullying the reputation of the family business, could we? They paid for everything but never let me forget it. My mother showed more affection for the stupid dogs than she did for me. Can you begin to imagine what that was like, Stella? Slinking off to get a secret abortion – not knowing if I would ever have a child of my own, a child I could keep." Vanessa paused to compose herself, but she wasn't finished. "And then to top it off, years later, who do I get for a neighbour? Ms. High and Mighty herself. I had to deal with it. Make nice to her. But when she went after Henry that was the last straw."

Stella closed her eyes to concentrate. "I can see why you'd be angry with Lillian, but –" She paused. Where was she going with this?

"Oh, grow up, Stella. Don't play the wide-eyed ingénue with me. Lillian's death was no great loss. Her time had come. She was old and half blind. Living on cigarettes and wine, pampering herself in every possible way. She was headed for a horrific heart attack. It was an act of kindness to kill Lillian – for Nina to kill Lillian. Death would have been quick and painless. I bet Nina barely had to spike her drink before she injected her with that syringe. With the amount of wine Lillian could put away it would have been absurdly easy to poke her with a syringe and get her back into the rowboat." Vanessa sniffled and poured herself another refill.

Stella said, "What do you mean 'back into the rowboat'?"

"What? I don't know. You know what I mean." Vanessa bit off a chunk of celery and crunched for a moment.

"You said it would be easy to poke Lillian with a syringe and get her back into the rowboat. As if she'd gotten out of the boat then returned to it," Stella said.

Vanessa shook her head, bit into the celery again. "How do I know what went on between those two."

Nice deflection, Stella thought. She tried again. "But how could anyone inject Lillian without her knowledge?"

"Sweetie! Show a little imagination. You could tell her she had dirt on the back of her dress – Lillian was nothing, if not vain. One or two swipes at her ass and she'd barely notice the needle go in. To a drunk it would feel like a mosquito bite. Mosquitoes are wicked that time of the evening." Vanessa gulped at her drink without removing the celery stick. It nearly poked her in the eye.

"Why insulin though?" Stella said. Trick question. The presence of insulin in the syringe on the beach was not public knowledge.

Vanessa didn't hesitate. "Nina's drug of choice. Although anyone can get their hands on it. I could get it in the blink of an eye." She was beginning to slur her words. "I've worked in that damn drugstore so long the pharmacists ask me where things are."

Vanessa had killed Lillian. Stella sat with that fact a moment. "This drink is yummy," she said, starting to stand up, "but I need to use your bathroom."

"Yummy? You've barely touched it," Vanessa cried. "Sit down, sweetie, please. I need to be heard. I need you to hear me out. You're the only friend I have."

"Okay, sure. I can hold on a bit longer." Stella conspicuously crossed her legs. Her eyes went to the canoe, the tote bag where she'd left her phone. "Um, that night she died." Keep it light now. "Lillian brought you flowers, didn't she?"

Vanessa laughed humourlessly. "Oh, yes, that was Lillian – a bouquet to smooth over every transgression. She knew I was onto her though. Knew I had my sus-pish-ons about her designs on Henry."

"In the end, the flowers were strewn all over the boat," Stella said. "Did she bring them up to the house first? I can see why you wouldn't want to keep them."

Vanessa started to finger her gold pendant, twisting it this way and that. Stella was almost mesmerized by the movement. She was beginning to think Vanessa had forgotten the question when she finally spoke again. "Kieran saw me. Always skulking around, that boy. He waited until the next day to mention it, after the police found her body. He'd seen me run to the beach with an armload of flowers but was too stoned to make sense of it. I told him Lillian had been drunk, that we'd argued about her drinking problem, and I was too mad at her to keep the flowers. I said her death wasn't all that surprising what with her smoking and drinking. Kieran and I have an understanding. Needless to say, I don't tell him everything but I know about his little habits."

"Speaking of Kieran, I heard… Well, it was probably just a rumour. But I heard Kieran took money from Nina's wallet the day she died." Stella looked away from the twisting pendant and tried not to give in to a pressing urge to close her eyes. God, she had only taken one swallow of the Caesar and lost track of how many glassfuls Vanessa had downed. Had she spiked the pitcher too? Maybe Vanessa was planning to kill herself but wanted to bare her soul first. Stella tried to concentrate on what she'd do if Vanessa keeled over and fell into the lake. There was a pole on the float; Stella could use it to pull her in then call 9-1-1. She would have to excuse herself soon, ostensibly to use the bathroom, so she could get her phone from the canoe then try to coax Vanessa off the wharf.

Vanessa gave a short laugh. "Silly boy. He didn't even know Nina was home when he poked his head into the cottage and took her wallet. The door was open and the handbag sitting there. He came to me in a panic when he found out she was dead too. I told him he didn't have to worry if he kept his head."

"You didn't tell him about the insulin – Nina's drug of choice?"

Vanessa made a dismissive gesture. "Insulin is too complicated for a stoner like Kieran. No, it wouldn't matter to him how Nina died. The point was he would have to keep his mouth shut about the wallet or he'd be a suspect in her death."

"But why...?" And now she chose the phrase Vanessa had used back at the coffee shop, the day Stella broke the news about finding Nina's body. "Why did Nina have to die?"

Vanessa exploded. "Because of that idiot Colette! She knew all about Clark and me. I talked to Nina the day after Lillian's funeral and Colette had been there, telling all sorts of stories about me. Before long Nina would have put two and two together and shot off her mouth to you. And you would have told McKean – I know you would have, Stella. Please don't insult me by denying it. No, I couldn't let that happen. As a diabetic Nina was the obvious suspect in Lillian's death. And Nina herself was more than ready to die. With Lillian gone she was miserable, and no one wants to spend the rest of her life in prison." And now Vanessa teasingly shook a finger at Stella. "You're asking too many questions, Ms. Smarty-pants Reporter. If you weren't my best friend in the entire world, I'd think you were trying to put words in my mouth."

Before Stella had time to respond, Vanessa abruptly stood up. Stella jumped to her feet too. "C'mon, Van," she said. "Let's leave the drinks and go inside. I'll make some tea." She was ready to lead Vanessa back to the cottage and keep her company until she sobered up. But she wasn't prepared for Vanessa to spring forward and shove her hard on the chest.

Stella stumbled backward over her chair and plunged into the lake.

45

ICY, BRUTAL WATER CHOKED her, blinded her, stopped up her ears. Leached into her panicked brain. Stella swallowed, spluttered, muscles seizing up as she fought to get upright, to tread water. *What drowning feels like…* Sinking, sinking, gulping, choking. *I can't die.* Tread water. Frantic, she kicked, flailed, and sunk. *I can't die.* She came up. Something sailed past her head. The pitcher. The pitcher hit the water and floated. *Kick. Kick. Sweep your arms.*

Ow! Shit! Her shoulder. The drinks table had banged into her shoulder. *Grab it and paddle.*

A pole stabbed her chest – she grappled for it. Lost the table. Vanessa pulled back the pole and jabbed her again. *I won't die.* Angry now, she dodged the pole, kicked her legs and swept her arms sideways, thought of her sons. In her head, she repeated "Matt, Nicky" with every stroke. There was a rhythm to it. "Matt, Nicky." Her head mostly stayed above water now. "Matt, Nicky." She swept with her arms, flutter-kicked her legs to get beyond Vanessa's reach. She rolled onto her back and floated, took a couple of breaths. Safe now, yes! She would alternate floating and kicking until she made it to the shallows.

"Leave her. Leave her, damn you!"

Who was she talking to?

An arm smacked Stella in the face. She struggled. Kieran. Trying to kill her. "I got you," he said. "Don't fight me." *Bastard!* She lashed out. He grabbed her neck and tried to throttle her.

"Leave her, you moron," screeched Vanessa. "Let her go."

Stella struggled as he grabbed at her, choked her, tried to push her under.

When she was almost too exhausted to go on, he yelled, "Stand up, stand up." She couldn't talk for coughing. "Stand up, Ms. Mosconi, stand up. You're in a fucking foot of water."

Liar! She yanked his hair – and then her back connected with a solid slab of sand. No more water in her face. She let go. Coughed, spluttered, turned around. Where did he go? Still gasping for air, she pushed herself up onto an elbow.

A short distance away Kieran was leaning over, his back to her now. She heard retching. He came back wiping his mouth. "You all right, Stella?" He called her Stella now.

Still unable to speak, she shook her head. Finally managed to choke out, "Where?"

"Took off in her car," he said.

"Oh, God, oh God," she whispered, easing herself into a sitting position. She wiped her eyes, cradled her sore shoulder. Snot dripped from her nose. "Thought you went home," she rasped.

"I was gonna go but she left the vodka and shot glass on the counter." He forced a laugh. "Tell your kids it's a bad idea to go swimming after you have a few shots. You'll puke your guts out."

She rubbed her shoulder and stood up to clear the water from her ears. But her mind hadn't entirely deserted her. She met Kieran's eyes. "On the counter in there – was there anything besides the vodka?"

"What do you mean?"

"I thought there might be drugs, some pills – something she used to spike the drinks."

"Oh, you mean the K? Nah, and it's not in the shed anymore if that's what you were looking for earlier. Few weeks back I found a little box of it on the top shelf. Gone now – all of it."

"Where do you think it came from – the stuff in the shed?"

He looked at her in disbelief. "You didn't know your pal's a recreational user? Lonely lady in a cottage in the woods… Don't look so shocked. Who doesn't need a little boost to get them through the day?" The boy sounded too world-weary for his years. "She has the stuff stashed all over. Doesn't smoke it though. Always nagging me about smoking." He smiled affectionately.

So, this boy had found a friend and possibly a mother figure in Vanessa. And Vanessa had found someone to fuss over – the son she never had.

Stella moved to the canoe on unsteady legs, retrieved her phone, and called 9-1-1. She must have garbled the report because the dispatcher said, "Is this an emergency, ma'am?" Stella disconnected and called Ben on his cell. He listened without interrupting. "Vanessa took off in her car and she's seriously drunk or high," Stella continued. "I bet she's headed straight for the border to try to reach Henry Sutton."

"We're on it," Ben said. "I'll be there with you ASAP. I'll come by boat."

Stella wrapped a beach towel sarong-like around herself and put on her lifejacket for added warmth. Even with it zipped to her chin she continued to shiver. "Kieran, listen," she said through chattering teeth. "I want you to think very carefully before you answer my next question. Have you seen or heard anything that might have a bearing on the way Lillian or Nina died?"

"Don't know about the housekeeper, but I think Ms. Fenniwick had a heart attack. She was drunk the night she rowed here. Vanessa was totally disgusted with her. Didn't even want to keep the flowers she brought. That's cold."

Stella bit down to stop her teeth chattering. "That night Lillian rowed here – did you see Vanessa help her back into the rowboat?"

"When I came by, Ms. Fenniwick was already in the boat, looking kind of wasted. I couldn't make out much in the dark but I saw Vanessa run down from the house with a bunch of flowers and throw them at her. Then she pushed the boat into the lake. She didn't want to talk about it, but she must have felt bad later when she heard Ms. Fenniwick died."

"Tell me what you saw tonight."

He glanced at her then looked away. "Never seen Vanessa that intense. A little high, yeah, but nothing like tonight. You two seemed to be having a good old yak out on the wharf." He chuckled. "Guess you pissed her off good though. I saw her bung you into the lake and start throwing things."

"That's when you came after me."

"I remembered you had a thing about water. From, you know, that time with your kids in the canoe. And you didn't look too good out there, I have to tell you."

"Listen, Kieran, I appreciate what you did. But if you wanted to help you should have passed me something to hold onto. You're not supposed to grab a person struggling in deep water. Trust me on that. I thought you were trying to kill me."

He smirked. "That's funny," he said. Then he stretched out on the beach as if warmed by the dying evening sun. Eyes closed, he looked like a kid again, a kid without a care in the world. And now for the first time, Stella noticed the little chunk of driftwood, hanging from his neck on a piece of purple raffia.

"Kieran, did you make that thing around your neck? Where did the raffia come from?"

He idly fingered the wood pendant as if just noticing it. "Oh, yeah. I made it for my girlfriend but she gave it back when we broke up."

"But the raffia – where did you get that?"

"You mean the string?" he said. "I found it here, when I was raking up flowers and stuff on the beach."

46

AT THE FAINT SOUND of a motor in the distance, Kieran got edgy. "Look, I gotta go," he said, sitting up, brushing sand off his arms and legs. "I gotta be going. See you."

"Wait a sec, okay? There was a reason I thought you were trying to drown me. Your arrangement with Vanessa – did that change after you lifted the cash from Nina's wallet? Did she start asking you to do things that went beyond yard work?"

Kieran sprung to his feet. "I told you – I don't know anything about a wallet."

"I think you do, Kieran. I think you saw an opportunity and took the cash without thinking twice. But Vanessa said you could be blamed for Nina's death, and that gave her a hold over you." The sound of the motor grew louder; the silhouette of a small boat was visible now.

"I don't know what you're talking about." Kieran put his hands over his ears and started to walk away.

"Did she call and tell you to let the air out of my tires? The tires on the Pathfinder?"

"No! That's just stupid."

"Did you key the Subaru too? Was the idea to scare me off the investigations?"

"It wasn't right you helping out that cop," Kieran erupted. "You being married and all. She said we had to stop you from destroying your family."

"I wasn't about to destroy my family, Kieran," Stella said, shakily. "But what about the tree? I remember Nina saying you were going to fall a rotten birch for her. Did you chop down the tree next to my house?"

"Chop down a tree? You're crazy." Back in control, he laughed out loud. *Okay, maybe not the tree.*

"Did you make the telephone calls, Kieran? Silent calls to my home and office."

"I got a right to remain silent. I got a right to a lawyer. You can ask your boyfriend." He bolted – dodging rocks, bare feet kicking up sand – and vanished into the darkening forest like a phantom.

The police launch powered down then came alongside the string of floats. Ben McKean got out and tied up the craft. He stepped lightly but swiftly along the makeshift wharf.

"You made it." Stella was almost giddy with relief. "Before I fall to pieces, let me give you the bare facts. Vanessa killed Lillian and Nina, and tonight she tried to kill me. In trying to frighten me off the investigations, she had a somewhat unwitting accomplice in a local teen, Kieran Corcoran, about sixteen years old. When he saw you coming he took off across the beach. Lives somewhere close by with his uncle."

"I'll follow up with the kid. We already have Levitt in custody. You were right about her escape route. US Customs stopped her at the border and Eberly picked her up." Ben looked hard at Stella. "You okay?"

"Sure." With the back of her hand she took a swipe at her nose and brushed back a dripping strand of hair. "Couldn't be better." Directly behind Ben, lights had begun to twinkle on the opposite shore of Kootenay Lake where the cozy green cabin waited just around a bend. Home. "Couldn't be better," she repeated, softly.

Two patrol cars sped down the driveway, sirens blaring. The driver from each walked toward the beach. Stella recognized Ray Eberle and Constable Naomi Lewis, the eager-beaver officer who had fingerprinted her the night of Nina's death. Constable Lewis exchanged a glance with Ben. Did she have a thing for him too? Ben stepped away to confer with his colleagues. When he came back, he told Stella that Constable Lewis would take her home.

Ben said he'd take one of the patrol cars to follow up with Kieran. "I'll go easy on him, read him his rights, interview him with a guardian present. We'll look after him. But later I want to stop by your house. Hate to put you through it, but I have to do a formal interview while the details are still fresh in your mind."

"Lillian's sunglasses," Stella said. "Before it gets any darker, take a photo of them there in the shallows." She waded into the lake. "Here they are. Right where they landed after Lillian threw them overboard. Even with her brain about to close down, she let us know she had been here that night. Without the sunglasses, we might not have found her killer."

* * *

By the time Ben arrived at the Mosconi cabin, Stella and Naomi Lewis had downed two pots of peppermint tea and run out of things to talk about. "Thanks, Constable," Ben said. "I'll take it from here." He looked comfortable sitting down at the kitchen table and setting up his recorder.

"I'd be glad to stay, sir," Lewis said, putting a subtle emphasis on "sir."

"Not necessary," Ben said. She seemed reluctant to leave but Ben didn't appear to notice. He clicked on the recorder and asked Stella to start at the beginning.

She began by telling him of her renewed suspicions about Henry Sutton, and her concern that Vanessa was seriously in love with a potential killer. When she talked about her solo paddle across the lake, she left out the part about her dad and his note – no sense getting off track. She described stopping and surprising Kieran in the garden shed. It was difficult to put into words her shock at discovering Lillian's sunglasses in the shallows.

She recapped the conversation on the wharf, including Vanessa's bitterness toward Lillian for supposedly stealing the affection of Clark Fenniwick. She noted Vanessa's unplanned pregnancy, the result of an affair with the much-older Clark, her dropping out of university to have an abortion and the years of blaming Lillian for pretty much everything that had gone wrong.

When she came to the part about Henry Sutton, Ben interjected. "Hold on," he said "Back up a minute. Vanessa killed Lillian Fenniwick to keep her away from Sutton?" He shook his head in wonder. "And here I thought greed was the motive for Fenniwick's murder. The valuable property."

"Never underestimate the human heart." Stella smiled. "But Vanessa's choice of insulin as a murder weapon was calculated to incriminate Nina. No offense, Ben, but you were inclined to buy it."

"Yes, I bought it." Ben raked his fingers through his hair. "But why kill Nina? Why not simply stand back and let her take the rap for Lillian's death?"

"I wondered about that too," Stella said. "It was Colette Fen-niwick, a niece of Lillian's husband, who set Vanessa after Nina. If Colette hadn't shown up in Nelson for the funeral, Nina might be alive today. But around the time of Clark's affair with Vanessa, Colette was a guest at his cottage. Vanessa assumed she knew all about the pregnancy and abortion and might have let Nina in on her secret. She was terrified Nina would realize she'd killed Lillian and then tell you and me. But Colette was a child when she visited her uncle. She probably had no inkling of the seriousness of the relationship between Vanessa and Clark."

When it came time to describe Vanessa's attack on her, Stella had to stop for a moment to check her emotions. She put a humorous spin on Kieran's rescue. "I thought he was trying to kill me," she said. "Vanessa's little helper."

Ben paused in his note taking. "I doubt it seemed funny at the time."

"No. You're right. It didn't," Stella said, subdued again. "But it's over now. And clear that Vanessa acted on her own to kill Lillian and Nina. She kept Kieran Corcoran close to her, but his crimes were relatively minor, if you don't count his drug use and the dam-age to Joe's Subaru. Yeah, on top of a lot of other mischief the kid keyed our car. Oh, and Kieran also lifted the money from Nina's wallet."

Ben held up the fingers of one hand. "Let's see: possession of illicit drugs, vandalism, robbery... how am I doing?"

"Kieran will be a useful witness though. On the night Lillian died, he was at Vanessa's in the shadows. He saw her toss Lillian's flowers into the rowboat and shove the boat into the lake. At that point Lillian would have been near death but Kieran didn't sus-pect a thing. Vanessa told him Lillian was drunk and she was too disgusted to keep the flowers. Later when he admitted to stealing the cash from Nina's wallet, Vanessa warned him to keep quiet or he'd be a suspect in her death. He didn't know anything about the insulin, by the way, or even the syringe found on the beach." Now she smiled. "You can thank the local press for keeping the official cause of both deaths from the public."

A flicker of acknowledgement passed over Ben's face.

Stella continued. "Oh, and get this: Vanessa is a quote/unquote recreational user of ketamine. Kieran said she had it stashed all over the place. She probably spiked her victims' drinks with ketamine to sedate them. How she got started with that stuff is anyone's guess. Even though she owned a drugstore, pharmacies have strict controls on ketamine so she likely turned to the Internet or got herself a dealer. Oh, and remember the robberies at the ferry slip and the vet's office? I doubt Vanessa would have been involved in either case but I wonder if Kieran knows anything about them?"

"Noted. I'll add that to my list of follow-up questions for the kid." Ben turned off his recorder. "You did good – more than good. This is enough for now but I'll want to talk to you again in the morning. You seem to be favouring that shoulder. Do you have any painkillers in the house? Or should I take you to the hospital, get the ER doc to take a look at it?"

"It's nothing. I'll take an ibuprofen or two. It's nothing. Really."

"Why don't you call a friend to come over and keep you company?"

"No, I'm talked out. I'll take the Advil with a glass of milk and sleep like a baby."

"That experience in the water is going to stay with you a while, Stella. You shouldn't be alone tonight. Call a friend."

"Hey, did you hear about the guy in New Zealand who fought off a shark then stitched up his own leg wound? Story was on some news feed. After his rescue, he went out for beer with his buddies."

"In other words, he let his friends support him. You had a close call, Stella. Let me get in touch with someone for you."

"No, no, I'm fine. Go. I mean it. I'll see you in the morning."

* * *

Stella felt kind of empty as she watched Ben's taillights disappear up the drive. Talking through everything with him had felt so good, so right. When they wrapped up it would have been natural to share a hug, instead of going through the awkward little dance that preceded their goodbyes.

Still chilled from her bout in the glacier-fed lake, her teeth began to chatter again. She stood at the sink and swallowed two painkillers with a gulp of milk. What an idiot she'd been to confront Vanessa alone. If she had drowned out there – well, the effect on her family didn't bear thinking about. Poor Joe – what was he going to think about his irresponsible wife?

She drew a bath and soaked until the water cooled, put on a flannel nightie and wool socks yet still didn't feel warm. She found the winter-weight duvet and pulled it up to her chin but was too revved up to sleep. Wrapped in the duvet, she hobbled out to the kitchen for another glass of milk, which she warmed in the microwave, her head still buzzing. What had happened to Vanessa that made her capable of murder? Even if her upbringing hadn't been warm and fuzzy… even if Clark Fenniwick had taken advantage of her, as he surely had … are those the kind of experiences that make a murderer?

Stella sat down at her computer, opened her browser, and keyed in psychopaths and sociopaths and narcissists until her head spun with all the bafflegab. She went back to bed. That was when the terror of her plunge in the lake came back. Her dad had tried so hard to teach her to swim – she should have tried harder. But, oh yeah, she had been a child at the time. And her dad had left. The pain of losing him flooded back.

Even now, his clumsy attempt to reconnect had caused her grief. He had to be the man with the brown dog who had approached the boys – he loved dogs. And then she flashed on a long-ago image of her and her dad in a car, windows wide open, New Kids on the Block belting out Step by Step. The radio request at the start of the long weekend, sent out to a special girl in Nelson. She was glad there was no one around to see her bawl like a baby.

At some point Stella dozed off and dreamt of water, her dad holding her, telling her to kick, her mom saying, "Leave her alone." The night wore on. When she heard the early morning train, she could have sworn she hadn't slept a wink despite the vague dreams. Maybe the scenes with her dad had been memories rather than dreams. She thought of him somewhere nearby, waiting for her call.

She got up and put on a pot of coffee. Checked out the sore shoulder. She had a blue-black bruise the diameter of a tennis ball, tender to the touch but not swollen. When she rotated her arm in a full circle, the range of motion seemed normal. A bike ride to work shouldn't be a problem – might even help her feel normal again. She poured a cup of coffee and sipped it on the porch as the sky lightened. At seven o'clock she called Ben.

"McKean," he answered, crisp and business-like. In the background, a radio was broadcasting the CBC morning news, a baby cooed and gurgled. A woman's voice said, "Is it her?" Ben said he would call right back. She didn't have to wait long.

"You wanted to talk this morning," she said.

"Should I come out to your place?"

"Let's meet at the park, near the wharf. Say, eight-thirty?"

"I'll bring coffee."

47

STELLA LEANED HER BICYCLE against the park fence, a short distance above the City Wharf. On the morning after her near drowning and the apprehension of Vanessa Levitt for two murders, it seemed fitting to return to the place where the whole tragic series of events had begun to unfold. The police float was deserted. A sprinkle of rain had all but a few diehards packing up and leaving the beach. Gulls circled and screeched overhead.

A patrol car pulled into the parking lot and Ben McKean got out and walked toward her, a paper cup of coffee in each hand. He asked whether she had slept.

"A little," she said. They sat down on a bench. She accepted the coffee. "I dreamt about my dad, or thought about him, anyway. Too bad he never managed to teach me to swim. Not for lack of trying though, and he never gave me a hard time for messing up – maybe he should have. Too soft hearted my old dad. He left though. Until yesterday, I didn't even know whether he was still alive."

Ben looked up. "Yesterday?"

She smiled. "Big day, yesterday. Along with everything else that happened, I found a note from my dad. After twenty-five years he seems to want to reconnect."

"How do you feel about that?"

She looked out over the lake. "Ambivalent." They sipped their coffee. "But we're not here to talk about my old man. When I had trouble sleeping last night, I went online to try to make sense of Vanessa's behaviour. She's had a tough life in many ways. I guess the family business preoccupied her parents. And she was barely out of her teens when Clark Fenniwick took advantage of her. I doubt she ever recovered emotionally from the abortion. That could have led to the alleged drug habit."

"You're overthinking, Stella. Who knows what motivated Levitt to act the way she did? The point is she killed two people."

"I know, I know." Stella looked out at the lake a moment. "I wonder if she simply dug herself into a hole. I mean, she believed Lillian had stood between her and Clark. And then she saw Henry Sutton as a last chance for romance. I think she honestly thought of me as a friend until I got too close to finding out about the murders... Did you get a signed confession?"

Ben shook his head. "We have a drunken rant on tape. Typist said it was a bugger to transcribe. Every second word an 'unintelligible.' But it shouldn't be too difficult to piece together the evidence against Levitt. For one thing, that length of raffia Kieran found at Levitt's is likely a match for the raffia in Fenniwick's garden shed."

Stella said, "I've never known Vanessa to drink the way she did last night. I wondered at first if she'd spiked my drink to make me forget the whole episode. Then when *she* slugged back glass after glass I didn't know what to think. One thing is certain: the murders were premeditated. Vanessa chose insulin as a weapon so she could implicate Nina. She probably filled a syringe with insulin and waited for an opportunity to use it on Lillian. Afterward she planted the used syringe on Nina's beach to incriminate her and dropped Lillian's cardigan into the trash burner for the same reason. Kieran expected to find ketamine in the garden shed. It's possible that planting ketamine in the shed was also part of the set up to throw suspicion on Nina."

A red kite dipped and soared over the lake as a bare-footed boy ran along the near-empty beach. Stella continued. "I thought it would be a massive relief to find out who killed Lillian and Nina, and in a way, it *is* a relief, but..."

Ben crumpled his empty coffee cup. "Don't try to make sense of murder, Stella."

She was quiet for a moment.

Ben didn't seem in a hurry to end the conversation. He leaned back on the bench. "I guess Max Huber will be free to claim the yellow cottage now," he said. "Seems he's joined at the hip with Colette Fenniwick these days. Talk about your odd couple."

"Odd, indeed." Stella laughed. "Colette must have something up her sleeve."

"Time will tell." Ben said. After a moment, he continued. "The ketamine connection is interesting."

"Is it ever," Stella said. "If the RCMP lab in Vancouver finds ketamine in samples from the victims, there we go. More evidence. I'm no scientist but I gather ketamine is quick to clear the bloodstream. I wonder if the fast-acting insulin in Nina's pump killed her before the ketamine could be fully metabolized. On the other hand, Lillian might have been unconscious for some time before she succumbed."

"You've done quite a study of all this," Ben said. "I'd like you to talk to Antoniak about it. Meanwhile we'll go over Levitt's property again. Chances are there'll be matches with the evidence collected from the bodies. Levitt manhandled the victims. I'd be surprised if she didn't leave a trace of something behind – a hair or fibre, a chip of nail polish. Locard's Exchange Principle has stood the test of time. Two people who come in close contact are almost certain to exchange or transfer trace materials. At any rate, your testimony and Kieran's should seal the deal with or without additional circumstantial evidence. And if this goes to court, Levitt is bound to trip herself up if she takes the stand. In view of her performance yesterday, I think we can count on it." He looked away then back at Stella. "When I think what could have happened to you last night..."

Stella closed her eyes a moment. "I should have beat it out of there as soon as I saw those sunglasses in the lake. It was unfair to my family to risk approaching Vanessa."

"When do they get home?"

"Three more days but who's counting? I'm going to bring in supplies for the mother of all beach fires. Wieners, marshmallows, you name it. Joe will be happy the lake has gone down. More than happy – I'm not kidding. He has a thing about beach fires." She felt a surge of excitement about her family's return, Joe included. Would he be happy to see her?

"You going to give him a second chance?" Ben said. "Your dad, I mean."

"I don't think I have a choice. If I don't respond to that note I'll probably go crazy wondering if I should have. I guess you could call that a second chance."

He smiled at Stella. "Well, you got your story."

"Patrick will have to give Jade the story," Stella said without rancour. "Which will thrill her to the tips of her ambitious little toes. One more reason to feel insecure about my job."

"You're good at what you do. Your boss knows that."

"You're good at what you do too."

"Best get back to it." Ben got up and began to walk toward his car, then looked back as if to memorize her face. She waited for another glimpse of the fleeting smile. "Expect I'll see you around, Ms. Mosconi," he said.

"Roger that, Sergeant."

He got into his car and glanced her way again. Stella thought of something she wanted to tell him and might have flagged him down, but her phone rang.

Joe. "On our way home," he said. "Figured you must be getting bored without us. The boys are flipping a coin to see who gets to talk next."

In the background Matt and Nicky sounded excited. Their voices brought a flood of joy. "Tell them we're going to have a big beach fire tonight," Stella said. "Hot dogs and all the trimmings."

"Great. A home-cooked meal."

She laughed. Ben was backing out of the parking lot; she waved at him.

Joe said, "I missed you, babe."

"Me too you," she said.

Nicky took the phone next, then Matt, but within a couple of minutes the line went blank. The car must have moved out of range of a cell tower. Never mind. At the end of the day they would all be together.

Stella threw a leg over the worn saddle of her bicycle and pedalled away from the City Wharf and up the hill toward the offices of the *Nelson Times*. She had a story to deliver, a real grabber. It was going to make Jade Visser's day.

Acknowledgments

I appreciate the teachers and mentors who shone a light along the way, especially Verna Relkoff, Nicole Parton Fisher, Deryn Collier, and the late Holley Rubinsky. A special shout-out to the Crime Writers of Canada for their Arthur Ellis Awards, in particular the Unhanged Arthur for best unpublished novel. Even to be shortlisted has jumpstarted many a crime-writing career, mine included.

The real Nelson, British Columbia, is rich in talented journalists. Thanks to Bob Hall, Kevin Mills, and Greg Nesteroff, along with Will Johnson, Tyler Harper, Bill Metcalfe, and Jennifer Cowan who permitted me to watch them in action at the *Nelson Star*.

Drs. Lee MacKay, Andrew Murray, and Sarah Merriman answered my questions about diabetes and insulin, and veterinarian Dr. Janice Gillis shared her practical knowledge of ketamine. Lawyers Erica Kleisinger and Michael Kleisinger offered guidance in legal matters. Shane Merriman, retired Identification Officer with the RCMP, provided information about police procedures, as did Chief Constable Paul Burkart of the Nelson Police Department (who bears no resemblance whatsoever to the police chief in my story). Any technical errors that might have crept into the manuscript are entirely mine.

Thanks also to Jennifer Steeksma, Lisa Nothling, Joanne Toews, and my trusty partner in crime writing Rachel M. Greenaway for their insights and encouragement. I'm especially grateful to Morty Mint, surely the kindest of literary agents, and to Matthew Goody, my superb editor at Mosaic Press.

This book is for my husband David, who cooks so I may write, and for our daughters Sarah and Erica and their husbands and daughters – all of whom make my heart sing.

* * *

This is a work of fiction, and while I've shared one or two personal hang-ups with Stella Mosconi, all of the characters and events are products of my imagination. Beautiful Nelson, BC, inspired the setting for the story, but I took many liberties with local geography, businesses, and other features of the area.

About the Author

JG Toews is a former health professional, technical writer, columnist, and non-fiction author. Give Out Creek is her debut novel and the first in a series of Stella Mosconi mysteries. It was shortlisted for the 2016 Arthur Ellis Award for Best Unpublished Crime Novel. Judy lives in Nelson, Canada. Visit her at www.jgtoews.com or follow her on Twitter @judytoews.

Photo credit: Lisa Seyfried Photography